Coffee Stains

a novel

Kat Caldwell

katcaldwell.com

Published by Ladwell Publishing, 2021

Cover Design by James, GoOnWrite.com

Print ISBN: 978-0-9995881-8-5

e-book ISBN: 978-0-9995881-6-1

Historical Romance:

Aurora's Dilemma

Stepping Across the Desert

Across the English Channel

Contemporary New Adult Romance:

Coffee Stains

Mythological Christian Fiction:

An Audience with the King

Contemporary Fiction:

Bended Dream

Bended Loyalty

Bended Love

To everyone who believes that their past doesn't define their future.

Chapter One

In the pitch black of an early December morning, a buzzing dragged Ana away from her dreamless sleep. It seemed an injustice to need to wake up so early. The buzzing called to her and, slowly, Ana reacted, turning to her right before sitting up. After a year of living in the attic room at her brother's house, she knew she had to move cautiously if she didn't wish to bump her head on the steep pitch her bed sat under. While she sometimes referred to her bedroom as Cinderella's room, she was grateful her brother and Elena had created a space for her to stay, especially since it was shaping up to be a longer stay than she had expected.

Her phone alarm buzzed again like an impatient mother yelling that it was time for school. *Vamos, Ana, levántate*! With no light yet coming through the window and the phone probably buried under a pillow or book or clothes, Ana had no choice but to open her eyes and sit up.

"Where are you?" she muttered as she wiggled her hands near the sound, patting down gently until her fingers hit something hard. Walking to the light switch might have been easier, but it required getting out of bed. "Aha! There you are. Please turn off."

The blazing blue light of the screen hit her pupils with force and suddenly her blankets weren't enough to keep her warm. Her blood turned icy at the notification from a newsletter she'd long forgotten about. Had she more self-will and self-compassion, she would have deleted it without bothering to open the email but clicking on the blue tinged box came as a reflex. Immediately, glossy pictures and emotionally gripping headlines bombarded her eyes.

We have your email address from a list that shows you might be interested in this new online magazine. You can make a difference! You can fight the system with us!

Oh, no. There she was, second picture down. All the efforts to erase any connection between her and the obscure activist group that she and Roberto had put together were no match for the internet.

Their group had hovered under the radar, even when they were at their most active, but they had attended some protests where a few journalists also came, eager to snap pictures of their frustration. Chosen for their shock value, she didn't have the rights to these photos to take them down, and she didn't know who took them. Not that they would scrub them from the internet just because she asked. Besides, she would have to admit the girl was her and Ana was trying to put those years behind her.

Reporters often used this picture, both in favor and against protests. The picture showed her dressed in black as usual in those days, with a scarf that had slipped just past her chin to make more room for her to spew insults at the people. Most wouldn't know it was her. The scarf still obstructed some of her chin. Ana peered closer. Her heavy eyeliner also made her look different since she rarely wore any now. The caption held no mention of her name, but that didn't matter either. Not to her.

Every time she saw it, rage and shame pushed every other emotion aside.

Scrolling further down, the third headline of the newsletter drew her in. Roberto stood with the girlfriend he had run away to Chicago with, now his wife, according to the caption.

Roberto and Nadia are ready and willing to do the work it will take to make Chicago better, was the caption under the photo.

Ana snorted, the reaction sending her dry throat into a coughing fit. Yes, certainly. Roberto was always willing to do the work to put himself in a place of power.

The second alarm, meant to get her butt out of bed if she had dared to sleep in, buzzed. It was the ultimate warning that she had only twenty minutes to dress and head out in order to arrive on time to work. She cursed herself for wasting time, found where to unsubscribe and pounded on the link, but that seemed to have no effect on her mood.

Ana sighed. That nagging, prickly sensation telling her she should be further along at twenty-three covered her skin, popping the hairs up in goosebumps. It didn't matter that she worked double shifts, or ran herself ragged taking more classes than she should to graduate earlier, or studied extra for perfect grades—the regret of wasting so many years would rear up regardless, the cruel voice pounding insults at the back of her head. Today was no different. Here she was heading off to serve coffee to students and professors while the guy who deserved no rewards in life was running for city council in Chicago. How pathetic.

Ana shoved the phone into her backpack and grabbed her work clothes. There was little time to spend pouting about where she wished she was in life. If she was late one more time with Nathalie managing, she might lose this job.

"What're you doing up so early?" Ana asked her sister-in-law Elena as she entered the kitchen. Elena was sitting at the dining table, filling out papers.

"Buenos días, Ana. I just couldn't sleep. Just filling out some paperwork. There's coffee there for you."

Ana's nose scrunched up at the sight of instant coffee. The microwave signaled the end of a warming cycle as Javier walked in.

"Are we ever going to buy a new coffeemaker?" Ana asked him as he kissed his wife. The coffee maker, the same one their parents had bought just weeks before dying in a car accident, had given up after five years. Even though she had been there when they bought it, and this was the same house she grew up in, Ana didn't feel like she could make any changes. Javier and Elena had been living here when the accident happened and took over paying for the house afterwards. It wasn't really her home anymore, even though she lived there.

"I'm fine with the coffee I make," Javier shrugged, giving her a smile and a wink as he stirred the dehydrated coffee granules into his hot milk and gave it a loud slurp. "Want more tea, mi amor?"

"No thank you, it'll just make me pee," Elena answered, patting her belly.

"Coffee?" Javier asked Ana. Always the older brother needing to tease a reaction out of her.

"I'll have some real coffee at work."

"Exactly! That's why we don't need to buy another machine."

"Do you mind if I go in and straighten up your room today, Ana?"

Ana looked up from looking for her mittens. All the winter things, once dry, ended up jumbled up in the large drawer of the enormous dresser they kept the television on. She peeked her head around the corner to look at Elena.

"It's fairly picked up, but of course. This is your house. Why?"

A strange look passed between Javier and Elena. Ana looked at the belly on her sister-in-law and wondered if they were hoping to use her room for little Sofia, once the baby was here. They would never kick her out of the house, but she knew she was in the way of their growing family. It was one reason she was trying to graduate as soon as possible and find a job that paid enough for her to rent an apartment. Her credit was too bad at the moment to get anything reasonable. Asking Javier to co-sign seemed not only unfair but embarrassing.

"Luis might come over later to look at the house," Elena said, referring to their landlord.

"To complete the papers for you guys to buy it?" Ana was back digging through the winter things and couldn't see her brother, but she could feel him hesitating. She wished he would just come out and say what she knew he was thinking. Javier had always planned on buying this house and growing his family here. Ana had no intention of imposing on them any more than she had to.

"Something like that," Javier said, as Ana emerged from the drawers with two scarves and thick mittens.

"Qué bien! And don't worry, I'll be graduating by next December, if not sooner, and be out of here as soon as possible."

"You aren't a bother," Elena told her, but Ana knew that wasn't true.

"She is sometimes," Javier said, giving her a wink.

Elena swatted at Javier as she stood and stretched. "Are you going to be here over Christmas break?"

"Claro. I'm working quite a few shifts at the coffee shop, but I'll be here."

"Ves, Javier? I told you she would be here."

"I thought maybe you'd be going away to the Caribbean or something with your rich boyfriend."

"Oh, stop. Between working and studying, I don't have time for almost anything else."

"Except sleeping at his house."

Javier ducked away from Elena, who swatted at him again.

"How's business?" Ana asked.

"Good. Much better than last year. Eric Mallard and I've formed a business. He does metal work and I do the wood to create these industrial looking pieces that people love. We just finished a wine cellar for a restaurant in town. It looks so good they did a piece on us in the newspaper."

"Seriously?"

Javier smirked. "Don't read the newspaper much? I left it out on the counter for you to see."

Ana looked where her brother was pointing, realizing she had seen the paper but hadn't bothered to look closer.

"After that, we won a bid to make the entire bar and wine area for another restaurant that's opening in May. Then we're doing a library wall for a house downtown and something for a new boutique down on Ellipse Street. One of those trendy boutique places you would like if you had money."

Ana laughed at the friendly jab.

"How much money did you make for the wine cellar?"

"About thirty thousand after paying for the material and the other hourly guys. It was a big wine cellar."

"Each?" The idea of that amount of money had her salivating.

"No, all together."

"Still, I wasn't expecting you to say that."

"And I didn't need a college education to do it, either."

Javier grinned, his white teeth gleaming. Ana laughed. Javier loved teasing her about not needing to go into debt to be successful, something her father used to say.

"Right, well, this girl needs an education because she doesn't know how to make beautiful wine cellars. And if you ever want me out of this house, then you shouldn't try to convince me to stop studying."

"He doesn't mean anything by it," Elena said, rolling her eyes at Javier, who grabbed her around the waist and kissed her noisily.

Ana laughed. "I know, I know. Bueno, me voy. If I don't leave now, I'll miss the bus."

"I'll take you, so you know I'm actually a nice brother. Just let me brush my teeth."

Ana nodded at her brother, grateful for the extra minutes to gather her books properly and make sure she left nothing behind.

"Take a snack," Elena said as they were heading out the door. She held out an apple and a large slice of banana bread. "You don't eat enough."

Ana gave her a quick peck on the cheek in thanks and headed out into the dark, frosty morning with Javier.

The sun slowly rose above the horizon as Marlon tried to finish his write up for his dispute resolution class. One other person in the coffee shop accompanied him, besides the workers behind the counter. Even the music coming from the speakers was slow and tired, encouraging his eyelids to droop. Every morning he regretted having taken the night court position. Setting his schedule up on paper at the beginning of the school year had been much easier than living it out.

Marlon shoved his body straight and rubbed his open palms across his cheeks, stopping just short of slapping himself. One hour ago, he felt wide awake as he left work, but now being up all night was catching up with him. The last drops of his cold cappuccino rolling down his throat helped perk him up a little, but it wasn't enough.

When the words on the computer screen started swirling before his eyes, Marlon jumped up out of his chair. He needed to move and wake up. He needed to sleep. The enormous clock on the back wall of the coffee shop told him he had less than two hours before class would start. Eyeing the couch shoved in the corner, Marlon thought about asking the girl barista if she would let him lie down for a few minutes, but decided against it. The morning coffee rush hour could start at any minute, which meant even if they allowed him to lie down, he wouldn't end up sleeping, anyway. Marlon shook his head at the couch, physically resisting its invitation. Anyway, Mama Rou raised him better than to sleep in public.

The music changed to some upbeat Columbian tunes. Marlon smiled in appreciation at the barista, who responded with a graceful swaying of her full hips and a wide smile back at him. It was the same young woman who had served him coffee a few days before. Lucinda. He remembered her catching him staring at her name tag. The Latin music filled his senses as he watched her, fully distracted from his paper.

A year had passed since he walked in on his girlfriend with his roommate in San Diego, clear by the strong reaction his body was having. Though his eyes were dry, he was now awake, but still unwilling to finish his project. Maybe it was time to jump back into the dating game.

Lucinda beamed at his request for a second muffin and continued to sing while looking at him out of the corner of her eye as she arranged the muffins on a tiered display.

Marlon leaned against the glass that protected the baked goods, trying to think of something interesting to say. *I like the way you dance* sounded too heavy. *Good morning* sounded too generic.

When she turned her attention towards him, he made sure he was smiling. His ex-girlfriend used to describe his smile as sexy, teasing, and mysterious. Her friends said it was an intriguing smile. Alana, his ex, used to compare him to a Greek god with his straight nose, shiny black curls he now had in dreads, and his tawny skin. The smile was his secret weapon, since the right words never seemed to come out. He could drone on and on just like some of his ancient ancestors about law and philosophy, but that did little to charm girls these days.

"Hey."

Marlon tried not to let his disappointment in himself allow his smile to falter. Thankfully, she smiled back, unruffled by his lame choice of greeting.

"Good morning," she said. "I've seen you in here before, haven't I?"

"Probably yesterday."

"What's got you out so early? Got a test soon?" she asked. "You look like you should be home sleeping."

"Just got off work." He ignored the habit of shifting his weight from left to right as he spoke, forcing himself instead to stay still. "Gotta finish this presentation and paper."

"Well then, you're gonna need another coffee, aren't you?" she asked with a wink. "How about a double shot latte?"

"Sounds like just what I need."

She headed towards the espresso machine as the front door opened, ushering in freezing cold air and a pack of black-clad goths. The taller one that banged through the door led the pack, his blood-shot eyes zeroing in on Marlon straight away.

"You gonna let me order?"

Marlon swept his arm to the side as he made way for the group. He grew up in this area, which had never been too diverse in ethnicities, but had been a good place to live. He had never had many problems being a kid with a mixture of background, including one of the dominant tribes in the Midwest, but there was always one or two who had something in for him from the beginning. One guy, Brandon, during their sophomore year of high school, had made it his priority to trip Marlon or make fun of him in front of others. Marlon ignored him until one day Brandon took a swing at him outside the bowling alley. His mistake. Marlon's dad had taught him how to fight back from the time he was four. After a duck and a quick hook to Brandon's jaw, the two of them called a truce and ended up talking for about an hour. No friendship came out of it, but at least Brandon left him alone after that.

This group of kids didn't look worth spending that much time with, though.

"Here ya go," Lucinda announced as she pushed the coffee towards to Marlon.

"You gonna service this guy before me?"

"He was here first, moron," was Lucinda's reply as she winked at Marlon. "Now I'll serve you."

"I'm here, Lu! Is Nathalie here?"

Marlon was already backing away but couldn't help turning at the familiar voice coming from behind the counter.

"Just in time, Ana. Don't worry, Nat isn't here. Just get in here and pretend you aren't half an hour late."

The new woman had her brown hair piled on top of her head, wide eyes, and a large smile that she flashed at Lucinda before setting to work making espressos. Marlon sat back at his table, but didn't start working again. There was something about the new barista that had him transfixed. He knew her, but he couldn't place where from.

More students and professors started piling in through the door and Marlon had to force himself to concentrate on his paper, which was difficult with the goth kids sitting behind him playing their music. Marlon slipped on his headphones, getting desperate to focus when something warm and wet splashed onto his pant leg.

"Hey!"

Marlon jumped out of his seat, finding himself face to face with a goth girl, her purple-lined eyes staring at him with contempt.

"Excuse me, you seem to be in the way," she said.

"Right."

"What did you say?"

This time, it was the leader talking from his place at the table behind him. Marlon flexed his fingers, reminding himself that violence wasn't worth the consequences. Before he could back away, the leader gave the girl a nod. The next second, the last bit of her coffee poured onto his notebook. The group erupted into laughter as they rose from their chairs and marched out, purposely bumping into Marlon on their way out.

Mama Rou's voice rose in the back of his mind. *It's not worth it*, her voice told him. Just *stay still and let the little people in this world pass you by.*

Instead of siding with his father and fighting this time, he obeyed his grandmother's voice and waited until the door closed behind the group before he moved to find napkins.

"I'm so sorry. What jerks," the girl with the familiar voice said as she rushed over with towels.

She handed him one for his pants, then set about mopping up the mess on the table.

"At least she didn't spill it on your computer."

"That was not an accident."

The woman looked at him, transporting Marlon back to his senior year of high school. Ana. She had been one of the few freshmen in math club his senior year. Though it became obvious that she and her two friends were there only for the extra credit points that Mr. Zanker always offered those that joined, Marlon hadn't cared. He had spent hours memorizing the outline of her mouth instead of the math formulas. They lost touch almost immediately after graduating, as happened with most high school friendships. And now she was here.

"Ana!"

"Yes?" She seemed startled at him knowing her name, but her eyes didn't register any recognition towards him

"I'm Marlon. From Mr. Zanker's math club. Remember?"

Coffee dripped from his notebook in her hands as recognition slowly filled her eyes.

"You look different. I haven't seen you in how long?"

"Four or five years now." Marlon brushed his hair back with his fingers, aware of the unruly dreadlocks pulled back into a ponytail at the back of his neck. He hadn't bothered to take care of them for over a year now. Ana looked as she did in high school, except for the tiny lines near her eyes. "How are you?"

"I'm—I'm good. I'm at the university and working, well, here." She shifted away from him a bit, then returned to cleaning the table.

"You studying your masters?"

"Um, no. I'm still doing my bachelor's. It took me longer to get to the university after my parents died."

"Right, I heard about that. I tried to contact you, but I only had your house phone, and no one ever answered. I'm sorry about your parents."

Ana gathered the coffee-soaked towels as Marlon wiped his pants and mentally kicked himself for always saying the wrong thing.

"Sorry about that again. I've never seen those kids before, but I'll make sure my manager hears about them."

"It's fine. No big deal."

"It is a big deal, Marlon. Their behavior is so gross. Done with that?"

Marlon handed the towel to her, meeting her gaze and remembered thinking her laugh was the most beautiful he had ever heard and spent too much time looking for ways to be funny when they were in math club together.

"I'd love to hang out sometime and catch up. I have yet to run into anyone else from high school."

"Yeah, for sure. We should do that."

"Ana!"

Another woman, looking like the manager, was calling her from behind the counter. Marlon saw his class was starting soon, of course, with his paper still unfinished.

"I gotta go."

Ana collected the towels and hurried back to work, leaving Marlon to gather his coffee-stained papers and head out into the cold alone.

Chapter Two

THE CLOCK ABOVE THE science building rang midafternoon as Ana made her way through the throng of students towards the Student Union. It was next to the Red Gym, named that because of the red brick they had used to build it eighty years before, and looked out over a small lake. Still feeling new and a bit out of place on campus, Ana avoided the Union. The space was so open and there were so many nooks that she felt lost the one and only time she ever went.

Daniel asked her to go this time; their first public meeting. Since there was an unspoken rule against professor-student relationships since a few crazy cases of Title IX a few years back, Daniel was skittish about meeting outside of his office. During the summer, with so few students on campus, they had met at his house. Their relationship had started out platonic, but as they spent more and more time together, it felt as though they were the old married couple. Romance was lacking, but Ana always shrugged the thought away. She didn't have time to have a romantic relationship. She could do that after graduation.

Usually, they met at his office to go over her essays or research papers, but this week the university was painting the hallways and Daniel said the fumes were giving him a headache. Though working in such a public arena was not her favorite, she wasn't about to turn down a coffee. Or the chance to figure out the Student Union without feeling like a fool.

Ana gathered her hair to one side and ran her fingers through the chestnut curls as she looked around. Just like the first time, there were posters and tables and people everywhere. Her stomach growled at her for skipping lunch, but she hated spending money on food when she could have just brought something from home.

"Would you sign our petition?"

Ana turned to find a group of three young women wearing *No Human is Illegal* t-shirts.

"What's it for?"

"Ay, hija, what do you think? The Dreamers need citizenship and people need to stop treating us like second-rate Americans."

"Us?"

The girls gawked at her.

"I agree with you about the Dreamers, but do you feel like a second-class citizen? We're at a university, after all."

"It isn't just about us," the girl with her hair pulled into high pigtails said. "it's about fighting for our people."

"You are Mexican, right?"

"I'm Argentinian—"

"I'm sorry. I shouldn't have just assumed. But at any rate, it's like the same thing. They just don't like us for speaking Spanish and for being different."

"Who doesn't like us?"

"Americans."

"But I'm American. My parents waited for their papers before coming."

"The white ones."

Ana and the girl with bleached hair had spoken at the same moment, both realizing at the same time where the other one was coming from, and where the conversation might go.

"I don't disagree with the Dreamers becoming citizens. I've fought for that myself, but—."

The girls dropped back before she could even finish, muttering insults in Spanish as they looked for another person more cooperative. She watched them for a bit, wondering who was sponsoring them. She had never come to the university when she was an activist, unless it was to attend a rally. Interestingly, she had never considered recruiting students from the university. Clearly a missed opportunity.

The magnetic sway of being part of a movement still called to her. *Un movimiento.* That's what Roberto had called it. Though it never got bigger than his eighty thousand followers, who watched his videos and read his articles and a few dozen people in town, it had felt *big*. He even made a bit of money from his videos, and she had felt genuine pride for him, for herself and their *movimiento*.

They had done a lot of good things at first: encouraging people to go out and vote, informing people about their rights. And then they had marched. For her, it was at the marches where she shined, wearing her provocative shirts, and yelling until her throat hurt. They went to all political and social marches, as well as a few others she didn't quite understand the point of being part of, since they had little to do with Hispanic rights and immigration. At first, she said nothing because she didn't care. Protesting was protesting. Yelling was yelling. And there was so much that needed to change, and they were the only ones willing to do the work.

One day Roberto insisted they go to a rally that had nothing to do with being Hispanic or their politics, even though all the chatter on the internet said a rival group that always started fights was expected to show up. When she asked what the point was, Roberto ridiculed her in front of their entire group, saying she was chicken. He said she and anyone else who was too chicken could leave, and never come near him again. Ana didn't say any more.

That night was the first time she punched someone in the face. The high that came with the punch was better than anything she got from marijuana. And she wanted more. The next night, it was she who insisted they attend. She was ready to teach a few people a lesson. Her anger ran high, swirling with alcohol and marijuana and culminating in her getting arrested for body slamming a young white girl to the ground as she left the speech where the speaker was advocating for stopping the flow of immigrants. Ana's memory was fuzzy on whether the girl had done or said something directly to her, but assumed she hadn't. Simply attending that sort of speech was enough to warrant violence from her back then. She knew she had gone looking for a fight that night. She got that and then some.

Roberto bragged about her for weeks afterward. He came to see her in jail but said he wouldn't post bail because that would be like her admitting she did something wrong. Which she hadn't. His voice came to her through the visitor phone, sounding hallow and much farther away than the three feet and plexiglass that separated them.

Surrounded by the gray walls and watched by a bored policeman, Roberto's impassioned speech did little to lift her spirits. She was tired and hungry and wanted to go home, but she didn't argue. The connection between the phones made it hard to hear, and she had no energy to repeat herself. Roberto finished the conversation by reminding her they needed to go deeper for the revolution. Then he hung up.

Alone and devastated, Ana played out her week in jail as though in a fog. She sat and listened to the stories of the other women, careful to stay away from those who talked to themselves more than to another person. Most came and went with payment of bail, but not after describing how bail was ruining their lives. Seven days in, Ana met Louise, who helped her secure a bail bond. It took most of the money she had in her bank account, but at least she didn't have to borrow from her brother. And being out of jail meant she could work. Louise even set her up with a spot in the local shoe factory to work nights. It wasn't ideal, but it paid over minimum wage.

The world was brighter the day she posted bail. Louise picked her up for an interview at the factory, which turned into Ana's first day. While picking shoe boxes off the conveyer belt and sticking labels onto them, Ana had time to think about her experience. If they could change the bail and bail bonds system, she knew they could make some actual change. It wasn't sexy or as interesting as some other topics. They would need to write letters and see representatives and learn about the law, but it seemed like a better idea than attending every protest and getting arrested. She thought they should focus on one topic at a time to make a bigger impact.

She still believed that and wished she had the right words to tell her story to the girls, though she doubted they would be interested. Roberto had told her that bail and bail bonds were boring and not enough. Since she had just finished paying off her bond with the interest it had accrued, she vehemently disagreed. Not that he would listen to her now, any more than he did then.

A wave from across the large space caught her eye. Daniel was at the end of the line, waiting for their coffee.

"Find a table," he mouthed to her. She gave him a thumbs up, leaving her memories for another day, and sat at the next available table she found, full of stickers and a few dents.

Once seated, Ana watched Daniel as he waited for the coffees. He wasn't sexy, but he had a nice smile, straight teeth, and a full head of hair. And he was economically set. His life was on a projection that Ana envied, and she figured it wasn't a bad idea to hang out with the one person she knew who had what she wanted. Plus, he was helping her get better grades.

She could figure out where she wanted to take their relationship after she graduated.

Ana pulled out her paper and shifted her attention to it. Though the noise of the coffee shop made her fingers tingle with nervousness, she would just have to put up with it. Wanting to be in control came from her grandmother. Her mother used to throw up her hands and exclaim she was "como Abuela Merce". And just like Abuela Merce, Ana didn't take well to noise.

It was impossible to retain any of what she was reading when three different conversations were within earshot: the most interesting one being between three girls talking about the fraternity party over the weekend. Keeping her notes tilted towards her, she pretended to study while eavesdropping on their description of the party's events. Only a few years ago, she and Roberto used to attend a party every weekend. If there wasn't one to attend, they would throw one themselves. Talking to people she didn't know and dancing all night had been easy with a little alcohol involved. Life had seemed perfect. Fun. Casual. Young.

Ana sighed and straightened her spine, refocusing on the study materials she had to read. A lot of time had passed since she had done any of those things. And anyway, looking back now, all she saw was time wasted.

Just as she reached for her phone, Daniel arrived with the over-sized mugs of coffee. He let out a deep sigh and shook his head in relief and frustration. Ana snorted at the absurdity that neither of them wanted to be here. Daniel said he came to the Union to stay in touch with the students. He claimed going to places students frequented helped him stay young. Going to the Union not only didn't connect him with the students, but it highlighted how old he was in comparison. Ana wasn't about to say that, though.

"It would have been quicker where I work," she said, deliberately antagonizing him as she enthusiastically dumped her sugar packet into the large mug and twirled the contents with her spoon.

He narrowed his eyes, his lips curling in disgust as he watched her spoon turn in the mug. Not once had he ever stuck a spoon into his coffee anywhere except his own home and the restaurants he deemed safe. According to him, college students didn't know how to clean utensils accurately, and college students ran all the coffee shops near campus.

Daniel dumped a tiny packet of cream into his mug and stared. The milk swirled lazily down the middle, but never combined with the coffee. He slumped back in his chair for a moment, then changed his mind as though remembering his headache. It was why they were meeting for coffee in the first place, after all. The two of them. In public. Daniel pulled out a clean tissue from his pocket, wiped the rim of his mug and finally took a sip.

"Aren't you having sugar with your coffee?" she teased.

Daniel shook his head with a sigh.

"There's a reason for health inspectors."

"Maybe. But I don't trust a compartment full of spoons. I wish they would hand them out from behind the counter."

"If it's that important to you, why don't you order a cappuccino with vanilla flavoring or something? That way, you won't have to add sugar."

"I don't like those syrups in my coffee," he replied, wincing as though the suggestion hurt him.

"Well, use your fingers then."

Daniel looked down at his mug, a thoughtful expression on his face, as though he was contemplating her idea. She couldn't help chuckling, the sound cracking his lips into a small smile.

"Being caught by one of my colleagues with my fingers in my coffee like a two-year-old. Right. Not what I was looking for," he said, making a face as she made an exaggerated groan of pleasure to tease him further. "Glad you're enjoying this."

"It isn't time to go yet," she told him as he looked at his wristwatch. "And you said you'd look over my paper."

"I know, I know. How's your coffee?"

"Wonderful. Thank you," she slurred over the rim of the mug.

Daniel chewed on his cuticles as he surveyed the cafe. His eyes swept rhythmically from one side to the other to catch anyone who might be watching and getting the wrong idea of what they were doing sitting together.

"Look, there's Professor Knight with a student. No one has the wrong idea about them, and I'm sure no one cares about us. Drink your coffee and relax."

Daniel looked in the direction that Ana was, relief fluttering across his face

"Why don't I look over your essay so that we look busy?"

That was all it took for the worry to slam back into her chest. She handed over the essay and tried not to watch as Daniel thumbed through the first pages, marking her mistakes with a bright red marker as he went, but she couldn't help looking from the corner of her eye. The more he marked on her paper, the faster her pen tapped against the table. Cold eyes greeted hers, then glared at the pen. Ana dropped it before trying to read again.

With a pleased grunt, Daniel returned to editing her paper. Every so often, Ana heard him sigh as he scribbled in red ink. After spending the summer correcting her papers and helping her with writing exercises, she was better, but according to Daniel, she still had a long way to go. Every time she mentioned going on for her master's, he smiled a strange, almost mocking smile before using flowery prose to encourage her to just finish her bachelor's degree.

"Ana! Change of venue?" a voice exclaimed over the noise. Several people turned to look towards them. Daniel's pale skin turned red. From embarrassment or anger, Ana wasn't certain which.

She looked up to see Marlon for the second time in one day.

"Hello, Marlon," Ana said, remembering that he had never been known as a smooth talker in high school. "You cut your hair."

Her old math club friend sat down with a thud, knocking the table and making the contents of her coffee jump dangerously close to the rim of the mug.

"Yeah, I'd been meaning to for a while," he replied, running his fingers through his inch-long hair that flopped haphazardly to one side. "Do you like it?"

"Well, I recognize you again," she replied with a smile.

The three of them sat in silence for a moment. Daniel sat as though awe struck, not quite believing someone else was sitting with them. As Ana struggled to find something to talk about between the three of them, Marlon leaned in with his hand stretched out to Daniel.

"This is a nice way to have a tutorial," Marlon said. "Hi, I'm Marlon."

Ana twisted her box of cigarettes between her fingers as Daniel shook Marlon's hand, muttering his name.

"My professors always did it in their offices. Tutoring, I mean."

Daniel smiled, his nose scrunching at the cigarettes. He tapped his index hard against the table twice, then jerked his head. Ana raised her brows at him but obeyed and put the cigarettes away.

"Well, I find it less intimidating this way," Daniel said. His smile smoothed itself out with the cigarettes gone.

"It's nice," Marlon replied. "What classes do you teach?"

"I'm a literature professor. What do you do?"

"I'm finishing my law degree here with an emphasis on dispute resolution. I have my undergraduate in journalism and pre-law. I'm an assistant to Professor Tuden on Thursday's."

Daniel grunted a curt reply. "I don't know that name."

"Guess it doesn't surprise me. The law school is way over that way. It's been a while since I've done any literature class."

"I'm sure you didn't need help like Ana here when you had one. At least, I hope someone studying to be a lawyer doesn't write a paper like a high school student."

The callous comment drew Ana's body away from the table. Perhaps he had said it out of nervousness. Whenever he thought someone suspected they were dating, he was always curt, sometimes mean. Still, with his quiet demeanor and typically low-key personality, his malice took her by surprise. Swallowing back her pride, she noticed Marlon's eyes widening, but he said nothing. Silence sat in the middle of them for a few beats. The only one that didn't seem to think anything was wrong with what he had said was Daniel, who drank his coffee with a wince and looked around the room, as though releasing a snarky comment allowed him to settle in better.

"Would you like more coffee?" Marlon tapped Ana lightly on the hand with his index finger, pulling her out of herself and back to the table. "How about you, professor? I'll get us some."

"No, that isn't necessary," Daniel said, making a face at his unsweetened drink.

"I'd love one," she replied at the same time.

Daniel returned to marking up her paper while they waited for Marlon to return. She desperately wanted to step out for a smoke but didn't move. Come New Year's Day, she was quitting all of it for good. The judgement and looks from people made the habit very uncomfortable.

"Where did you study your undergrad?" Daniel asked once Marlon came back. "You should capitalize this word, Ana."

"San Diego State University," Marlon replied absently. Ana looked up to see him focused on her paper, still under Daniel's hand.

"You said you were focusing on dispute resolution?"

Marlon nodded. "Yes."

"But you already went through law school?"

"Pre-law," was the absent-minded answer before Marlon changed the subject entirely. "There is no reason to take out that entire paragraph. In fact, that's the basis of your argument. While I don't agree with the point of view, if you take out those five sentences the paper would become boring."

Irritation flared in Daniel's eyes. She knew he tended to correct her papers to coincide with his opinions on each subject, but since she always received a good grade for them, Ana always overlooked the breech of manners. In front of her, Marlon and Daniel argued politely about their differences of opinion, but it was impossible not to notice how Daniel's voice turned icy when she took a pen out of her bag and started noting down some of Marlon's points. She kept her eyes on the paper to keep from making contact with him.

"But this is an opinion paper, isn't it?"

Ana looked at Daniel, who tilted his head and exaggerated bringing his watch up to look at.

"I have a class I need to prepare for. Ana, will I see you later?"

"Probably," she said, standing as well. "I have to go to class, too. It was good to see you again, Marlon."

"It was good to see you, Ana. I hope we run into each other again."

Ana wanted very much to run into him again, though she avoided answering the suggestion with nervous laughter.

Before she could form an appropriate reply, Daniel ushered her out the door, before leaving her to walk to her class across campus alone.

Chapter Three

Ana flashed her student identity card to the guard inside the library, keeping her head down. The person on duty only ever looked for the blue university symbol and never at the picture, but her heart still fluttered each time she entered. If ever someone were to ask her to justify the difference in the eye and hair color, she just knew she would freeze up. The fear of that confrontation kept her from daring to check books out until she found the self-check-out at the end of the hall. Still, walking past the bored students at the counter always made her heart beat a little faster. And anyway, she preferred to study at the library, where it was quiet, and she didn't feel in the way of her brother and his family life. She needed complete silence to concentrate, especially for her real estate law class and microeconomics, two classes she would be happy if she simply passed. At home, she felt obligated to hang out with Javier and Elena and catch up on their lives.

At any rate, she often told herself that after three semesters sequestered in the back of the library, the space was more like home than the house she slept in with her brother- and sister-in-law. Ana breathed in the tangy smell of decaying paper. If intelligence and knowledge had a smell, it would be that of old paper.

With her notebooks spread across her usual table, Ana walked to the other end to find the grammar book Daniel has suggested. She could have sat at a computer, but there was so little space. She supposed she was old-fashioned, in some sense, still preferring a book. Besides, the internet was too easy a distraction, and she didn't have time for distractions right now.

Not when she was finally on track, moving forward in her life into a successful future. Soon she would have a career rather than serving coffee or working at a factory. A tingle of gratitude rose within at the thought. The smell of the books meant she was going somewhere.

Not being able to pay the tuition was the main reason for her not going to college right away, though once she and Roberto started their *movimiento*, she had given up completely on the idea of ever going. The result was that she was one of the oldest students in her classes, though she wasn't the oldest at school. That honor was reserved for the seventy-year-old that made the town's paper's as being the university's oldest undergraduate student ever. He was in her microeconomics class and was killing it. She tried to ask him to explain something to her one day but ended up leaving more confused than before he started talking. He had learned everything as an entrepreneur his whole life, but he wasn't a teacher.

Ana sighed in admiration. Owning her own business seemed like an impossible dream. The idea of being her own boss was appealing, but she couldn't come up with an inventive business idea, try as she might. Then there was the fact that she was terribly awkward as a salesperson, which seemed to be a necessary skill in the business world. Despite all of that, she dreamed of being on the cover of Success Magazine one day. Or perhaps Forbes. Thirty under thirty probably wasn't going to happen. Ana smiled to herself. At this point, she'd be happy to get out of her brother's house and into her own, not owing anything to anyone.

Grabbing her real estate law book from behind the potted plant, her student badge fell. Green eyes stared up at her from the floor, piercing her daydreams with sharp guilt.

Fate arranged the night she and Ana-Maria met. Anyone could dispute her sentiment, of course, but she was convinced. Everything lined up too neatly to be just a coincidence. First, there was her manager's mistake that forced her to work the evening shift instead of her morning shift, which forced her to take the 254-bus home whose stop was on the opposite side of the plaza than her usual bus stop. Then there was the wind that blew the snow hard, which forced her to tuck her chin into her coat and consequently look down as she walked.

Guilt zipped through her chest again as she relived tripping over Ana-Maria passed out in the snow that night, but Ana clamped down on it quickly. She deserved to be at this university. It was something she had always wanted. Ana-Maria died too young, but she had done everything she could to help her. Ana hadn't given her the drugs. And the doctor had warned Ana-Maria not to try them again.

At least in some way Ana-Maria's memory was living on since Ana was using her scholarship and place. That's what Ellen said when she suggested the idea. It was more than most overdose victims got.

She hadn't dragged Ana-Maria out of the snow, thinking she'd get her scholarship as a prize. She had done it because it was the right thing to do. After recovering from her initial fright from finding her lying face up in the snow, Ana had dragged her into the first bar she saw.

The bouncer was nice enough to let her in. Ana-Maria had woken up enough in the struggle to stumble inside, sitting herself down on a bench in the entryway. When the manager came in screaming that they both leave, Ana was in the middle of trying to work out with the bouncer what to do next. They both tried to explain that neither of them knew the girl, but the manager wouldn't listen. With a taxi at the ready for the bar, Ana found herself left in charge of taking the half-unconscious girl home. A task that had changed her whole life.

Ana shook the memory out of her head. She moved past one aisle and walked into another. It seemed impossible that finding that girl had gotten her into this library with all expenses paid. It was a strange string of events that she marveled at still.

"No!" The last book she needed wasn't there, which meant she would either have to pay for it or do the work later.

"What's the matter?" The voice boomed from the other side of the aisle. Several people shifted in their chairs at the disturbance. Ana dropped her shoulders to peek through the books, though she knew who it was even before her eyes looked straight into the black pools of Marlon's pupils. She remembered looking into them in math class a few times, soaking up his attention.

"I need a book that isn't here," she whispered, signaling him to join her at the end of the aisle.

"What book were you looking for?" he asked, this time his voice lowered to a murmur which gave it a certain mid-night DJ quality, bringing back memories of sitting in math club with Marlon's breath brushing across her cheek as he gave her instructions. Memories she had forgotten long ago; memories that made her blush. The same shudder that flowed down her spine just a minute before used to run down her every time she felt his presence near.

She cleared her throat to concentrate on the present. "A Spanish book. I'm finishing my language credits."

"I can't help you with that. If I remember correctly, you were quite good at speaking Spanish back in high school."

She shrugged. "That's why I didn't want to buy this book, but I guess I'll have to."

"I tried not buying my books for exactly half a semester, but I could never find the things I needed. It was so frustrating and law professors have very limited patience on excuses."

Ana laughed.

"I found a way to make sure that all the books I need are always here." Ana wiggled the books she had in the air. "I hide them so that no one can find them. The real problem is when they assign a book that isn't on the syllabus, which is what happened today. I might just have to splurge and buy the book. The aide assured us it wasn't that expensive."

Marlon's eyes glowed as he laughed.

"Don't you have grants that help pay for your books?"

"Umm, no. Not enough anyway." All she had, in reality, was Ana-Maria's name. Ana-Maria's scholarship paid her tuition, but she was in charge of the rest, including books. If she could get through one more year without having to give anyone the specifics of her financial situation or position at the university, she could graduate and move on before anyone found out anything.

"I thought you would have found some scholarships." Marlon stood still, his word slowly fading as they both grasped at something to say. Ana chose to ignore his last statement.

"Are you planning to stay here and study?"

"At the university? Yeah. I have a scholarship."

Ana shook her head. "I meant at this moment in the library. Are you planning on studying right now?"

Marlon looked down at the books in his hands, but shook his head.

"No, I was going to go to a coffee shop. I've been here for three hours already, and the heat is making me want to sleep more than study. I thought colleges kept libraries cold to keep the students awake. They were always freezing in California."

"It's the middle of winter in Michigan. Every place cranks the heat beyond what the norm should be," Ana laughed. "Don't you remember? I usually sit over there by the window where it's a little cooler."

Ana's cell phone buzzed, splintering the library's silence. A sharp hushing noise came at her from across the room.

"I'm sorry," she said, running to the table to shut off her phone. "Were you going to say something, Marlon?"

"Oh, no, I mean, I was just thinking that, if you wanted, if you needed any help with essays or something, I could help you. I mean, if you have time."

"That's nice of you," she answered slowly, trying to concentrate on Marlon and the text screaming at her from her phone screen. All capital letters usually meant frustration and annoyance, not excitement, from Daniel. Apparently, he had invited her for dinner and she hadn't answered. "I actually have to leave. I, um, forgot about something. Maybe we can meet up again on Friday. I'll probably come here after work to see if that book came back."

"Yeah, sure. No problem. What time will you be here?"

"Around five o'clock, I guess. And I'll probably stick around to study a bit and use the computer. See you then?"

"Yeah, see you then."

Ana watched him go as she tried to shove her books into her bag. His shoulders seemed broader than they had been in high school. In her mind's eye, Marlon Jones had the slight build of a teenager, was gangly and awkward. This Marlon was not only all grown up but filled out. She wasn't one to swoon. Since Roberto, she had rejected the very idea of swooning, relegating it to romance novels. Skipping lunch had her feeling light-headed, that's all. It had nothing to do with the boy she used to have a crush on in high school coming back to town a full-grown man, looking like a Greek god.

Rushing out of the library, an icy dread oozed over her body. She stopped suddenly in her tracks, almost running into the bored young man at the reference counter. Her phone buzzed again, but she brushed it aside. It wasn't Daniel that had her worried. It was something else.

She glanced back at where Marlon had once been. Something about Marlon.

Ana tried hard to place what was causing her body to panic, not noticing she was giving her back to the bored working student behind the check-out counter.

"Ready?"

"Uh, sure," Ana replied, placing her books down and handing over her id card, still looking back at where she had just come from. If she could just place the moment that the dread had washed over her, maybe she could place her finger on it.

"All set," the girl with bleach blond hair replied, her gum cracking as she picked up her phone again.

Ana stared dumbfounded at the id card she had handed over without thinking and then at the books.

Ana-Maria. That was the problem.

Ana quickly gathered her books up, keeping her brown eyes down, even though it was obvious the girl at check-out was much more interested in scrolling her social media than anything else.

Finally, out in the frosty night air, Ana gulped in oxygen while trying to smooth out her panicked thoughts. Marlon knew her as Ana, not Ana-Maria, but technically, she was at the university as Ana-Maria. If Marlon ever pointed out to someone at the university that she was plain Ana Sanz and not Ana-Maria Lopez, she could lose everything.

This shouldn't be happening. This shouldn't have been a problem. She could lose her scholarship. Her dreams.

Down the road, a half-empty bus trudged its way towards the bus stop. Ana clutched her bag and ran on tiptoes through the newly landed snow, jumping onto the bus just in time. She would have to leave her worries for another day. Or just hope nothing ever came of them. She was so close to graduating. She only needed one more year.

Chapter Four

Outside the front window, the world was a giant snow globe. It was the perfect snowfall; slow, steady, virtually silent. The small flecks that fell from the heavens were sturdy enough not to melt instantly when they touched the snow already on the ground, though Daniel hoped they wouldn't accumulate too much and ruin his morning jog. He hated running on the treadmill at the gym, which is where he went when the ground became too slippery or too soggy. He grimaced at the glaring light his neighbors set up to the left to capture their annual nativity scene. Only one week had passed since Thanksgiving. What a shame people still believed in a baby being special enough to make plastic figures as replicas. Such an archaic belief system belonged in the Middle Ages, when people only had their superstitions to give them a semblance of hope. In the twenty-first century, humans should have evolved enough intelligence to have a grasp on the earth and its system without needing a god. Of course, those same people with the plastic nativity probably didn't even believe in climate change or recycling. It almost convinced him to vote for outlawing freedom of religion. Or having a required intelligence test before being allowed to vote.

His stomach growled louder than before. The irritation already built up by his fanatical neighbors only increased with the signs of his hunger. Almost an hour had passed since Ana answered she was coming. Contrary to his normally laid-back manners, he was watching for her through the window. Reserving his right to growl at the empty street, Daniel swiped his phone from the charging depot near the door, but the screen was blank. No messages. It was good to know he was coming out on top of the argument this time. Strictly speaking, he had come out on top last week when he pointed out it was impolite to be twenty minutes late to a dinner appointment.

"I sent you a message," she had said in an agitated, mocking tone. "Don't you ever check your phone?"

Of course, he found the message when he picked up the phone, but he wasn't ready to give in. He reminded her he never looked at his phone after seven o'clock. It was a steadfast rule of his and she knew it, and yet her face turned a strange shade of red after that comment. Just when he thought she was going to screech like a hyena, he apologized, and she calmed down. In his experience, apologizing was what a woman actually wanted in a fight, because it made them feel they were right. To him, it didn't mean he was wrong. He hadn't changed his thoughts about being late, nor had he changed his rule about not checking his phone. In reality, he was apologizing for the escalation of the conversation, not for the subject of the fight.

It seemed he would have to confront her on this again. Ana's lack of time management made him worry, which was not good for his health and reminded him of his mother, which was also not good for his health. With each passing minute, his nerves tightened and tingled.

Another ten minutes passed before Ana finally came into view, walking down the sidewalk towards his house. By that time, his pride had vanished, as well as his anger. The only thing left was his bitten-down fingernails. As soon as he saw her red hat under the streetlight, Daniel jumped away from the window and sat on the couch. He hoped to pretend that he hadn't been watching, but quickly abandoned the idea when he realized he had left the beige curtains open.

"Hi," he said, opening the door before she could knock. "I thought you'd be rushing over when I texted you I was cooking."

"I'm sorry. I tried to hurry, but I was at the library talking to Marlon, that guy that you met today. It just took me a little longer to gather my things."

"Did you walk the entire way?"

"No." She rubbed the cold from her face, then rubbed her hands together. Daniel stood at the ready to take her boots to the garage when she finally took them off. "But I caught the first bus, which leaves me on Oak Street. I walked from there."

"It's probably late enough to call an Uber." Her choice of transportation was another subject of disagreement between them. He didn't know why he had brought it up when she had already apologized for being late. Ana only smiled at him, refusing to take the bait and fight.

"Are you hungry?" he asked as they entered the living room.

"Famished."

He frowned at her as she sat down on the couch and placed her backpack next to her.

"Ana."

Annoyance flittered across her face, but she controlled it quickly, smoothing her brow out and smiling again as she took the snow-covered bag off the couch and placed it on the floor. Daniel swallowed, disappointed in himself. That terrible counselor after his marriage dissolved told him that his tendency to control everything was partly responsible for his ex-wife choosing to divorce him. He had vowed he would change, vowed he wouldn't be so fanatical about where things were put or not put. When it was just him, he could see the reasoning behind changing, but tested in real life, he almost always failed. Hot yoga and writing in his Acceptance and Tranquility Journal, as he called it, helped calm him and recenter on trying to change again, two things he hadn't done in a while. He made mental notes to do at least one in the morning.

"What did you make?"

"Hmm? Oh. Yes, mushroom stuffed chicken breasts, wild rice, and broccoli," he said, steering her elbow towards the kitchen. "It's a new recipe that I've wanted to try for weeks. I hope you like it."

"It smells amazing."

Daniel held his breath as she leaned in and moaned in delight at the smell that wafted up from the opened oven. Gripping the pan firmly, Daniel turned, only to find such a look of ecstasy on her face that he instantly felt ill.

"It looks like you outdid yourself tonight."

Another man would have dropped the pan, pulled her close and kiss her passionately. Perhaps feed her with his fingers after making love to her. After all, food was a complement to passion. But as much as he often wished he were like a main character in a historical romance novel, he wasn't. Trying to be spontaneous and romantic had always failed him. He tried a few times with his ex-wife, only to end up either startling her or making her laugh. A man's ego could only take so many beatings. It took effort to accept the fact that he was not a great Casanova or James Bond type. After all, admitting that called for settling into a love life that was comfortable and soothing rather than tumultuous and exhilarating. But accepting oneself was a vital part of life, according to his tranquility coach. And he would conquer that lesson.

Besides, trying to become passionate now would only be more awkward and feeble than a decade ago with his ex-wife. They had been each other's first and along with that came room to forgive awkwardness. Trying to be passionate with a younger woman would probably end with her laughing in his face, or worse yet, physically harming his lower back. Assuming she was much more experienced than him is what scared him. Everything he heard throughout the university halls convinced him that every young woman these days was more experienced sexually in their two decades of life than he was in his three and a half. Still, someday, he hoped to change his and Ana's platonic relationship. Somehow.

"What would you like to do tonight?" Ana took the e-cigarette out of her back pocket before sitting down, flipping it over her fingers as they sat.

"Homework. I have to re-write that essay. I really want an A on it."

"Right. Well, that's fine. I can grade those papers I've had for a week. We can go into the living room after dinner and work. That way, if you need help, I'll be right next to you. Doesn't that sound nicer than the library?"

His eyes landed on her hands, which were busy flipping her e-cigarette over and over.

"Ana—."

"I wasn't going to smoke; I was just fidgeting."

Daniel kissed her forehead as he placed the plates down. "Good girl."

Ana didn't bother to suppress her sigh, but Daniel ignored it. With her youth, he must grant grace.

The plates finally served; Ana dug straight into the dish.

"This is delicious. You should teach me how to cook someday. We could do it some Saturday when neither of us is very busy; maybe during the summer."

He closed his eyes, reveling in the idea of being with her during the summer. The comment was enough to eliminate his complaint that she hadn't waited for him before eating.

"You don't know how to cook? I thought cooking was a big thing for Hispanic families."

Ana's fork paused for a moment, but she quickly squared her shoulders back and continued eating. Daniel sipped his wine. Just recently, he had been told by another student that it was impolite to bring up the heritage of others, so he wondered if that was the issue. But then also Ana had made it clear that she disliked talking about her family from the beginning, especially her dead parents. Perhaps he had committed a double hitter, then. When she answered him, he accepted it as a peace offering towards him.

"Yes, well, my mama taught me some things, though I don't remember them very well," Ana said. "When I was younger, I never wanted to learn much about the kitchen. It seemed so boring to me. I wanted to be with my brother and my father at the shop. I loved the smell and the beautiful furniture that came out of irregular pieces of wood. But whether or not I liked it, helping mama in the kitchen was considered my job and helping papa was my brother's job. Since I showed such disinterest in everything, I usually ended up either messing up the recipe, catching something on fire or hurting myself. We had a very old stove when I was little in Argentina, and it wasn't much better when we moved here. Even with an electric oven, I tended to burn myself. As a result, I know how to peel every kind of vegetable, especially potatoes, and how to chop, though that was something they allowed me to do later on after I learned to pay attention to what I was chopping. In the summer, I learned how to skin fish when Javier and papa would come back from their weekend fishing at the lake. That was fun, though. That I liked."

"Ana," Daniel said, interrupting her stare into the past.

"Yes?"

"Are you going to eat? Everything on your plate's getting cold. Don't you like it?"

She tapped her wine glass lightly against his in answer to his question and smiled. He had already finished his plate while it was warm, so he observed her as she caught up. Though elegant was not a word he would use to describe Ana, there was something delicate in the way that she ate. It was what consoled him when he dared to think about a future with her. If he ever ended up introducing her to his friends, he would do it during a dinner. That way, they would see that though she wasn't as cultured as they were, she knew how to eat like a lady. He knew that had to count for something on the part of her parents even if they had never taught her about opera, classical music, or literature.

"What? Why are you looking at me like that?"

"No reason," he replied, moving his eyes up from her breasts to her lips. "I was just noticing that you have a beautiful mouth."

Words never failed him, even if action did. That was one benefit of having read too many Jane Austen novels where the young woman falls in love with the sensible and established good guy.

Ana took her last sip of wine. Flattery caused her to blush.

"Thank you."

His chest swelled at the sight of her glowing cheeks, reminding him of his ex-wife, Gloria, and the day that he dared to let her know she looked beautiful in her sundress. Nothing before ever caused him to feel so powerful as that first time his words triggered her to blush and stutter back a reply. In a matter of days, the two of them were lying naked in bed talking about philosophy and literature instead of hanging out as friends on the campus lawn. Things were easier back then, with Gloria. Being young and lustful had filled in for his lack of confidence.

Remembering his time with Gloria sent a shiver of invigorating power through him. Before he had time to think about what he was doing, he rested his hand lightly on Ana's thigh and leaned his body closer.

Ana turned at his touch. Their bodies were now close enough that their breath mixed in the air between them. It was the perfect moment to draw her close to him, to kiss her, to let her know he had a desire for their relationship to take on a physical nature, but as quickly as that power tingled through his body, it abandoned him.

Ana was beautiful, young, and vibrant, everything that his wife used to be. There was no reason for him to not be able to make love to her. He wanted to; he knew that much. He even dreamed about it. But when she was physically near him, he couldn't drum up enough... desire. Once he tried picturing Gloria to see if he could power through, but the guilt of thinking about one woman while holding another inhibited him from going on. There had to be a way to eradicate those feelings about Gloria, but he still hadn't found it.

He pulled away, abruptly picking up the dishes.

"You need to finish eating," he said. "Are you going to stay the night?"

"Would you mind if I did? The last bus leaves pretty soon and I really would like to get some work done on that essay," she said, stepping up behind him with the glasses. The heat of her breath sent a shiver down his back, urging him to try again. Perhaps this time his body wouldn't fail him, but reason whispered the opposite and won again.

"Of course, I don't mind. The guest room is all made up for you."

"Perfect," Ana said, reaching for her backpack.

For the last fifteen years, Daniel had woken up at five-thirty in the morning. He started the routine back in college while living in a house that was quiet only in the mornings. His roommates were night people, partying all night, and sleeping very late in the morning. Once he finished his eight years at the university with the same routine, there was no option to change it. As a young professor, Daniel spent his early morning hours jogging and reading the newspaper. And perfecting coffee brewing in his steel French press.

While they were dating, Gloria used to make fun of his steadfast commitment to this routine. Though secretly he dreamed of her joining him once they were married, he thought it would be better to bring up the topic after the ceremony. A taste of his perfect French press coffee and a promise from a blushing bride was his plan, but that hadn't worked. A few months later, the perfect time came when she asked him what he wanted for his birthday. Again, she refused to commit to waking up early, but after a week of insisting it was what he wanted, she finally agreed.

The first week was painful. He'd never seen anyone so glum and irritable than Gloria before six in the morning. She had sat at the table with her coffee mug in her hands, staring out the window in silence. Every time he tried to speak, she snapped at him and complained about how tired she was. The third week, her mood was a little better, but she still threatened to sleep until noon every day once her promise was completed. By the end of the month, she was singing in the shower and waking up five minutes before the alarm went off. His plan had worked.

For four years, they woke up at five-thirty every morning. It was the best time of the day since there were many days in which prior commitments kept them from seeing each other until late at night.

It wasn't until she had suddenly become pregnant that his dream fell apart.

Originally, they decided they were going to wait a while before having kids, but nature had a different plan. Although she complained about being exhausted, she didn't give up on him and their mornings for the first few weeks. But around the tenth week of her pregnancy, a severe case of morning sickness kept her in bed until right before she had to be at work.

The morning he had his coffee alone for the first time in four years, it was raining, which had perfectly aligned with his mood. In a fit of frustration, he had donned his running shoes and dove straight into the pouring rain. He understood the theory of a pregnant woman needing more sleep, even so, he couldn't help feeling deserted. The only consolation was the assumption that babies were normally early risers, which meant all three of them would soon be back into the routine.

Then came the day that she entered his office sobbing that the university had cut her job due to budget cuts in the department. Secretly, the news thrilled him. Since she wasn't one who often let him take care of her, he saw this as his opportunity to do just that. Plus, he thought she would most likely go back to their morning routine to spend more time with him.

A miscarriage a few weeks later shattered everything. The world stopped at those words. His heart ballooned in his chest, restricting his breathing. When the baby was an unseen blip on Gloria's smooth belly, he hadn't thought much about what being a father would be like, putting all of that off until the birth. He assumed he would step into the role as though it were as easy as turning a page in a book.

The instant the doctor took away the possibility of a birth, though, he realized just how much he had been looking forward to being a dad. It was as though someone had taken an electric beater to his insides. While the doctor droned on about how normal it was and that they could try again soon, he tried to restrain himself from crying. Gloria, on the other hand, seemed fine. He tried to talk to her about it, but she waved him away, saying that it was nature making better decisions for them and quoting the doctor that it happened all the time.

Thus began more months of him waking up alone, but not because she slept late. Instead, Gloria took to rising earlier than him and setting off for two-hour-long runs through the city. Then, about a year after the miscarriage, Gloria found another job, which required she spend half of her time in Colorado. Her excitement convinced him it was something she needed, so he didn't protest even once. She hadn't asked for his consent and to oppose her would give the appearance that he didn't support her.

A colleague, one he didn't particularly like, clapped him on the back and joked that it was the start to his divorce. Daniel had never been so angry in his life. Had they not been in the university teacher's lounge, surrounded by other professors who gave him pitiful looks, he might have punched him in the nose. When Gloria started making up excuses not to come home on the weekends, the truth of his colleague's words hit him like a brick.

For four months, she traveled every week. Then she skipped coming home some weekends. By the seventh month, she was staying in Colorado for three to four weeks at a time. When the legal separation papers arrived at the year mark, he didn't even blink twice. The reasons that came to him through her letter were surprising. Apparently, what he thought of as a comfortable life had become dull and cramped to her. She needed adventure suddenly. And he was not adventurous. The worst was that the colleague he hated didn't even gloat when Daniel announced it at work. As though that guy had the right to take some higher ground.

Daniel stared at his reflection. Every time he allowed his thoughts to go back to that year, his lungs became heavy, and oxygen deprived. Taking air deep into the bottom of his lungs, Daniel absently stroked his freshly shaved chin as though the pain could somehow be rubbed away. Remembering Gloria drained him of energy, but for some aggravating reason, it also awoke desire within him. He only needed to think about Gloria, and he was ready, but when he had the opportunity to hold Ana close, his body failed him.

Processing the situation exhausted him and, for the first time in years, he considered going back to bed. He had pushed his run harder that morning, but that was no excuse. Daniel tapped his razor hard against the old porcelain sink, giving himself a shake of his own head. He wasn't about to throw away seventeen years of routine because of his wife's ghost.

Having learned from his mistakes with Gloria, he negotiated early on to Ana: if he waited to wake her until after his run and shower, she would get up without any complaints. Usually, he was already on his second cup of coffee before she made it downstairs, but he was willing to compromise a little if it meant not pushing her away.

"Did you sleep well?" He had slowly entered the guest room after hearing a groggy answer for him to come in. If they weren't physically together, he didn't think it fair to have to share his bed and worry about whether he snored or drooled or hogged the covers. Those were worries that came in exchange for sex. Which was why she slept in the guest room, he reminded himself every morning. Also, the way he convinced her to stay the night the first time was by offering the guest room.

"I slept very well, thank you." She was already standing, her oversized sweatshirt hiding her body, her eyes puffy from sleep.

"I had your wool skirt and that red sweater cleaned for you. They're hanging on the back of the door." Daniel smiled, pleased at the surprised look on her face. Before he could think himself out of it, Daniel forced himself to kiss the tip of her nose, holding his breath against her morning breath. "I'll see you downstairs."

Chapter Five

TURNING ONTO HIGH OAK Street, Ana pulled her chin out of her scarf to see the houses. The brick walls, steps up to the front doors, the garages at the back, the iron fences, all contributed to the old-fashioned feel of the neighborhood. Each house had a unique architecture except for the block at the end that were all colonial style. All were taken care of, unlike her neighborhood, where parents worked too many hours and had too little extra money to paint the trim or scrape off the moss growing on the roof. This had been the neighborhood of professors and middle management fifty years ago. Upper-middle class.

In the middle of High Oak Street, stood a brick house with a decorative peaked roof over the front door. The windows were large, looking into the living room and a formal dining room, divided into twelve rectangles each. The house was beautiful, but lonely.

Ellen Lopez, an old lady born in Cincinnati, got her last name from marrying a man from Mexico City. Ellen compared herself once to Lucy Ricardo, which Ana had to look up to understand what she meant. Though Ana never met Ellen's husband, the vision she had of him was of Ricky from the '*I Love Lucy Show*'.

The doorbell echoed through the heavy door, audible outside where Ana waited on the cold front steps. Almost a year ago, she had shown up here in the dead of night with Ana-Maria. It had taken three rings of the doorbell for a light to turn on that night.

Ana pressed the doorbell one more time. Some things stayed the same no matter what time of day it was. After a moment of silence, Ellen's heels echoed down the hallway as she made her way to the door. A few days before Thanksgiving, she noticed Ellen's steps falling heavier and slower. Ellen had offered her a job cleaning her house once a week to help Ana financially since she couldn't work the shoe factory hours while attending school. Slowly, though, she had started coming more often. Not for extra pay, but because she liked Ellen and felt she owed Ellen a little more than just stopping by once a week to dust. The older woman needed human contact, something Ana also craved after the last few years.

After what seemed like an eternity in the bitter cold, the front door burst open. Ellen stood tall at the door; her thin body framed by her dark house. The desolate picture made Ana hesitate on the steps for a moment.

"What's the matter?" Ellen demanded. "It's freezing out there! Aren't you coming in?"

"Nothing's the matter." Ana picked up her feet which were strapped into her heavy snow boots and stepped inside. She had to wait as Ellen shuffled backwards into the formal entryway before she could sit on the polished wood bench to take off her winter things. "How are you today?"

Ellen either ignored the question or didn't hear it. She was already halfway to the living room again. There she settled onto an antique sofa covered with an old patch blanket which smelled slightly of mothballs and a book with her glasses marking the last page she read.

"I was trying to read a bit, hoping to get a nap in. I almost don't sleep at all at night now. Too many noises," the older woman said with a sigh.

Ellen no longer had a living relative. Everyone she loved now lived on glossy paper inside a frame. Ana glanced at the piano where

Ellen's family now lived, before placing the blanket over Ellen and propping a pillow behind her back.

"Could you sing to me while you dust, dear? Maybe that will help me sleep."

Ana stood speechless for a moment.

"Well? You sing all the time while you work but just low enough so that I can't enjoy it. I'm just asking that you sing a little louder."

"Really? I assumed you wouldn't want to hear me."

"You have a nice voice," said Ellen with her eyes closed. "I just wish I could hear what the words are."

"Do you understand Spanish? All the songs are in Spanish."

"I don't mind what language they're in. It's better than what's on the radio these days."

Ana laughed. She could almost hear her abuela or even her own mother saying the same thing if they were alive. Picking up the duster, Ana allowed herself to plunge into the memories of her abuela, the one who taught her most of the songs she liked to sing.

The smell of baby powder and boiled potatoes filled her nostrils as she thought about the small woman with olive skin. Wrinkles covered every inch of her face, a sign she had not only lived by the sun but had worked under its rays all her life. Ana could see her eyes, darker than a moonless night, smiling down at her. She could almost feel the leathery fingers stroking her hair and caressing her face.

Tears filled her eyes as she remembered waking up one morning to be told that her grandmother had passed. They had only just gotten her permission to stay in the States the year before. After a lifetime of hard work and little food, her abuela had finally grown round in her hips during her last year, but her heart had not gotten better from a birth condition. There was nothing the doctors could do but give her medication and tell her not to exert herself. Ana always believed the exertion of sheer happiness and the lack of worrying had taken her abuela away. Believing that seemed easier than thinking there was no justice in the world.

Ellen snored lightly on the couch as Ana took a moment to sink down into a chair to allow a few more tears to roll down her cheeks.

Twelve years had passed since her grandmother's death, and yet sadness still crushed Ana at the mere thought of her. She sat quietly for a minute, her heart too heavy to sing, but after a few tears, Ana pushed herself back up. It was time to do her job. That's what her grandmother would have said, had she been there. Never one to shirk her duties, her grandmother had worked hard all her life.

Ana continued cleaning, remembering the wonderful moments during the last year her grandmother was alive. The many afternoons her abuela took her for ice cream cones at the Mexican fruit stand. Or the times Ana would hold the yarn while her abuela knitted, her abuela spinning stories of her childhood while creating a blanket. And the many times her abuela defended her from the chore of cooking from her mother.

Ana looked around her with a sigh, realizing how much her life had changed in the last few years. No real friends to go out with, an inexplicable relationship with her professor that could fit into her plan for a comfortable future but didn't stir up any genuine excitement in her, a job cleaning and another serving coffee. After that, all she had was a shaky grip on her classes and the hope that she would graduate soon.

It was her fault she was alone; she knew that, but the truth brought no consolation. She had left Roberto after all, and while she understood why most of their shared friends felt obligated to choose sides, she had expected one or two to stand with her. At least Alicia and possibly Sam. Or maybe even Thalia and Roberta. Instead, they either chose him or simply faded away. No one called, texted, or came to the hospital when she was there. Gossip travelled too quickly in her community for her to believe no one knew she was back home.

For the first year after running away from Roberto, all she did was work every hour she could pick up at the shoe factory to pay off her bail bond. Slowly she folded into herself, as though she stopped taking joy in being with people. When Elena had Sofia, Ana was ecstatic on the outside and heart-broken on the inside. Her niece would have had a cousin were it not for her allowing Roberto to bully her into getting rid of their baby.

Her heartbreak was a steppingstone to another job, which turned out to be the one at the coffee shop. The one that caused her to meet Ana and eventually Ellen. The job that brought her to her fate with Ana-Maria.

Ana walked past Ellen's family pictures, running her fingers over the frames. Her eyes spied a picture on the piano of Ana-Maria, with her playful green eyes that looked beyond the camera. Ana tried to feel a connection more than guilt for this feisty girl whose place she was taking, but she hadn't known her in any real sense. There was a part of her that thought she should feel bad about taking her scholarship and her name, or at least possibly grateful for the opportunity, but that just seemed too morbid to think about.

Ellen shifted. Ana snapped out of her daydreams and quickly put the frame back. Her nerves tingled at the possibility of being caught wandering about the house with no work left to do, but Ellen continued to sleep peacefully. Ana watched her out of the corner of her eye as she put the cleaning things away, tidied up Ellen's book and glasses, then picked up her bag. But when she was halfway to the door, Ana stopped.

There was probably something to do upstairs. Though she had never been, she couldn't imagine Ellen doing much cleaning. She could re-listen to the lectures through her headphones while helping

Ellen more. Walking out of the house without a word seemed a strange thing to do, especially as they were becoming closer.

A real granddaughter would stay. If it were her abuela, she would stay.

Perhaps it was time Ana did the work of Ana-Maria and be a true granddaughter to Ellen.

Ana gave a satisfactory nod as she looked about the upstairs rooms. Just a few hours earlier, she had started her war that saw dust bunnies flying and now could finally claim victory. The next step was the attic, since her work of cleaning out the grills would be to no effect if the filters remained filthy.

"What are you doing up there?" Ellen demanded as Ana reached the top of the rickety attic ladder.

Before Ana could answer, she heard the ladder moan.

"Ellen! Don't you dare climb up here. I'm changing the filters. I'll be down in just a second."

"It's my home. I can climb whatever I want."

"No, you can't. The railing is split, and your balance isn't good enough. Now, move away so I can come down." Ana glared at her from the top rung and Ellen's frail hand gripped the split railing until her knuckles turned white. "It's already done, Ellen. No need to come up."

The older woman finally stepped aside to make way for Ana's descent. Ellen clicked her tongue when Ana hopped off the last rung, smiling triumphantly. The entire episode was both absurd and hilarious, just as many moments with family should be, but her vibrating phone cut her desire to laugh short.

"Sorry," she said, whipping her phone out as she pulled off the red and black handkerchief, certain of who it was before she saw the message. Ellen tapped her foot. Several times she had made her distaste for mobile phones and the younger generation's addiction to them known to Ana.

"I'm sorry, Ellen, I should go."

"But I have coffee and cookies set up downstairs. Why would you have to go now?" Ellen crossed her arms, blocking the hallway. "Who called you?"

"I just have to go."

"Is it an emergency?"

"No."

"Then you have an obligation to me first. You shouldn't change your plans because something better comes up. That, my dear, is lack of integrity."

"I already finished my work and stayed on to do more while you slept. I could have left an hour ago."

"Well, you didn't. And you're still here and I already set up the cookies. It'd be rude of you to leave."

Ana snorted, then backed up a step when Ellen didn't move.

"Ellen, I will come back tomorrow, alright? It's this man that I'm seeing. Sort of."

"He's sort of a man, or you're sort of seeing him?"

Ana made a face at Ellen.

"Not funny."

"Well, which is it?"

"I'm sort of seeing him," Ana said with a sigh. "Could you please let it go?"

"But you're going to just leave me in the dust because he sent you a text?"

"I'm leaving because I'm finished here and the man I'm seeing is asking me to meet up with him."

Ellen sniffed.

"You shouldn't run after a man at his every beck and call. Believe me. A man gets used to that behavior, but one of these days you'll tire of doing everything he says and he'll be stunned at your attitude, thinking you're just 'that way.' Humph. I thought my generation fought long and hard for you youngsters not to do that sort of thing."

"Are you saying I'm not a feminist?" Ana asked, following Ellen into the kitchen. Though she knew she should go, the conversation had taken a turn she felt needed a finalization to.

"I'm saying you are standing up for yourself and what you should do. And you aren't making him fight much for you."

"And how should I make him fight for me?"

Ellen poured the decaf into porcelain cups, then took her time to sit down before answering. Ana stood with her hands wrapped around the mug, waiting for an answer.

"Is this man the one that you're seeing? Is he in love with you?"

The question stirred resistance in Ana. Probably a poor sign. She ignored it and sipped her coffee as she decided how to answer.

"Our relationship isn't at that point yet."

Ellen didn't back off.

"Where, exactly, is it at?"

"I don't know where it's at. Right now, I'm just focused on finishing school, you know? I changed majors from what Ana-Maria was doing, so no professors would recognize me using her name and worked hard last spring and this summer to raise her grades. I got a paper back last spring that had all these marks on it. The teacher said it wasn't college material and suggested I go to see Daniel for some tutoring. It all started with him helping me with my homework, but then summer came and the week they were painting the hallway where his office was, he suggested he tutor me at his house. Little by little, we've divided up the time between his office and his house. And then a few weeks ago it got late, so he made dinner. And then the next time I missed the bus, so I stayed the night."

Ellen's eyebrows rose.

"The problem with young people these days is that they get involved physically too soon."

Ana looked away, her cheek warming at the implications of the comment.

"I stay in the guest room, actually. And yes, I've slept there a few times, but the relationship hasn't really escalated physically. He's concerned the university would discipline him, or even fire him."

"You aren't attracted to him, then?"

"What do you mean?"

"Well, you don't seem in any hurry to push the relationship further than a strange friendship between a professor and student."

"He's a nice-looking man," Ana said. "And he's kind and treats me well. What's more is that he has his future already figured out and isn't in the middle of finding out what he wants, like most guys my age. He's educated, has a good job, and he's financially stable. I know that doesn't sound very romantic, but my parents were the romantics who couldn't ever seem to get ahead financially. I don't want that for me."

Ellen nodded. "Nothing wrong with being a little practical."

Ana's phone buzzed again. This time, Daniel was calling.

"Hello?"

"Hi." They had never spoken on the phone before. Ana noticed his voice lacked the self-assurance it typically had in person. "I just wanted to know what your plans were. Are you coming over?"

"I'm not sure I can. I'm at my other job, the house cleaning one. I was helping with changing the filters and things Ellen can't do—"

"But you're done now, right?"

"I'm just having some coffee with her. We're winding down the day."

"So, you're coming later? I thought you wanted my help with your essay."

Ana looked at her watch. It was almost six o'clock. Daniel continued talking, but she wasn't listening.

"Are you listening, Ana?"

"Sorry, I got distracted. I feel like I'm forgetting something."

"Are you actually at work?"

"Oh no! I forgot. I can't see you today, Daniel. I told Marlon I would meet him at the library after work. I'm so sorry, I totally forgot."

Silence met her.

"Marlon?"

"Remember Marlon? The guy—"

"I remember. You're meeting him?"

"I thought it'd be nice to catch up with him," Ana said, unwilling suddenly to share that they were going to go over her essay.

"Right. Well, that sounds fine. Of course, you have other friends. I would love to see you this weekend, but of course that all depends on whether you're free. Just let me know."

Before Ana could answer, Daniel hung up. To save face in front of Ellen, she said goodbye to a silent phone, then put it away.

"You have to go?"

"I forgot I said I would meet someone. He's a guy I went to high school with. I don't know him very well, but we had math club together."

"Math club?"

"I know. It's geeky, but I enjoyed it. Anyway, we were in math club in high school for one year and we ran into each other at the coffee shop where I work the other day. He said he would help me with my essay."

"And Daniel is ok with that? I thought he was helping you with your essays."

Ana washed her porcelain cup out slowly as she thought.

"Daniel seemed mad, but I just thought it would be nice to have another opinion about my work. I know I've gotten better because my grades are better, but Daniel can be so critical sometimes. Like every paper I write should be at the level of a dissertation."

"Jealousy will kill a relationship."

"I'm not sure it's jealousy. I mean, there's nothing to be jealous of. I'm not looking to date Marlon."

Ellen sat back into the cushions on the couch and looked lovingly at the picture of her husband hanging over the mantel. A distant smile clung to her lips and there was a light twinkling in her eyes. The look reminded Ana of her mother and father, who swooned over each other till the day they died.

"Jealousy that rages or turns ugly ruins a relationship."

Ana's mind flashed to the whiteboard with all the signs of an abusive relationship. Roberto had been jealous and abusive, but Daniel was nothing like Roberto. Categorizing him in that way would be unfair.

"I better go. I'm already late."

Ellen caught her hand as she walked by to get her coat. "You don't owe me any explanation, Ana, but I think you owe yourself one. What do you want and who do you want it with?"

"Thank you, Ellen," she whispered, kissing the old woman's soft cheek. "I'll see you in a few days."

The sun was down completely, the streets now dark and cold.

"What's wrong with me?" she asked herself, stepping out into the dismal Michigan winter. She pulled her scarf around her neck, secured her coat buttons, and trudged on. Determined to change her mood, she tried to smile underneath her scarf, but it didn't help much. It didn't matter if she was in love with Daniel or if he was in love with her, she tried to convince herself. That wasn't what she was looking for. She had no time for love in her life. What she could accept was safety and security and a life that had a future.

She approved her thoughts with a sharp nod before trudging forward into the clear, frosty night.

Chapter Six

THE LIGHTS IN THE library twinkled off and then on again, waking Marlon from his sleepy trance. The sun was now below the horizon, and Ana still hadn't showed. He craned his neck to make sure her usual table was still empty, then stood up to see if she was sitting somewhere else. He didn't want to stray too far from his books and table, but then who was going to steal law books and books on dispute resolution cases? Still, in case Ana was looking for him, he didn't want to wander too far.

For the last few hours, he'd been telling himself that meeting at the library was hardly a date, but her not showing was eerily similar to being stood up. He had come in excited to see her again, talk to her again, see if maybe she would go on an actual date with him... and then she hadn't shown. She could have had something else to do; something better than studying across the table from him. He was the one who foolishly took her words as seriously as though it were a date, even though he told himself it wasn't.

Marlon slumped down in the chair, exhausted from the debate going on in his head. A little over two hours before he had to go to work and still fifty pages to read.

Soon his eyes drooped, and his head nodded down to his chin before he could catch it. To save himself more embarrassment, Marlon set the timer on his phone, crossed his arms, and pushed back his chair. If he was going to sleep instead of study, he might as well do it right.

"I thought libraries were for studying."

Marlon jerked his head up the instant her breath tickled his neck. Ana's eyes glistened, giggling at his reaction.

"Hi. I didn't think you were coming." The release of pressure in his chest at seeing her caught his attention. He hadn't noticed just how tense he had become waiting for her.

"I'm sorry. I forgot about it until just now."

"No problem." Trying to find a place to put his hands, which were suddenly too large, distracted him from saying much more. He finally opted to fold his arms across his chest and hide them altogether. "It's always good to know what level of priority I am on people's lists."

Ana blinked at him before giggling again. Marlon smiled at the pleasant sound.

"I see you've kept a sense of humor in California," she said. "But apparently, you've lost the Midwestern ability to forgive a slight lapse in memory."

"Ah, is that what it's called?" he asked with a smile. "Anyway, I've gotten, let's see, a fifteen-minute nap in, along with three unproductive hours of reading just faffing about."

"Is that something they say in California?" she asked, her small nose scrunching up.

Marlon laughed uneasily.

"I had an internship in London two years ago. Some of the vocabulary's still stuck in my head."

"I would love to have an internship in London." Ana looked away, as though able to envision herself in London across the room. "I can't imagine you over there with their accents and tea. Do many Englishmen have dreadlocks?"

"A few," he said, gathering up his books. "England is probably more diverse than you think. It's almost as diverse as America, just with a funny accent."

"Where are you going?"

"I have to work at eight, but I need a coffee before I go. You can sit here. Or would you rather come have a coffee?"

"I don't know."

When she hesitated, he continued talking. "You don't have to come. We can catch up later. I'll see you around."

Marlon stood still for a few seconds, suspended in that space of the unknown, of possibly changing minds, before heaving his bag over his shoulder, mumbling a goodbye, and ducking out of the library as fast as his ego would let him.

Three blocks away from the library, Marlon finally slowed down. The afternoon sun had heated up past needing his puffer coat. The sun and walking quickly while carrying four heavy law books caused beads of sweat to form on his forehead. Thinking about his inability to flirt well didn't help lower his body temperature. He was inching closer to thirty than to twenty. Surely, he should know how to convince a girl to have coffee or dinner with him.

Marlon wished he could soothe his anxiety with a gin and tonic, but he couldn't leave Jennifer, his co-worker to clerk alone. Night court was a long line of people paying off fines and taking care of small misdemeanors, with little time for a break even when there were two of them. While people waited their turn to face the judge, Marlon usually gave advice to people who were trying to represent themselves, which he enjoyed. As tired as he was, working would satisfy him more than nursing a drink by himself at a bar.

"Hello, Marlon."

The voice was so close behind it startled him. Daniel, the professor who had been sitting with Ana the other day at the Student Union was standing right next to him.

"Professor Hardiwick."

"Please, call me Daniel. You aren't in any of my classes." The man had a jittery laugh that sounded as though it should come from a puppet. "I was just coming from a meeting. What are you doing wandering around here? Shouldn't you be at a party or something? It's Friday night, you know."

"Right. I would've been during my undergrad," Marlon answered. "Now I'm on my way to work."

"You don't look like you're in a hurry."

"No, I have another hour before I start. Just taking a walk and getting a coffee."

"Are you working third shift?"

"I guess you could call it that. I clerk for Judge Boughtsy for night court." The two of them fell into step, though Daniel had to lean in to keep up with Marlon's longer stride.

"Night court? That's an actual thing?"

Marlon laughed dryly. People vote for their judges while knowing nothing about the judicial system. Didn't seem like a win for anyone.

"Yes, it's a thing. Most people have to take a day off to go to court, so the city's required to work around that and help facilitate their ability to show up for their court date. Especially for hourly workers. We have to make things easier for workers, right?"

"Right. I agree with that. Or they could simply follow the law and not have to show up for court," Daniel said, shrugging his shoulders. Before Marlon could manage a reply that didn't include a questionable insult, Daniel changed the topic. "I admire you students who work your way through college. I only worked during the summers and tried to live off that money throughout the semester so I could dedicate as much time to studying as possible. Ten-hour days in a shoe factory with no air conditioning; that's not a job I would want to go back to. Definitely made me study harder."

"You must have been very good with your money then," said Marlon. "Because with rent and books and a little entertainment every once in a while, I'd never be able to just work through the summer."

"College wasn't half as expensive back then. I did work during my master's degree, though I was getting married by then. Guess that's normal."

As they shuffled around each other and got into line, Marlon tried to think of something else to ask, but came up short. Awkward silence stretched out before them, reminding Marlon of a few bad blind dates he'd had back in California.

"What would you like, Marlon?"

"Cappuccino, please."

"Don't worry about it," Daniel said. "I'm buying this time. What with the fees and books for college? I know you're working, and I don't mean that you can't pay for your own stuff. I just want to pay this time. Once you graduate and have an actual job, you can pay."

He was never one to say no to a free coffee and telling the professor who insisted on paying that he had already paid over half of his debt back through working and scholarships seemed ill-mannered. Mama Rou always said to just smile, say thank you, and accept the gifts people offered. So, he did just that.

"Tell me, how do you know Ana again?" Finally, a topic of conversation as they sat down.

"We don't know each other that well. We met in high school in math club."

"I would have taken you for a football player or basketball player."

"Football was never my thing. I really liked science and math and all that, so I was always joining those clubs. My mama made me play tennis and do track. I think she did it so I wouldn't only be a geek."

Daniel laughed. "Seems like it worked."

"Not sure about that. I'm pretty sure I still come off as a geek when talking to women."

"Well, I know how that feels. I don't envy you younger men the way things are these days. Dating seems very complicated."

"Are you married?"

Daniel frozen. The wrong question to ask, it seemed.

"Not anymore."

"So, you're as single as me."

Daniel nodded, though he seemed distracted. "I guess I was talking about the dating apps and all that these days. My wife, my ex-wife, and I met in college, and it was just normal to be looking for a relationship that would become long term, you know? When I hear the students talking these days, it seems like no one is really looking for long-term at all."

"That might be true, sometimes," Marlon said. Afraid the topic might swerve into the weird, he changed it quickly."When did you decide to become a professor?"

Daniel looked up in surprise, but then smiled. Marlon settled back into his chair, ready for a story that could be summed up in two sentences but would instead probably be a tome.

"At first, I wanted to be a high school teacher," Daniel started, "but soon found that the mind of a young person during their college years is more malleable, so I got my master's and switched. I wanted to influence the college kids, since they're the next generation. It feels rather powerful, you know? Like holding the future of the world in your hands. Especially when you see the kids swallow everything you say."

Marlon shook his head in a double take. The idea that this rather dull, middle-aged man had a sense of humor was disarming. As Daniel continued laughing, Marlon slowly waded through his surprise to give him a smile. Something about the man had him questioning whether it really had been a joke.

"I'm kidding, I'm kidding. I never really thought about becoming a professor. It just happened. I started working as a teacher's aide and soon became the teacher. It's a good job, what with tenure and all."

"You never thought of being something else?"

"I never was the person who thought too hard about what I wanted to do. Teaching seemed appropriate, so I never looked anywhere else. What are your aspirations? A white-collar, jack-of-all-trades?"

"I might get involved in politics. Right now, I'm happy to clerk for a judge and write on the side. I have my business of sorts and I'm excited to see where that takes me."

"You're a journalist as well?"

"I write, yes. Perhaps it isn't true journalism. I don't go investigate things as you might think. I started off writing about laws; new ones and old ones and how the courts are interpreting them across the country. It bothered me that so few people understood the laws and the system and I enjoy writing, so I started a blog. Then I got into the social media thing and set up a video channel to talk about the same things I write about, but to an audience that prefers video. Then I started the podcast. I have a fairly big following now."

"You sound busy. What's the point of still working that clerking job?"

Marlon shrugged, finishing his cappuccino.

"I'm in my mid-twenties. It isn't like I shouldn't be working. A lot of ideas come to me through this clerking job. Plus, I had a commitment made already to the judge. I don't want to back out on my commitment."

"But then why go back to school?"

"I enjoy learning things and they offered me a scholarship to study here. Apparently, they wanted to diversify more," Marlon said, laughing before clarifying. "They wanted more ethnicities in their doctorate program. I'm one-quarter Ojibwe. It's an American tribe, concentrated mostly in Wisconsin and Canada."

"Huh. So, you got one of those lottery scholarships."

"Yes."

"You don't look Native American."

"American Indian," Marlon corrected. His grandmother certainly smiled at him from the other side of life, but guilt hit him in the chest for taking pleasure in the correction.

"Do I look more African? Or more Greek? My grandmother left the reservation and her people when she was seventeen. She travelled with the circus for a while, then stayed behind in Massachusetts, where she married an Italian man who was a doctor. She attended college to become a nurse. After she graduated, she and my grandfather made their way to Ohio, where they settled. My mother went to Chicago for work, where she met my dad. He was part Ethiopian, part Greek. So basically, I'm a mix like any other American, right? If you saw my grandmother's picture, you'd see the American Indian in me. We look alike."

Marlon stopped talking, realizing he had just given away a lot of information about himself. It felt unorthodox to say so much to a man who annoyed him.

But Daniel didn't seem to feel the same as he leaned in to listen.

"Those DNA tests are a marvel. I took one a few months ago just for fun. Turns out I'm Jewish. I had no idea. My mother didn't know either, though things started making sense when we looked over little quirks about our family culture," Daniel said, chuckling to himself.

"Do your parents still live here?"

"My parents moved to Florida as soon as my dad retired. One of those couples," he answered with a smile.

The front door of the coffee shop flew open, the wind chime in the corner ringing loudly as the wind caught its strings. Daniel sat up straighter when he looked towards the door, his laughter dying, his face tightening. Marlon checked his watch, grateful to see he should start heading to work.

"Ana." Daniel's voice was flat, as though unhappy to see her.

Marlon looked up in surprise. Ana stood frozen in the doorway, bundled up with two scarves and a hat. Some snowflakes gathered on her coat.

"Hey, Ana," Marlon said, standing to gather his things. He motioned to the barista for two more lattes.

"What are you doing here?"

"I told you I was going for a coffee. I ran into Daniel on my way here. Anyway, nice chatting with you, Daniel. I need to grab a few more coffees and go. I don't want to be late."

"Right, you did. I just didn't realize you were having coffee with Professor Hardiwick. Anyway," Ana said, shaking her head as though clearing her thoughts. "But I'm glad I ran into you."

"Why?"

Ana shifted her stance, looking at him and then the professor.

"Ana."

"Right, sorry. I was wondering if you would look over an essay of mine if you have a moment next week? Professor Hardiwick has been nice enough to look them over so far, but I don't want to keep bothering him when he's so busy."

"Of course. I gotta go. We could meet here on Monday to discuss it between classes."

"Sounds good. One o'clock?"

"Fine. I'll see you then. Daniel, nice talking with you."

"Yes, it was fun. We should do it again soon. I'd love to hear more about clerking for a judge."

"Sounds good."

"I'll get your number from Ana, then."

Marlon saluted with the two new lattes and headed out the door. Daniel inviting him to hang out again seemed very odd, and there was also a strange stillness between Daniel and Ana. He had assumed they were friends the first time he met them, now they seemed frigid towards each other. Something was off, but he had no time to figure it out if he didn't want to be late.

Chapter Seven

"ANA!"

Ana turned toward Marlon's voice, trying to find him in the mix of hundreds of other students leaving and entering different classrooms. Before she found him, another male voice, this one stern and cold, hissed her name from the other direction.

"I didn't see you all weekend," Daniel said through firmly closed lips, as though a ventriloquist, looking around him instead of at her.

"I've been busy."

"Doing what?"

The incredulity in his voice shut down any desire she had to share her weekend with him.

"Professor Hardiwick, Ana, what's up?"

They both turned to find Marlon jogging the last steps toward them. Before allowing Daniel to answer, Marlon looked down at Ana. "Are we still on for today? Or if you're free, we could go now."

Ana felt Daniel's eyes drilling into her. Typically, they met in his office if both of them had free time to go over any essays or presentations she had coming up. She always had a few typos to fix or some sentences to tighten up.

"I'm sorry, I can't right now, I have—um, a few things to do, but I'll meet you later."

"Great. I'll see you then, Ana."

The way he said her name caused Ana to pause for a moment. The measured way it left his lips brought up something within her she couldn't quite place. As though he meant for her entire world to close into this moment.

Daniel shifted to turn towards her, pulling her attention to him.

"Come with me to my office. Please?"

Ana followed him to the elevator. Her obedience irked her. It was something she thought about over the weekend. After her conversation with Ellen about jealousy, she started looking back and trying to analyze Daniel through a different lens, resulting in some old nightmares coming back. All weekend she woke up out of a dead sleep gasping for breath, a foreboding filling her.

As the elevator climbed, the tension within her dumped itself into her temples, throbbing intensely and demanding her attention. The last time he brought her to his office in this mood was to lecture her about treating him with indifference while in front of his colleagues, to make sure they suspected nothing between them. That wasn't an example of jealousy, but it could be an example of control. Something Roberto had a problem with. Or it could just be Daniel's vanity. Either way, a quick glance at her watch told her she didn't have time for any type of lecture. She needed her business tax law presentation looked over and another paper to finish.

As was usual, Daniel chatted along with one of his colleagues in the elevator, making sure he didn't pay too much attention to her.

Whenever they sat in his office to correct her papers, Daniel always left the door open. Today he closed it, his face clouding as he sat in the chair behind his desk.

"Are you seeing him on the side?" Daniel's voice was quiet, yet unyielding. A voice Ana imagined a cop or government official would use when interrogating.

"Who?"

Daniel sighed as he turned to her.

"Marlon."

Ana laughed in surprise.

"I think he likes you."

"Why would you say that?"

"Because I can see it. It isn't hard to understand why. You're pretty, smart, fun. You don't know it, but it's true."

"Are you complimenting me or accusing me of something?"

"You're eluding the question."

"Is your question whether I was with him or whether I was sleeping with him?" When Daniel didn't answer, Ana went on, spurred by frustration and lack of sleep. "There's no need for me to answer such a stupid question. I don't have time for this. Right now, all I need to do is study and graduate."

"Why do you need to graduate early?"

The unexpected change in topic surprised Ana. For a moment, she didn't know what to say, unsure if he suspected something or simply wanted to know.

"Because that's my plan, Daniel."

"But if you slowed down, perhaps we could pursue an actual relationship."

"I thought we couldn't do that until I wasn't a student?"

"You're graduating early for me?" His face smoothed into a smile. The comment was meant to remind him of what he had said months before, not as a declaration of her desire to build a relationship with him. The problem with giving in to her frustration and stress was that it kept her from thinking before speaking.

Daniel motioned for her to come closer. Ana stood where she was, still grappling with what the implications might be from her comment. He stood up and walked over to her, cupping her face with his hands. She could tell him now that she wasn't at all sure if she ever wanted a romantic relationship with him, which would probably ruin any relationship they had, even the tutoring-type relationship, or she could keep her mouth shut. It was possible that Daniel would be the best she could catch. And he wasn't bad.

"I like you, and I know other men may be attracted to you as well. I just thought we should both understand where we are going. I guess I just wanted to make sure you were on the same page as me. Maybe it's archaic, but I would prefer you all to myself." The heat from his breath covered her face; a sweet mint aroma filling her nose.

Daniel's words triggered something foreboding within her.

"I don't think it's too much to ask you not to see Marlon anymore."

Ana pulled away from him, anger building in her chest.

Jealousy. Possessiveness. She had seen these in action before.

"Ana, I didn't mean to offend you. I just want you to be careful."

"I think I know how to handle myself, Daniel. It's nice to have an old friend around, and it's nice to have someone to study with."

"Sure, but we started out with me tutoring you. Anything can happen. Right?"

Ana hesitated. She didn't want to answer that question when she was angry.

"You don't know his intentions. He's a guy—"

"The only intentions I can control are my own, and I have every intention of continuing a friendship." Ana steeled her gaze on his face. Her voice had grown an icy touch to it. No denying that.

"You're still going to see him?"

"You don't get to tell me who I can see and I need his help." Ever since leaving Roberto, Ana had wondered if she could stand up for herself better the next time around or if she was too shattered. It seemed she could. "And I wouldn't mind the company of someone who doesn't accuse me of things I haven't done."

"Do whatever you want." Daniel turned back to the window and waved his hand over his shoulder. "But you can only be with one person, you know. I have a class to prepare for now. I guess it's a good thing you can go to Marlon for help with your presentation."

Ana stood for a minute, staring at his back. She wanted to demand specifics on what exactly he thought he could do to her, but decided against it. Any more time spent on the subject was a waste. This was her chance to leave the discussion and return to studying.

But she didn't take it. Instead, she left his office quietly and headed down the stairs. She needed a moment to think before heading out to study.

Once outside, she pulled out her e-cigarette and headed to the designated area, ignoring the looks of disgust from half the people who passed by.

Before and after Roberto seemed to be the order of her life. Back when she was with Roberto, she considered herself to be strong; an intellectual who had come to her own conclusions about the world. Someone who stood up for herself in a world that was not created for her.

You should have left before.

Those words rolled back and forth in her head each time she got caught up in reminiscing about those years with Roberto. Back and forth they would roll until she felt beaten up by them.

Being the woman next to Roberto as he built his ethnocentric pride movement had been exhilarating. She had fought both with her words and her fists for things that were important to her. Together they had dreamed of making change, actual change, in their community. But everything started falling apart after her arrest. He had been so proud of her arrest, as a symbol of her dedication to their cause, but when she paid bail after he said not to, his behavior towards her changed. He became angry, volatile, and mean. He had never been violent against her before, never hit her. The first time happened a few weeks after she came home.

The day she had to show up for her court date, Roberto refused to go with her. Which was better. He would have hated to hear the apology she read to the judge following her lawyer's advice. The apology worked in her favor. Because the girl she punched had recovered well physically and didn't want to press charges, Judge Fabic handed her ten weeks of community service and a fine of $6000 to be paid to the girl. When she arrived home from her court date and told Roberto about her sentence, he laughed it off.

"You don't need to do nothing."

No matter how many times she tried to explain the situation to him, he ridiculed her.

"Just let them try to force you," he had said while taking out another beer from the fridge.

The comment sent chills down her spine. The Judge had looked at her with such intensity that she believed him when he told her he would never be so kind to her again if she ever showed up in his courtroom again. Plus, the attorney had negotiated a clean record in exchange for completing the community service, the fee payment, and not getting arrested again for five years.

No one in their right mind would defy that sentence and condemn themselves to a different outcome. To get a job that would put her on the path of financial stability, Ana knew she couldn't have a record. But because she refused to defy the judge and the system, Roberto gave her a new nickname: capitalist coward. The first time he said it, he threw a bottle of beer at her head and left the apartment; the walls shaking from the force. The glass bottle hit the edge of her ear, causing a pain that stunned her for a few moments, but it was nothing to go to the hospital for.

Roberto refused to talk to her for three weeks. She was a traitor to their cause for working in the system they were trying to dismantle. During these changes in her relationship with Roberto, she started her community service at a homeless shelter, which was something else entirely.

Being amongst people who had nothing was jarring. She had grown up listening to her dad talk about his neighborhood in Argentina during the economic collapse there, but she never imagined what she saw at the homeless shelter. Though her family had always been part of the lower income class, compared to the people in the homeless shelter, she felt rich and greedy. Starved for some human contact, the men and women were always telling a story, no matter if someone listened or not. At first, Ana ignored them, assuming at least half were mentally unwell, and not wanting to get too close to them, but soon she couldn't help listening. Arrest, drugs, alcohol, risky money investments, war or other violent pasts were usually their reasons for ending up homeless, but despite being left behind by the governments and most of society, they were kind, patriotic and self-reliant people. Many she spoke to took responsibility for where they were. Even when she pointed out where they could lay blame with someone else, most waved her away. Frustratingly, they seemed either a-political or almost conservative in their beliefs.

One day, frustrated by what she perceived as a lack of passion for change, she started arguing the points of immigration in America with an older white veteran. When a Hispanic man joined them, she wrongly assumed he would agree with her on open borders, free housing, instant green cards and access to Medicare, but he pushed back on all of her point until she was out of arguments. That was when her tamped down anger boiled over into insults. Both men looked at her like she was a spoiled child, speaking another language.

Pablo, the Hispanic man, demanded Ana apologize for her insulting his friend, leaving her speechless.

That was the same day she went home to find Roberto pacing back and forth amongst three strange women. Once Roberto finished a beer, the girl with bleach streaks in her hair and heavy eyeliner would immediately exchange it for a full one, while the other two who were Asian or Native American lounged on the chairs, watching Roberto as though waiting for a genius to speak. Her hands and voice shaking with rage.

"Are we becoming a multiracial group now?"

Of course, the question was meant to mock Roberto, but she had never expected to see the murderous glint in his eyes.

"Sit down and shut up or get out." Those were the only words he said to her.

Ana shuddered outside on campus. She looked around and reminded herself that she was safe. She was at the university. Roberto was long gone to Chicago and didn't pose a threat to her anymore.

Interestingly, if she hadn't gotten arrested, she wouldn't have ended up at the homeless shelter, which meant she never would have entered the free abuse survivor counseling session they held for women every Thursday.

She could still hear the first words she ever heard the counselor say, "Signs of an abusive person are fits of rage, extreme jealousy, mood swings, needing to be affirmed and agreed with, isolating the other person from friends and family, ridicule and disrespect, always blaming someone else or the partner and never taking responsibility, and of course, harm."

Ana squinted into the sun, checking her watch again. Daniel had said he didn't want her to see Marlon, but that could just be jealousy. There was nothing dangerous about him. He was all words and smooth talking, sipping coffee while reading the newspaper and making sure he kept his daily schedule.

She couldn't imagine him ever hitting her.

But if he couldn't allow her to have friends, what would come next?

The first time Roberto hit her with his hands was the day he had a sudden drop in listeners online after being flagged for hate speech. When she tried to calm him down, his open palm met her cheek with such force she thought a tooth might be loose. The pain was so intense she fell to the floor in shock. Roberto apologized after he calmed down and swore he didn't know what came over him.

But the outbursts started happening more often. The more she accepted his apologies; the more explosions seemed to happen until there was no containing them at all and no getting away from them. Roberto wanted what he wanted and if he was told no, he simply took it.

When Ana found out she was pregnant, she started looking for a way to leave. Unfortunately, she became distracted from that goal the day he came home and announced he had accepted a debate with a local political activist with very different views on how to create change named Dwayne. Roberto online, the one Roberto claimed was un tonto que no sabe su nariz de su culo. *A man who didn't know his nose from his ass.*

Roberto had spoken so badly of him that Ana took for granted Dwayne was stupid.

Looking back, Ana realized what she wanted was to believe Roberto. Every week, people at the homeless shelter and at the factory bombarded her with views didn't line up with hers, but which seemed to make sense. Sometimes more sense than hers. Eventually, it got to where she needed some sign that her life wasn't being turned upside down, that she and Roberto were right.

The debate took place at a hip-hop club. Ana stood defiantly and proudly next to her man, aggressively shouting at any woman who stood with Dwayne. The atmosphere pulsed with tension. The debate started with so much noise in the crowd that it was difficult to hear anything. Roberto called for calm, and his fans eventually followed suit. Assuming he had power, Roberto flexed his muscles and dove in, only to have every intellectual punch he threw easily tossed to the side by Dwayne with facts and statistics and questions Roberto couldn't answer. When Roberto compared the black American community to the Hispanic American community, the audience booed and mocked him so vehemently that Ana became afraid they might start throwing things at him.

Had there been swords, it would have been a bloodbath. Dwayne knew Roberto's arguments before he said them. Within a few sentences, he could interrupt and leave Roberto stammering from a comeback.

With each passing minute, embarrassment and shame overtook her senses until she could no longer look Roberto's way. Ana tried to conjure up better replies to Dwayne in her head, but the only words that came to her were insults, which she was soon shouting, along with the others in the crowd.

"A man who insults is a man who doesn't think," Ana's father used to say, but she was no longer listening to his sage advice. She yelled and jeered until she ran out of words. Then she pushed the button of her foghorn so hard her fingers turned white and the bone bruised from the force. Rage ran through every vein in her arms at Roberto and his idiotic pride. Rage at the crowd, who seemed so simple and stupid in their pathetic insults. Rage at Dwayne with his smug smile that smoothed his black-as-night skin back from his teeth. Rage at his ideas that clung to the traditional ways and gave little room to progress. Rage that some of his arguments made more sense.

The question a woman at the factory had asked her played over and over in her head, "Wouldn't we get more done if we all worked together towards a common goal? If we listened to one another and treated each other not as enemies, but as people?"

Half of the crowd supporting Dwayne had been on her side of a protest many times, but that night they were enemies. It all suddenly seemed so stupid. Roberto left the debate without her and never showed up at home.

Ana tried to let the debate go, but she couldn't. The next day at the homeless shelter, she spilled her thoughts and frustrations to Bob, a war veteran who was always willing to listen. When she finished, all he said was, *"Aun el necio, cuando calla, es contado por sabio."*

Even a fool, when quiet, is counted as wise.

That night Roberto came home drunk and took his frustration out on her. When he started hitting her stomach, she reminded him about the baby, forgetting he had demanded she get an abortion.

His rage seemed to make him grow three times his size.

"I don't have time to be burdened by a baby!" he had screamed. "If you won't take care of it, then I will!"

After a few rounds of punches and kicks, Ana agreed to the abortion. Roberto drove her to the clinic, and walked her in, but he didn't bother to go to the back with her. Alone in her clinic gown, Ana hoped a nurse would notice her lip swelling and let her slip out of the clinic without Roberto knowing, but no one said a word. They finished with her in a matter of a few minutes. She couldn't even remember speaking much the entire time. The only interaction she remembered was asking what the baby looked like and being sternly told that the fetus was little more than a blip.

That idea worked for her until she went with her sister-in-law, Elena, to see the ultrasound of her niece at twelve weeks. That baby was much more than a blip. Though she tried to believe that two weeks changed everything, a sinking feeling within her always said she was wrong. Now, every once in a while, she had dreams of a small, baby-like creature that would come to her and snuggled against her chest. Each time she would wake up gasping for breath as though being smothered.

Chapter Eight

The frigid air stung Ana's ungloved hands. She cursed herself for forgetting them again. The last few days, her head simply hadn't been where it was supposed to have been. Instead of focusing on her finals, she'd been overwhelmed with Daniel and dwelling on her past and, for some reason, Marlon.

She needed to pull off all A's in order to raise the failing grade that Ana-Maria had left her with. But focus was in short supply and sleep was even worse. Two nights the week before, she had woken up with nightmares of Roberto forcing her to get back together with him. Then last night she had a dream about kissing Marlon. Daniel's strange behavior didn't help any of it, either.

His appearance in her political science class that morning had been an unpleasant surprise after another restless night. Daniel chided her for not knowing the political history of South America. She tried to remember what her abuela used to say, but couldn't quite find the words. Before that moment, she'd never looked into the political past of her first home. The self-proclaimed communists in her class who spent most of their time mocking anyone who didn't wear Che Guevara t-shirts joined in chiding her, though that didn't bother her as much. She was pretty sure they knew nothing about Argentina, either.

Shoving her freezing hands deeper into her pockets while ignoring the pain her shoulder bag was giving her back, Ana noticed she was close to Lincoln Street. In less than a mile, she could be at Ellen's house. Despite the cool wind coming off Lake Michigan, Ana was sweating. Reliving that morning and the stress of finals were causing her sweat glands to go into hyper-drive.

The smell of smoked meat wafted through the air, and Ana's stomach grumbled angrily in response. With that simple sound, almost all her anger dissipated, her attention now to food. *Feed a man and change his mind*, her father used to say. Since he grew up with hunger all around him, Ana believed him. Many times throughout her childhood, he recounted stories of what hungry people would do for a scrap of meat.

It was unfair to compare her situation to that of her father who grew up in the slums of Buenos Aires, but she couldn't help thinking that if she wasn't fighting with Daniel, she could be having lunch with him.

Today Ellen was not expecting her, but Ana didn't have time to go home before her late afternoon classes and she didn't feel right showing up for her tutoring lesson in Daniel's office. Going to Ellen's was a simple solution that could give her some food. Plus, she didn't want to be alone.

"Hello, dear! What a delightful surprise." Ellen shuffled to the side to allow Ana through the door.

"I know you weren't expecting me today, but I was taking a walk and found myself near your house, so I thought I would pay you a visit."

Ellen looked towards the living room and back at Ana.

"Come in. I'm having someone for lunch. Why don't you join us?"

Ana hung up her coat with relief and followed Ellen's steps into the living room. Immediately, Ana's focus shifted towards the silver tray filled with sandwiches, apple slices, and crackers.

"Ana," Ellen was saying, as she entered the living room with another glass of lemonade. "I want to introduce you to Marlon, the grandson of an old friend of mine."

"Hello, Ana."

Ana dropped her apple slices on the carpet at the sound of a deep, slightly mocking hello. Marlon was sitting in an armchair, the one she sat in sometimes when reading to Ellen.

"What are you doing here?"

The question came from both at the same time, and the silence that followed. The first one to answer would be on the defensive. To not be that person, Ana occupied herself with picking up the apples to wait out the silence. But she forgot about the third person in the room who wouldn't know to let the situation ride out until Marlon lost.

"How wonderful that you two know each other! I guess probably from the university," Ellen said. "Sit down, Ana! You're making me nervous hovering around. And, please, eat something."

Ana obeyed immediately. Then stood back up for her plate of food. Shaking hands made it much more difficult to bring the food back to the couch without dropping something again. To avoid Marlon's stare, Ana took notice of her sandwich, like it was going out of style. Unfortunately, it tasted like sawdust on her nervous tongue.

"So, Ellen, my grandmother says that your granddaughter is attending the university here," Marlon said.

Her overactive nerves sent her head snapping up as Marlon sat waiting for Ellen to answer. The question seemed innocent enough, and yet the fact that so much hinged on him accepting that she is not only the Ana from high school but also Ana-Maria, Ellen's granddaughter made her unable to tell if she was being overly conspiratorial or not.

The last bit of sandwich stuck to her throat despite the gobs of mayonnaise in it. Ellen ignored the choking noises and the gulps of lemonade. She handed Ana a napkin without ever taking her attention from Marlon.

"Yes," Ellen said.

"What's she studying?" asked Marlon.

Ellen looked at Ana with a soft smile.

"Why don't you ask her?"

Ana's heartbeat rose again. To buy time, she sipped again on her lemonade, noting Ellen must have forgotten the sugar. The tension within her eased somewhat, but her tongue seemed glued in place. Loosening it caused her temples to pulse. This was the moment Marlon could just accept everything and move on.

"You're Ellen's granddaughter?"

"Yes." She cleared her throat, attempting to wet her vocal cords. "Why else would I be here?"

"It's just weird that we never figured that out in math club. That we knew each other, I mean."

That was not the answer she expected. Her palms began sweating, her tongue clamped up again, and her mind slowly churned to a halt.

"There was a certain family quarrel that kept Ana and I from each other while she was in high school. It was silly, really," Ellen said. "Right before her parents died, we all made things right again. It was a good thing, too; otherwise, we would both have been left alone."

Ana smiled with relief at Ellen's quick thinking, but still not trusting herself to speak the right words yet, she bit into another apple slice and chewed slowly. Keeping her mouth full might help keep all the lies at a minimum. Or so she hoped.

Marlon followed Ana as she walked out of the house. Even though she refused to wait for him while he bid Ellen farewell, he caught up with her easily enough. There was no way he was about to allow her off the hook.

"Where's your car?"

Ana finally stopped to turn to look at him, the lines in her face easing into a smile.

"I don't have a car," she answered, pulling out her cigarettes. The wind made lighting it difficult, which gave her something to focus on. He could have leaned closer to block the wind, but he stayed back. Uncertain of who she was, he just didn't know what to make of her. A gust of icy wind swept between them just as Ana finally inhaled. The way she rolled back her shoulders, trying to ignore the coughing attack that came, he found endearing.

"Are you coming down with something?" he asked, pushing a lock of hair away from her face. It had been instinct, but he instantly regretted the move. Her eyes rolled to where his fingers were, her cigarette hung midair until he dropped his hand to his sides and looked away.

"No, I don't think so. I just need to quit smoking."

"It seems strange that you're Ellen's Ana." The discussion needed to be had, and he wasn't one to wait around for it. The dots just didn't connect.

Ana looked away

"It's strange but Ellen seems to forget that you and I knew each other."

"What?" she asked quietly.

Marlon watched her closely, but her face revealed nothing of her thoughts.

"Don't you remember we used to play together in the summer?"

"When?" she asked. "How old were we?"

Marlon shrugged.

"About seven, eight and nine," he said, emphasizing each consecutive number more than the last. "A couple of times we coincided at our grandmother's houses. They used to have tea on the porch while we played. Your hair was lighter back then, and you were... feistier."

Ana forced a laugh. She stubbed out her cigarette on the ground before placing the butt into a metal box, then looked him in the eyes for the first time all afternoon.

"Everyone changes a little from the time that they're young," she said.

Marlon watched her shift her eyes away, looking at anything else but him.

"Well," she said, "I'll see ya around."

"Are you seriously walking back to campus?"

"Of course. I'm too impatient to wait for the bus and it's cold. Besides, walking is my only exercise."

Marlon grabbed her elbow and steered her back to the street they just passed.

"What're you doing?"

"I'll take you back to campus, Ana. The wind is so cold I can barely feel my face."

He thought she might try to resist him, but she didn't. One more block down the street, he stopped at his pickup truck.

"I expected a Prius," Ana said, her teasing lost in the teeth chattering.

"Ana, I might not look it, but I'm black enough not to buy a Prius. I like powerful engines."

She laughed out loud as she slipped into the passenger seat. There was something about making a woman laugh that could clear a man's mind and steer his thoughts in a different direction entirely.

"What are you doing later?" Perhaps he could convince her to tell him the truth about what her relationship with Ellen in a more relaxed setting. And he could find out if the woman he was thinking of pursuing was a fraud, and perhaps a thief. He wasn't sure Ellen had anything to steal, but he'd seen some crazy things at night court. Enough to make him suspicious of Ana's behavior now.

"I need to study," Ana was saying as she held her hands up to the vent. "And I have a couple of extra credit projects I need to finish. What're your plans?"

Marlon paused before answering.

"I have to work later tonight. I picked up an extra shift. Before that, I guess I'll hit the gym."

That wasn't a full lie. Truth was, he did plan to hit the gym, but he would have much rather take Ana to dinner or coffee, find out the explanation for everything. It sounded better than lifting weights with a bunch of sweaty guys, but he couldn't find the words that sounded right to say so.

For the next few minutes, Marlon concentrated on the traffic as Ana sat quietly, watching the view outside her window. Glancing at her as he switched lanes, it struck him how very different she was from the girl he played with as a kid. It seemed impossible that they never figured out the connection when they were in high school, either. But then, he couldn't think of why Ellen would lie about it.

He shook the thoughts away as his truck pulled up next to the school library. After saying goodbye to each other, Marlon sat for a moment, watching Ana enter the library while waiting for his brain to catch up.

Just as he was about to pull away, a lost memory came back to him. One that was almost a decade old. It was Thanksgiving, and he was an awkward sophomore in high school, eager to turn sixteen as the youngest in his class and be able to drive like everyone else.

That year he visited his mother's mom for the holiday, the one who was friends with Ellen. Ana-Maria had been with Ellen there that year. Her parents had just moved her out of state, and she couldn't stop talking about being a freshman at her new high school. She even asked Marlon for tips about getting a date to the winter formal. She was not the same Ana who had just entered the library. It was as a freshman that she showed up in math club.

But Ellen herself had introduced Ana as her granddaughter. Marlon sat stumped in his truck, wondering what he should do. Involving anyone else, at the moment, seemed dramatic. He didn't even know what was happening, but nothing was adding up. For Ellen to lie seemed out of place. He couldn't think of a motivation for her to do so. He looked towards the library doors again, remembering the stories his grandmother told him about the troubles Ellen's granddaughter had with drugs. Perhaps he was missing something.

Marlon shook his head and turned in the gym's direction. If the gym was good for anything, it was to let go and think. And tomorrow he could at least run all of this as a hypothetical situation with the judge. Hopefully, he might have some advice to give him.

Chapter Nine

DANIEL OPENED HIS DOOR to an empty house. He took care to put the snow-covered scarf and jacket in the laundry room before making his way to the dark living room and his favorite over-stuffed couch. Never had he felt so tired. Going to bed straightaway was the responsible option, but the liquor cabinet held a much more interesting prospect. Usually, Daniel scoffed at the idea of drinking alone. 'Drinking alone led to ending up like Hemingway,' he liked to joke. But tonight, was different. He opened the beautiful Vietnamese liquor bar and took in the sparkling bottles. It seemed a shame to let them go to waste.

During his marriage, Gloria and he used to make a fire and sit next to each other on the couch with a glass of whiskey in one hand and a book in the other. Daniel tugged on his tie as he pulled out the abandoned bottle of whiskey. He and Ana had never gotten into the same habit. She seemed to only drink wine, and only drank it moderately, and flat out rejected his favorite nightcap. The few times she had stayed over, studying, or writing late into the night, she only ever accepted herbal tea as a drink.

Tonight, though, there would be no tea. His relationship with Ana was, after all, on the rocks.

Even he couldn't laugh at his own joke.

The house was cold. He would have liked a fire, but the wood was in the garage, which seemed very far away at that moment. Gloria had always made the fires. Looking at the dead fireplace through the caramel-colored liquid, Daniel realized he had never built a fire in it. That cast a strange, gray light on his life, nothing of which he wanted to ponder further. Many cultures in the world categorized firework as a primarily female undertaking, Daniel reminded himself as he turned up the thermostat. Between central heating and whiskey, he would warm up in no time.

The sun set completely, but Daniel stayed where he was. At one point, Daniel reached his hand up to pull the chain on his reading lamp, but his hand found the whiskey bottle instead. The darkness fit his mood much better. If he was going to brood all night about his failed relationship with Ana, he couldn't have a light shining in his eyes. Acting reasonably might bring critical thinking, which was no good when brooding. He had no evidence of her cheating, that was certain. It certainly didn't seem like she had time to cheat, but the obvious fact was that the moment she had time to think and choose, she would choose Marlon. He was younger, more handsome, and had never been divorced. Psychology and history were on his side.

Daniel laughed out loud, the sound echoing through the discouragingly empty house. A house that was never supposed to have been empty. The current state of it rankled him.

Catching his image in the mirror over the mantel, Daniel stopped for a moment. The darkness covered most of his likeness, but he knew what was staring back at him: a man with forgettable looks, though not altogether unpleasant to look at either. He had a strong jawline, and his eyes were still the bright blue that caught Gloria's attention years ago. His lips were too thin perhaps and his hair might have lost some of its thickness, but he certainly wasn't going bald. Besides, since he never ate sweets and ran almost every day of the week, his body was in shape, more or less.

The last drop of whiskey slipped down his throat as he ruminated on his dark reflection. The option of going to bed reentered his mind and again he discarded it. Getting drunk seemed a much more fun idea.

This time as he reached for the bottle a frame from the top of the cabinet crashed onto the floor. Daniel picked up the broken frame, his former wife's face looking back at him with a wide smile.

As the etched-crystal tumbler filled with golden liquid again, Daniel took a moment to sneer at the woman he thought he would be with for the rest of his life; the women he thought he was so madly in love with, and she with him. They seemed so perfect for each other when they first met.

Perhaps too perfect.

That thought alone turned his blood cold. The whiskey no longer held any lure. What lingered on his tongue now tasted of ash. Daniel left the remaining liquid unconsumed in the glass before making his way upstairs, and made his way straight to Gloria's closet, thrusting the door open so violently he fell backwards. Though the carpet caused little harm to his back, the first thing Daniel saw as he looked up stabbed him directly in the heart.

The silk robe swinging softly from the only hook on the door gleamed warmly from the sliver of hallway light that made its way into the room. Daniel's throat constricted and for one awful moment he thought he might cry out with grief. Ana wore that robe just the other day, and yet now it was here. Rational thinking told him that Karina, his housekeeper, put it back where she thought it should go. But with too much whiskey in his system, it was easy to conjure up conspiracy theories of the universe playing tricks on him. Much more fun as well.

It didn't matter how the robe got back to its rightful place. The piece of silk seemed to personify his life. Gloria hadn't even worn it the Christmas morning that she opened it.

"I want to save it for warmer weather," she had said. "Being silk and all."

He had drowned his disappointment in lukewarm coffee.

In just a few weeks, he would have to experience his third Christmas as a divorced man. The thought was humiliating. Demoralizing. Never in his life had he imagined himself a divorced man. Never. With the way things were going, he wasn't even sure he and Ana would make it until Christmas, which meant one more year of imposing on friends and staring at other couples kissing under the mistletoe.

Six weekends ago, he and Ana had made their first fire of the season together. It was a Saturday morning, bright and early. She braved the cold while he made them breakfast. It was the first time in many weeks that she hadn't taken on a shift at the coffee shop, and they spent hours reading. It was also the first time since Gloria moved out that he thought it would be possible to move on with his life.

Now that possibility seemed to have shattered with the arrival of this Marlon character. How he hated the fact that in literature it was always the older, wiser, more mature man who won. It gave false hope to men in real life. The reality was that the girl always went for the younger, more handsome catch, even if it meant less stability. Had he been born in the eighteen-hundreds when woman valued a man more for what he could offer than for how he looked, Daniel was certain he would never have been lonely.

From some corner in his mind came the reminder that he had not yet lost, but he gulped it down anyway, along with the cries of his stomach to rid his body of the whiskey. It seemed he might never win with women; after all, he had already lost the one he wanted to keep until death. In a fit of rage, he tore the robe from the hook, ripping the seam of the collar. Daniel marched down the stairs to the trash. The robe hovered over the open can, but his hand wouldn't let go. It was an expensive robe, after all.

Daniel lifted his foot from the trash lever and watched the lid slowly lower, the robe still safe in his hand. There was a better way of doing things. The robe had done no harm. If he could keep Ana, the robe could still be useful. Daniel closed his eyes as he hung up the silk, imagining it clinging to Ana's full hips. There was still Marlon, of course, and something had to be done about him. Some convincing of sorts.

Daniel stumbled down the hallway and stairs, arriving at his phone with the perfect plan. Keeping enemies close had worked throughout the centuries, so there was no reason to think it wouldn't work now. Instead of brooding over Marlon, assuming instead of knowing, he would become his friend. His confident. He would find out his plans. And if Ana was part of them, Daniel would gently steer him away.

Simple as that.

Daniel jumped from his couch. Something was ringing. But his phone was black. It rang again, echoing all throughout the house. Daniel rubbed his face vigorously with his palms to wake up. The ringing happened again, this time clearly coming from the front door. Quickly, he slammed the rest of his drink, dropped his whiskey glass at the next table he could reach, and ran to the front door. As he got to the door, he realized whiskey was dribbling down his chin onto his flared out collar. He wiped his chin with his sleeve before shouting hello into the black, snowy night.

"Hi." The voice was male. Definitely not Ana's. It came from someone tall, a scarf and hat shadowing most of his face.

Daniel stepped back in surprise, allowing Marlon to step into the empty foyer. He closed the door automatically to keep the cold out while still trying to work through his confusion. Through the fog in his brain, he could only think of one reason that Marlon would seek him out: to take away Ana, but that didn't seem rational since Ana wasn't there at the moment.

"What're you doing here?" Daniel tried to focus on his pronunciation, but he had a feeling it wasn't working.

"You sent me a text saying you wanted to continue our conversation from the other day."

Daniel stared at him.

"I was just down the street when you texted. My grandmother lives near here. I could go if you've changed your mind."

Keep your enemies closer. Daniel smiled, finally understanding where he was and what was happening.

"No! Come on in! I'm sorry, I must have dozed off a bit. But come in, come in. Have a drink."

"Thank you."

Daniel walked over to the liquor cabinet and poured another glass, refilling his own as well. "Are you a whiskey drinker?"

"I like it, but my preference is gin. Or tequila."

Daniel paused for a second, scouring the bottles organized alphabetically.

"I have tequila, though I don't know if it's any good. No vodka though."

"Don't worry about it," Marlon said, taking the whiskey. "Whiskey is fine."

"Well, I think I'm ahead of you on the drinks, but cheers."

"I could try to catch up." Marlon had that irritating kind of smile that pasted on his face like a bad art project. Daniel smirked, accidentally sucking whiskey up his nose. The ensuing coughing fit helped take away most of Marlon's smile.

"You ok?"

"Yes, fine," Daniel gasped. The depth in his voice from the phlegm gave him a boost of confidence he hadn't had in a while. "Went down the wrong tube. Sit down, sit down. Let's talk."

"I like your house."

Daniel grunted, still boring his eyes into Marlon's head. Marlon. Like Marlon Brando. A namesake this kid didn't deserve. He wasn't macho enough, didn't look like he could get into a fight at any second. He seemed intelligent though, and he was easy to look at. Daniel could see how Ana would find him attractive. Even so, there was something missing that made the name stick awkwardly to him instead of melting into place.

Marlon sipped his drink and looked around the room.

"I like this room." Small talk grated on Daniel's nerves.

"My ex-wife decorated it. She liked the feeling of being in an old, English study."

"I was going to say that it reminds me of my grandfather's study."

"There you go," he said, with false bravado. "That was her plan."

The two men lapsed into silence once again, each drinking to occupy themselves. The clock ticked loudly, encouraging them to take more sips until they found their glasses empty quicker than they should have been. Daniel moved to fix the situation.

"So you were married before?" Marlon asked.

"Yeah, I was."

"Is it worth it?"

The question startled Daniel. His hand stopped midair from taking another drink.

"I beg your pardon?"

"You know, marriage. Is it worth going through with it? Like the whole wedding and all?"

"Your parents aren't married?"

"They were. But they split up when I went to college. My dad went out to California, which is why, you know, I went there for my undergrad."

"I've heard your generation doesn't think marriage is worth it."

"Why would we? I mean, I had it pretty easy with my parents sticking it out until I was out of the house, but most people my age come from single-parent homes. I see mess after mess at night court with divorces and cheating and child support and all that." Marlon paused. "You guys never had kids?"

"No." Daniel stared somberly at the empty fireplace. It took great concentration to pronounce his next words. "But it was absolutely worth it."

"Even though it didn't work out?"

"I'd do it all over again."

"How long did you know her before you married her?"

"I dated Gloria for a year before we got married. No, before we got engaged. And we got married six months later," answered Daniel, suddenly animated. He swept his hand across the room. Luckily, it was his empty hand.

"Do you think you knew everything about her?"

"I knew I wanted to spend the rest of my life with her. Of course, that plan didn't work out exactly how it was supposed to. If you want to know my opinion, I say be careful. I thought I knew the woman I married and look what happened."

Daniel's body moved too far to the right than he was ready for as he stood up. His shin meeting the coffee table helped keep him from falling completely.

"Careful."

"Yes, exactly. Be careful. Take your time getting to know someone. But then, anything can happen in the end, right? What about you? Are you seeing anyone? A fancy lawyer or judge?"

"No," Marlon laughed. "The judges I work for are much older than me. Anyway, I came out of a three-year relationship back in California."

"You never thought to marry her?"

"Sure, I did. But then I caught her in bed with my roommate."

"That sucks," Daniel said, though it sounded more like 'shucks'.

Daniel squinted to focus while commanding his mind to concentrate on why he had wanted Marlon to come over in the first place.

"What about Ana?"

"What about her?"

"She's nice. Good looking. And you know her, right?"

"I know her some. We were in math club together, but our friend groups never really crossed. I always thought she was nice, though."

Daniel threw his head back and laughed as he made his way back to the liquor cabinet. How good it felt to laugh in the face of his own adversary; to keep this young man on his toes. With a grand sweep of his hand, Daniel snatched up the whiskey bottle and filled both of their glasses with a flourish. A large splash of it fell onto the carpet, but Daniel pretended he hadn't seen it. He would try to remember to clean it in the morning. "I think you like her."

"She's nice," Marlon said was a shrug, looking at Daniel straight on. "But I'm not sure I really know her."

"So why do you think you're in love with her?"

"I'm—not. I'm not sure I said anything about her and love."

"But you wanted to know about marriage."

"Yes, I'm interested in what people think about marriage. It was just a conversation."

Daniel relaxed his shoulders at the last statement.

"Weren't you hanging out this week?"

"I saw her a few times. We ended up being at the same house for lunch. My grandmother asked me to stop by her friend Ellen's house, and Ana turned up there as well."

"Ah, yes, she cleans her house."

Marlon's eyes clouded at this statement, which allowed Daniel to grow taller. He knew something about Ana that Marlon didn't know. But then, he remembered, he was supposed to be pretending that he and Ana were just tutor and student. His chest deflated.

"What did you say?"

Daniel waved his hand. "Sorry, was thinking of something else. What were you saying?"

Marlon didn't have time to answer before the doorbell rang.

It had to be Ana. Daniel ran to the door and wedged his body into the opening to muffle any sound she might make.

"What the-?"

Daniel's eyes bulged at her to shut her up while his hands took their time in obeying his mind. At least before she could say any more, his fingers were against her mouth, though clumsily so. He walked forward, forcing her to step back from the stoop.

"Why are you coming outside?"

"You can't come in. Marlon's in there," Daniel said, his tongue working with difficulty.

"Then I guess I'll go."

Daniel cried out before thinking. "No!"

Both looked towards the house, almost expecting Marlon to appear. Daniel lowered his voice to a whisper.

"I want you to stay. I haven't seen you for a few days," he said, his voiced sounding a bit like a four-year-old's to his ears. "Just go behind the house and hideout until I get him to leave."

"Are you insane? It's freezing outside! How long until he leaves?"

"I promise it won't take long." Daniel leaned in to kiss her lips, but Ana turned away too quickly and marched to the side of the house. When Daniel leaned too far out to watch her go, he stumbled right into the snow-covered bushes.

"What's going on?"

Daniel looked up from his struggle to stand up to find Marlon darkening his doorway. The snow was seeping into Daniel's pants, but he had to admit the cold felt good on his face.

"Come on, man. Let me help you up." A large hand appeared in Daniel's. He gripped it and felt himself pulled up without hardly helping move his own bodyweight.

"Are you ok?"

"Yeah, I'm fine. Let's go back in. It's cold."

"Who was here?"

"Just, um, some carolers. Every year they try to sing for me. I told them to go away."

"Okay. I think I better go."

"Don't worry about it. Why don't you come to my office on Monday, and we can finish our talk?" The minute the words were out of his mouth, he wished he could take them back. If only he could have learned to be more like Gloria and only give invitations to people he liked.

"Sure thing." Thankfully, Marlon didn't sound very sincere. Or perhaps it was the alcohol hearing for him. Daniel shrugged. Marlon allowed himself the last of his whiskey before taking his coat from Daniel.

"Good night, professor."

"See you," Daniel called out from the doorway as Marlon walked towards his truck. The minute the engine blared, the bushes around the corner rustled.

"You're lucky you got rid of him so quickly." Ana's voice was like a growl, emphasized by the roaring of Marlon's truck driving away down the road. "I was just about to go home."

Ana pushed past him into the entryway of the house. The force she exerted almost put him into the bushes again, but he caught himself on the short iron railing this time. He followed her inside, the effects of the whiskey somehow amplified now. From the entryway he watched Ana as she pulled off her coat, then hung her things back in the entry, then returned to the living room.

Her constant motion had his head spinning. Needing a place to focus on to not pass out, he concentrated on her breasts. But that didn't work once she bent down to take off her boots.

She finally stopped moving, standing with her hands on her hips. "So. Are you drunk?"

"I might be slightly affected by the amount of alcohol I have had to drink," he drawled. He needed to escape her stare. The fire popped. As though a direct call to action, Daniel grabbed a log and marched forward.

"I will do that!" Ana shrieked, grabbing the log. "You just sit down."

Daniel smiled and sat down. Her lips consumed his thoughts. He wanted to kiss them and have them kiss him back. He imagined himself grabbing her suddenly, passionately, and whispering beautiful things in her ears. She would melt into his arms, telling him she had been waiting for this moment. Their bodies would fuse into one, an act that would be more passionate than a harlequin romance novel come to life. Afterwards, once they moved in together, they could make love at any time of day. He imagined them going on vacation to beautiful places and every other man being envious of him.

Ana turned her back to the roaring fire, her face filled with impatience instead of passion. Anxiety zipped through him from his head to his midsection at her look. Despite her angled eyebrows, the time was now or never.

He jumped up and grabbed her at the waist. Unfortunately, Ana impulsively jumped away, sending his body forward with nothing to stop it. His lower back overcompensated for the fall. Though he worried he would pay for it dearly in the morning, he couldn't let some back pain stop him.

"What are you doing?"

"Shhh," he slurred, sliding onto the brick ledge of the fireplace.

"You smell like whiskey. Have you had dinner yet?"

"I was waiting for you," Daniel said from the floor. He rose to his knees and wrapped both arms around her waist. He couldn't seem to stand up. "Why don't we go upstairs and talk about it."

"Anything to make you happy."

The words were good, but her tone was flat. Ana didn't move, didn't even look at him. Not willing to give up his dream of a night of passion, Daniel pushed himself into standing, his torso swaying from side to side, pulling Ana closer to him, almost toppling them both to the ground.

"Daniel, what are you doing?"

"Shhh," he slurred again, spit flying from his lips. He pulled her against him and kissed her. His mind said it was passion, but the way she pulled out of his grasp said otherwise. Or perhaps, she just needed more persuasion. Daniel pulled her closer to run his tongue over the nape of her neck. His teeth grabbed playfully at her earlobes. In his chest, his heart beat wildly with lust.

She stood still, not joining him in the petting, but not moving away either. When he ran his hands up her sweater, he heard her sigh, though it sounded more like annoyance. Still, the sound sent a wave of heat spreading over his legs. When her bra came unclasped, a shiver ran down him. It was time to act, and fast. Just as he had hoped, the alcohol had taken over his emotions rather than rationale, and he was physically ready this time to make love to her.

He pushed her body away from his, grabbed her hand, finished the last swallow of whiskey in his glass, and pulled her up the stairs.

Chapter Ten

ANA STARED AT DANIEL. He was stretched across his bed, arms and legs flung into an X, passed out. Downstairs, his movement had been so clumsy she had simply stood still until the alcohol took its effect. It was a trick she learned when Roberto started drinking more and more. Sometimes, he would pass out while trying to have sex with her like Daniel, and sometimes he would pass out while threatening to beat her. Either way, it worked for her so long as he passed out.

She looked around Daniel's bedroom for a large pillow to keep him on his side. Pushing his dead weight to the right was no small task. He wasn't a big man, but she was sweating by the time she had him partly turned. The last thing she needed was for him to vomit in his sleep.

Checking the clock on his dresser, Ana was disappointed to see she had missed the last bus home. Her choices were to call her brother or stay the night. Her brother would have so many questions. Plus, he might be already in bed. He woke up so early these days for work.

Ana tiptoed downstairs and into the kitchen. It was a half galley kitchen with the fridge and stove against the wall. A long counter with the sink separated the dinette area with its bay window and round table. Everything was so clean, shiny, and perfectly in order. Quite the opposite from the tiny kitchen at her house. Or rather,

Javier's house. Ana tapped the granite countertops and tried to wire into her memory to ask Javier about Luis and buying the house.

Looking around, she saw no remnants of dinner, which explained Daniel's inebriation further. There wasn't much in the fridge either that didn't need to be cooked. To settle her hunger, Ana took out the milk and rummaged through the pantry until she found some granola bars. Then she set herself up at the round table and enjoyed pretending the house was hers for a moment. The sensation made her smile. Owning her own house was a goal that seemed so far into the future, at times pessimism overwhelmed her senses with the thought that it would never happen. Of course, if she could find some passion within her for a life with Daniel, this house had a possibility of becoming hers.

Chewing the last bits of the granola bar, Ana contemplated that thought further. The problem with her was that she didn't know what she wanted.

As she trudged up the stairs, hearing the drunken snoring coming from Daniel's room, Ana couldn't find any sort of feeling for him except worry that he might vomit and die. Not a great sign. But as she undressed and slipped into the guest bed, Ana couldn't help wondering if she was just tired. Maybe she would feel differently in the morning.

Ana woke up with a start, her body flying into a sitting position from deep sleep. A strange feeling of desperation and confusion fogged up her sluggish brain. She had been dreaming again of the tiny baby that kept falling out of her arms, its cries sounding so far away, no matter how much she tried to run towards them.

Desperate to move the dream away, Ana shook her head and checked the clock. It was almost six in the morning, time enough to go back to sleep. But as she sank down into the pillow, a strange sound caught her attention. She laid very still, listening. Daniel snorted again, then settled into snoring. Ana sighed with relief that he wasn't waking up.

Now fully awake, Ana threw back the covers and shuffled to the bathroom. The reflection of a woman who didn't sleep or take care of herself enough shrugged at her from the mirror. She sighed and dismissed the night before from her mind. Everything other than schoolwork would have to be put off until after exams. During Christmas break she would have time to figure out what her relationship was with Daniel. And if she wanted to keep pursuing it.

Once dressed and downstairs, she relaxed and allowed herself some time to enjoy the morning. Reading the news on her phone, leaning up against the granite countertops, Ana again found it easy to pretend the house was hers. Two hours passed by quickly as she played in her imagination, only to be brought back to reality suddenly when Daniel started moving around upstairs.

There was nothing she wanted less than to face Daniel and what happened the night before.

Ana threw her dishes in the dishwasher and ran out the door. Arriving at the sidewalk, Ana scowled at herself but didn't slow down. Every few seconds she glanced back, her teeth clenched ever tighter, expecting to see Daniel jogging after her. It wasn't until she had crossed three streets and was at least a quarter of a mile away that she slowed down and relaxed her jaw. The voice in her head was right, she was acting crazy. She didn't have to rush to the library to study. She could head home. Or she could just try to enjoy a slower walk.

But no matter how much she tried to relax and listen to the snow falling off the trees, she couldn't shake the feeling that someone was following her. It was ridiculous. The hangover Daniel was sure to wake up with would keep him indoors all day. He was far too vain to be seen with bloodshot eyes. It was just old paranoia and narcissism that had her thinking someone was behind her.

Ana breathed again, then counted down from five. A therapist taught the trick during an anxiety management seminar on campus last spring. It worked. Sometimes.

Grabbing the blank space in her mind before paranoia took over, Ana thought back to the psychology books she read after leaving Roberto. *Feel. Analyze those feelings. Dig deeper to find the source that connects them.*

It was good advice. Advice that kept her from spiraling into chaos before. Again, Ana slowed her pace and forced herself to sit in the discomfort she felt with Daniel the night before.

Perhaps some of it was guilt.

That was an interesting thought. As much as she tried to tell herself that she was not using Daniel, now this thought forced her to face that possibility. Maybe she was using him as an excuse. If she was honest with herself, she felt no attraction to him. And if she felt no attraction to him, it wasn't fair to keep seeing him. And if she did, she was using him.

Those truths led her deeper into questions she hadn't yet bothered to ponder. Why did she entertain the idea of staying with him? Why did she spend the night if all she wanted was to sleep in the guest room?

A branch snapped behind her. She jumped, her backpack almost pulling her off balance.

The instinct to be on high alert from her days as a political protester was still strong. Many times, they got themselves into standoffs with other protestors or police that vibrated with tension and violence. She had learned to be always prepared to run to not get caught.

By now, she was less than a mile from the campus. There was nothing to run from. A branch snapping could be a squirrel or a car heading to work. Still, Ana couldn't help walking a little faster. Dread that Daniel might follow her had Ana glancing over her shoulder. There was someone behind her, but it wasn't Daniel.

A few blocks back, Marlon was walking, his head down. They were about five blocks from the main strip of the campus, State Street, where all the shops and restaurants were, which led directly to the enormous law building. She had somehow taken the longer route to the business school, which was another six blocks south, but Marlon was probably heading to the law building.

A strange happiness zipped through her just at the thought of walking with him. Just to be with someone, not alone.

The thought was so startling that she had to say it out loud, though quietly. *She didn't want to be alone.* Perhaps that was true, but the uncomfortable fact was that she was happy to see and walk with Marlon. She hadn't been happy about the idea of seeing Daniel.

Not a good sign. And something she would think about more after exams. Right now, there was nothing wrong with wanting to walk with Marlon.

"Why so slow?" Ana called out once he was in earshot.

Marlon raised his eyebrows as he pulled off the large headphones that Ana was pretty sure cost more than she made in a weekend at the cafe. The sunlight bounced off the metallic blue color, shining right into her eyes. Raising her hand to ward off the glare, Ana thought how she would have assumed he would have opted for sterile gray.

"I'm sorry, what did you say?" His tongue ran over his lips to swipe away the rogue snowflakes that landed on them, the movement strangely jarring and appealing. Too much sudden change in her mind for one morning was a bit terrifying.

"Why are you walking so slowly?"

Marlon looked past her and shrugged before continuing. Ana fell in step with him, unwilling to let him go on without her.

"No reason. Just got time."

Ana nodded. "When are your last exams?"

"I'm here right until Christmas vacation. My last paper presentation is on Friday at two in the afternoon."

"I have them until Friday, too. Friday at noon is my last exam."

They walked in silence for a few minutes until the tops of the buildings of the university came into view.

"Would you like to have breakfast together?" Ana asked, noting her voice sounded much too hopeful. "I have time before class starts."

Marlon shook his head.

"I really need to study. I have so much to do and not enough time for it all."

His eyes shifted away from her.

"Marlon, can you have lunch sometime soon?"

"Sure, that'd be a good idea," he said, looking at her for the first time. "I think we should catch up on a few things. I'll call you later. I gotta go."

Ana lifted her hand in a wave, but he turned and walked away before seeing it. His tone of voice, the distance he placed between her and him, all showed he wasn't very excited about spending time with her. And then there were the words he had used. *I think we should catch up on a few things.*

As she headed towards the coffee shop she worked at, Ana hoped Marlon wasn't questioning her name and relationship with Ellen and Ana-Maria. But that hope diminished when she watched

Marlon make a sharp turn into another coffee shop at the end of the street, well before the law building entrance.

Chapter Eleven

ANA'S WERE THE ONLY footsteps that disrupted the smooth snow on Ellen's stoop. There was a subtle, soft beauty to the surroundings she was about to disturb. For a moment, she allowed life to stand still, watching her frozen breath blast into the cold. Every fresh snowfall reminded her of the first time she saw it; thirteen years ago, on Christmas Day. After living her first few months in America in Arizona, Ana and her family had come to Indianapolis in a van, driving for two days straight. She still remembered her grandmother whispering through the dark that they had arrived, her strong father lifting her from the van and the blast of freezing air that hit her belly where her shirt had wrinkled up.

Throwing her backpack onto the porch, Ana grabbed a shovel out of the garage and got to work. The icy breeze swirled flakes into her scarf, which melted instantly against her hot skin. The crisp air hit deep into her lungs, giving her a clean, healthy feeling, though the occasional cough had her vowing once again to quit smoking come New Year's. This time for good. Ana closed her eyes as the sun peaked out, reflecting strongly off the snow's crystals, just like that first morning.

She had woken up on a strange couch; a tall, lush Christmas tree the first thing she saw. It gleamed with tiny lights and glass balls with presents wrapped in gold, silver and green paper spilling out from underneath it. First, she thought she might be dead and in heaven, but then her mind caught up and remembered being carried inside. Not fully understanding why they moved in the first place, Ana's next thought was that her family had left her here. After all, she had been whiny about the move. Mama had said so. And she hadn't been helping with her chores like she was supposed to.

Trying to be brave about her new fate, Ana remembered sliding off the couch while swallowing back frightened tears. Just when she didn't think she could hold in her weeping, her foot caught on something solid and warm, almost sending her down to the floor. Through blurred vision, Ana saw her brother's sleeping bulk covered in blankets, snoring softly against a blue pillow. Able to breathe slightly better, Ana tip-toed down the first hallway until she found her parents in a bedroom off the living room. Fully awake by that time, but no longer afraid they had left her behind to be a servant girl to a strange family, Ana looked around.

The sky was then turning from pink to blue outside the windows, but something even more beautiful than the sunrise caught her eye. Ana pushed a chair up against the sink and climbed up. A fluffy layer of beautiful snow topped everything outside, just like in her favorite Christmas movies. There was even a misshapen snow man in the corner of the yard with charcoal eyes and a carrot nose.

She stood there staring, ignoring the draft cooling her bare feet and the rumbling in her stomach. When the sound of shuffling feet came from behind her, Ana froze. Her mother never shuffled. Grandma did, but her shuffles were heavier.

"Buenos días, chiquitita."

Tia Leticia, a small, shapeless woman with brown eyes and caramel hair, sung her words more than speaking them as she stood behind Ana.

"Beautiful, no?" Tía Leticia, who was not her mother's sister, but in fact her mother's best friend from childhood in Argentina, pointed outside. "Have you ever seen snow before?"

Too shy to speak, Ana could only shake her head.

"Later we will go out and fix that snowman. I think Andrea's old snow pants might fit you."

Ana didn't have the courage to ask what pants earned the right to be solely for snow. She turned back to the window as Tía Leticia fussed with the hot water boiler and some mugs.

"Ven, hija." Tía motioned to Ana to join her, where she sat on a rug with two large mugs full of hot chocolate in front of her. "This is my favorite place to be during the morning."

Together they leaned against the radiator covered in an old, handmade quilt to keep themselves warm as they drank their hot chocolate and watched the wind swirl the snow.

Those days were some of her favorite memories of her move to America. Before then, everything was fuzzy and disorienting. Her father was always the stranger who would come visit once a year from the States as he worked to get his family their visas. Then one day, she came home from school and found him in their home in Argentina, her mother standing with their bags packed. They moved to the states three days later. From the arid climate of Salta, in the northwest of Argentina, to Arizona. She couldn't remember feeling confused by the difference in language or opposite seasons. At six, it was much more important to play and make friends.

The door of the old house opened abruptly, sending Ana's backpack flying into the snow.

"Ana! What are you doing out here?"

"Goodness, you scared me! I was shoveling the stoop for you in case you wanted to go out." Ana picked up her bag, now covered in snow, and pecked Ellen impulsively on her cheek.

Ellen's eyes widened in surprise, her hand touching the place Ana's lips had just been. When her parents were alive, kissing had been such an integral part of her day-to-day life.

"Well, I'm not sure who would want to go out in this weather."

"Not all of us can stay indoors," Ana said with a laugh. She threw snow in the air and smiled at Ellen. "Merry Christmas."

"It isn't Christmas yet," scolded Ellen.

"Close enough, Abuela. It's the Christmas season."

"What did you call me?"

The two of them stepped into the warm house as soon as Ana noticed Ellen's shoulders shivering, though she wore a wool sweater over a long sleeve shirt.

"Abuela. I thought you spoke Spanish."

"I never learned my husband's language. He only spoke it to his mother. She didn't speak English."

"You remind me of my grandmother, but I'll stick to Ellen if you prefer."

Ellen's face lit up with a rarely used smile. "I think being compared to your grandma is probably a nice compliment. I don't mind it at all."

"Right. Well, what would you like to do today? There isn't much cleaning left to do. Should we play cards?"

"No. We're going to bake cookies. Christmas cookies."

"I thought you said it wasn't Christmas yet." Ana couldn't help teasing her as she followed Ellen into the kitchen.

"I normally disapprove of making anything Christmas until the week before, but these are for my church. We have a bake sale every year to make money for the choir. Since it's mostly the church members that end up buying each other's cookies, I always thought it would be better to just give more money in the offering. But no one wants my opinion. So, I make my share of cookies every year without complaining."

Ana clicked her tongue.

"Well, maybe I should call you 'Scrooge' instead."

"That wouldn't be very nice of you."

"Abuela!" exclaimed Ana, laughing. "Don't you have any sense of humor?"

Ellen looked at her in surprise for a few seconds before chuckling.

"You've got some spunk in you today, don't you?"

"I should be more worried about my exams coming up, but outside I was thinking about the first time that I saw snow, which led me to thinking about my parents. It just reminded me that life can be good to you sometimes."

"Hmm, yes. I remember the first time that I taught Ana-Maria to make cookies for Christmas. She was about four years old and made a bigger mess than I had seen in my life!" Ellen laughed, her small body shaking as she sifted through her well-worn cookbook. "She was always a spunky little girl that didn't want to listen to anybody. Instead of putting the flour directly into the bowl, she stood on her stool, and laughed with glee as the flour mushroomed out and all over the counter. She yelled out 'snow!' and then clapped flour into the air."

Ellen hadn't spoken of Ana-Maria since her death. Ana had always been grateful not to speak of the dead girl, assuming the conversation would be awkward, reminding them that the bond between them was fragile and based on death. She was certain that any reminder of why they even knew each other would catapult them into an uncomfortable class system: Ana as the cleaning woman and Ellen as the lady of the house.

There was no uneasy silence, though. After the story ended, Ana found she wanted to know more. Ellen chuckled again, but she offered no more stories, and Ana couldn't place the words in the right way enough to ask.

"Take out the mixer, would you? It's on the shelf over there."

"This thing?" Ana lifted the heavy mixer onto the counter, bending her knees so she could lift the giant appliance. "It's positively vintage!"

"It still works. Why should I buy a new one if this one still mixes?"

Ellen gave an indignant shrug. Ana laughed because of course she was right and because she was exactly like her grandma, though the two women had come from such different backgrounds and lived such different lives.

For the next hour, Ana followed orders, enduring gentle ridicule for not knowing the difference between teaspoons and tablespoons, why brown sugar had to be packed down into the cup, and what 'creaming the butter' meant. When one batch of cookies was finally in the oven, Ana found a Christmas vinyl and slipped it onto the record player, another one of Ellen's vintage things that still worked.

They both sang along with Bing Crosby, butchering the tune in good humor as they put batch after batch of cookies to cool. After all that time, Ana found she still wasn't ready to go home. Instead, they shared left over stew for dinner, then played rummy, where Ana beat Ellen four times. Unwilling to play a fifth game, the two of them enjoyed a few cookies until Ellen started falling asleep in her glass of milk. With gentle pleading, Ana got Ellen to bed, tucked under the heavy quilts, then stepped out once again into the cold.

'White Christmas' was still running through her head as she entered her childhood home. The lights were off except the blinking ones wrapped around the tree. Ana tip-toed to the kitchen and placed the box of cookies on the counter along with her weekly addition of fifty dollars placed on top.

Just as she was turning out the lights, a paper with glossy pictures of her childhood home caught her eye. The paper was a real estate document stating all the square footage and amenities. She could instantly tell the picture wasn't professional, which went against everything she was learning in her marketing class, but once her eyes fell on the price, her attention refocused. If her brother was thinking of selling the house, he was looking to make a good amount of money.

For a moment, she wondered if any of the money would be hers. After her parents died, Ana had refused to show up to the legal meetings and Javier hadn't made her. Since he kept the house, she assumed she owned part of it. Not that she wanted it, but if he was going to sell, then she assumed some of it was hers. Which could certainly help her move out.

Perhaps that was the real reason Luis had been over, though it seemed strange that Javier told her it was about him buying the house.

Ana set the paper down with a sigh. There were so many rules to real estate law that she was certain the meeting with Luis was more about formalities than anything else. One thing she knew for certain was that Javier wouldn't lie to her.

For the next few days, she needed to concentrate on taking her last few exams and working the extra shifts she'd signed up for. Then it would be Christmas and she could ask Javier and Elena what was going on. It could all wait until then.

Chapter Twelve

"MERRY CHRISTMAS!"

Ana looked up from her register with a smile. Marlon was standing in front of her, his scarf and coat covered in tiny snowflakes.

"Well, you seem happy."

"Done with the semester! How about you?"

Ana looked at the clock, then tapped her notebook.

"I'm done with exams, but I still have a paper to turn in."

He couldn't help being disappointed. The plan was for her to be done so they could have dinner. Straighten some things out. He had come in earlier to find out when she was working, so he could put it all together. Knowing who Ana was and why she visited her professor's house at night would be the best Christmas present. He needed to know those things before he could decide what kind of relationship, he might pursue with her. He'd prefer to know before the break.

"Dang. I thought we could have a coffee before I head out. But I could wait until you're done with your test."

"No need. I'm done here in five minutes. Carla, can you take his order and let me finish up in the back?"

Marlon busied himself with answering questions to his latest law video while he waited for Ana while sipping on his peppermint mocha Carla had made him. It was too sweet, but a nice treat.

"Are you tired?" Marlon asked, as Ana finally sat down next to him.

"Exhausted," she admitted. "But it's almost break, right?"

Marlon nodded; all of his introductory arguments suddenly gone out of his head. He had exactly what he wanted to say in his head the entire afternoon, and now he couldn't remember how he was supposed to start.

"I saw you at Daniel's house the other night."

Ana's body froze.

"What do you mean?"

"He invited me over for a drink that evening. I was curious why he would do that, so I went. The funny thing is, the doorbell rang while I was there and he never let the person in. I left soon after and saw you coming out from behind the house as I drove away."

"I was just there to drop off my essay."

Marlon's happiness sank at her words.

"Don't lie, Ana."

"Ok, I go over there because he helps me with my essays and homework. No, it's true. And that night I went because he had wanted me to stop by. And it was late, but nothing happened. I mean, sometimes I go because he's nice enough to make me dinner and—"

She stopped. Marlon was sure his face had a look of disbelief.

"That sounds crazy, doesn't it?"

"Yep. So, are you involved with him or not?"

"I wouldn't call it involved."

"You were walking from the direction of his house the next morning."

"We're friends. I stayed to make sure he didn't vomit and die."

"You stayed the night?"

"It isn't what you think."

"It's none of my business. I was just sorta hoping there was another explanation."

He took in a deep breath before drinking his coffee. That was one subject down, with an answer he had hoped would be different. She wasn't free. And he should leave it at that. If he wasn't careful, not keeping his mouth shut was going to get him in trouble. It would have done him some good to haul himself over to the mirror and remind himself that what Ana did with her life wasn't any of his business, all in his mama's tone. But of course, he couldn't.

"Why do you even mess with him? He isn't even nice to you."

"He's helped me out a lot during the last two semesters. My grades are so much better thanks to him. I just feel badly telling him I want nothing to do with a relationship with him."

"I don't think he's very nice to you."

She didn't answer. They sat in silence, each finishing their lukewarm coffee and wishing the other would put an end to the agonizing silence.

"I'm not sleeping with him."

"Like I said, it isn't any of my business," Marlon said, although her words gave him hope.

"Did you know I had a crush on you in high school?"

Marlon raised his brows and leaned in closer.

"I'm interested," he said, smiling, genuinely grateful at the turn of conversation. "When?"

"Sophomore year, when we were in math club. I thought you were so funny and cute. And you were with that stupid blond girl who played on the volleyball team. I honestly thought that you were going to ask me to the prom instead of her."

"Why would you think that?"

Ana shrugged, her cheeks still flushed.

"I guess I thought you liked me, too."

Marlon relaxed back into his seat.

"I thought you were pretty and funny. I was just a math geek who liked to go see rock bands downtown. I didn't think you would go with me. You were dating someone by the time prom came about, don't you remember?"

Ana's shoulders drooped as though the word deflated everything within her.

"The things we need to do in order to find ourselves," she said with a sigh.

"You guys seemed pretty good together, doing all that Hispanic stuff. I thought it was great how proud you were of your heritage. I remember you giving that speech in front of the entire school in Spanish. It made me wish I spoke one of my grandparent's languages."

"It was international week or something like that."

"I have to admit I was surprised to see you doing your undergrad now," Marlon said after a pause. "I assumed you were doing your masters or your doctorate. You were so passionate in high school about so many things."

"Yes, well, I got sidetracked. Roberto, the guy I was dating, and I got a bit caught up in politics. For a while, I thought my activism was better than a degree. Or at least as good. I mean, looking back, it really seems idiotic to me. It's like I changed my own thoughts, because before that I was on track to start at the community college. A degree had always been important to me before Roberto. But then, my parents died, which hit me pretty hard. I was so angry, I guess, is the right word. I don't know. I took it out on the system and the people and things around me. I thought I could change them for the better. Or like I had an obligation to change them. But also, the way I did activism was a great way to release my anger. I could yell at the people who represented what I thought, sometimes still think, was wrong."

"Well, that explains some things."

"What do you mean?"

"I saw some videos and articles about you, and I've seen a few of the videos your old boyfriend made. What I saw of you was well said, very impassioned, though I didn't agree with your stance."

"Oh."

Memories of watching the videos of water gushing and objects flying and lots of people screaming until two in the morning moved like a movie reel through his brain. In one video, Ana was front and center, screaming at people who were leaving the building. When one woman stops to in front of her, Ana clocked her in the head. It was shocking.

"Which ones did you see?"

"One where you scream and end up hitting someone."

"Right." Ana's face was bright red. She sank deeper into her chair. "I don't do that anymore. I mean, that was the only time I hit someone, but I also don't go to those kinds of protests these days. The ones where you know it's going to be violent. Actually, I haven't been to any protest in two years."

"I liked your argument for minimum wage. Not that I agree with you, necessarily, but I could tell you had thought a lot about it."

Ana paused. "Thank you. That means a lot. It wasn't usually me debating. That minimum wage video is the only one that Roberto had me on."

"Probably because it had a ton of views and the comments were more complimentary to you than to him."

"Oh? I had no idea."

"You never checked?"

"I was usually too busy getting high or planning the next rally," Ana said, her eyes still not rising to his.

"Are you and Roberto still friends?"

Her skin took on an ashy color and her eyes glistened as though about to cry at that question.

"I'm sorry Ana, I didn't mean to upset you."

She pressed her lips together as though to squeeze her emotions tightly within herself.

"It's fine. It's been over two years already. No, Roberto and I aren't friends. He became more violent after he lost a big debate and quite of few of his followers. That should have been the end, though I didn't realize it at the time and still stayed on. But activism doesn't pay much, and I felt a bit lost and trapped after getting out of jail. The only place I could go was crawling back to my brother. Which I eventually had to do, anyway. It's just that prolonging it got me a few more punches. When Roberto lost this one debate, he just started acting different. Like he was losing everything. I mean, he was losing his audience, but he took the loss as a sign he was losing his status in our group."

Marlon's chest tightened, but he ignored it.

"Wasn't it against Dwayne?"

"How'd you know about that?"

"It was a pretty big deal on the internet and I'm on the internet all the time. Besides, I know Dwayne."

"Oh."

Their silence allowed the background music to slide in between them. Ana smiled, her face more relaxed than a minute before.

"What?"

"This song was on the first CD my father ever bought in America. It's a Spanish singer, Julio Iglesias. He used to make us listen to it every Sunday morning as we cleaned the house and my brother,

Javier, would complain the entire morning about having to listen to the 'old-world music', as he called it. He said that listening to a singer who was past his prime, with predictable songs that all seemed to have the same rhythm, hurt his ear." Ana chuckled. "Javier bought some earmuffs and would wear them around as he swept the floors. That only made my dad turn the volume up higher."

"The old world?" He leaned in closer to her, though not too close that her defenses would go up again.

"Argentina," Ana answered with a perfect accent. Marlon leaned back as she sang, his lingering question now answered. He took a moment to revel in having figured it out.

"Ellen's husband is from Mexico and your parents are from Argentina."

Ana stopped swaying and fell silent.

"My father is Argentinian. He grew up there," she said, stammered. "He came to the States when he was twenty-two."

"So, your father taught you Spanish?"

"He and my grandmother. My father's mother, that is."

Ana's hands started shaking as she fiddled with her box of cigarettes, dashing his hopes she might finally admit she was lying. Marlon's sympathy for her was wearing thin.

"Ana," he said, grabbing her hand. "What is going on? Ellen's son was Ana-Maria's father. You're getting the entire story wrong."

"I don't want to talk about it right now."

"Ana, just tell me. Are you in trouble?"

"I have an exam, Marlon. Please. Just let me try to get a good grade on this exam. Please let me go."

Marlon let go of her hand without another word and watched as she gathered her things quickly, without looking at him. Just as she started towards the door, Ana came back. Before he understood what she was doing, Ana placed her gloved hand behind his head and drew his cheek to her lips. Her lips were dry and warm.

"Ana—"

"Merry Christmas, Marlon," she whispered before walking away.

"Merry Christmas," he answered to an already empty room.

Chapter Thirteen

"You're home!" Javier shouted over the banister from the upper split level as Ana entered the house on Christmas Eve.

"Of course! And I have presents!" Ana shouted back, turning her smile on, determined to enjoy herself.

She had somehow survived her last exam, even after the fiasco with Marlon. The last few days at work had been a nightmare of stress and nerves because she stupidly kept looking for Marlon to come in, wanting to talk. She wasn't sure what she would say, but she was desperate to give some sort of clarification that wouldn't leave her looking like a horrible human being. She hadn't yet come up with anything.

Marlon had never come and never texted, and she was too chicken to text or call him.

It was Christmas Eve, and Ana would not spend any more time worrying about what to do with Marlon. As she tugged her coat off, Ana rolled her shoulders back and got ready for Christmas with her family.

A shadow from overhead darkened the entryway.

"Catch," Javier said, dropping an empanada down to Ana. She caught it with the ease of a sister's second sense. He had trained her well.

"I can take your regalos back to the store. Or better yet, give them to my rich boyfriend."

Javier appeared on the stairs with an enormous grin on his face.

"You wouldn't do that. Your rich boyfriend can buy his own presents."

Free finally of her winter clothes, Ana ripped off her soggy socks and went to find refuge with her sister-in-law, leaving Javier to place the presents under the tree.

"Mine is way too small," her brother yelled from the living room. "And Elena has two!"

"Great things come in small packages, Javier." Ana winked at Elena, who stood stirring a pot on the stove. "What can I do to help?"

"You and Javier can set the table, and then you can help me put the food on the china platters your brother bought me. Mira! Javier bought me all these new plates and dishes and silver serving spoons and forks. I don't even know what half of these things are for, pero son hermosos, no?"

Elena waved her hands over the assortment of plates and platters and silver serving spoons.

"They're gorgeous." It had never occurred to Ana to throw out the plates and cups her mother had bought when they first moved into that house that were now chipped and worn. Mama had been so proud of the deal she got that day. It was as though Christmas had come early that year. She had never seen her mother act like a little kid before that.

"How come you got to open your present early?"

"She didn't open anything!" Javier exclaimed. "She wouldn't let me pick it out myself. Apparently, she didn't think I would choose a pattern that was pretty."

Javier playfully spanked the back end of his wife as she bent over to look into the oven. She jumped up; her face flushed pink.

"Get out of here!" Elena waved her spatula as though to threaten to hit him, but she was giggling at the same time. Javier chuckled at his wife's threat and kissed her instead of obeying. Sofia joined her parents by shrieking with delight and throwing her bottle on the ground in the excitement. The happiness tugged on Ana. It was easy to let go of her worries in the middle of such joy.

A gurgle from the floor drew her attention. Chubby little Sofia stared up at her with wide black eyes and a smile that dimpled both her cheeks. When Ana knelt at her level, Sofia's fat, dimpled hands reached out to touch her cheek, melting away her frustration instantly. Her hands smelled of milk and graham crackers, the sweetest smell in the world. When Sofia smiled, her eyes crinkled with a familiar look of mischief twinkling in them.

"Have you noticed that Sofia looks like Abuela Silvia?"

"We have a picture of Abuela in our room right next to one of Sofia. You should see it; Sofia's the spitting image of her. We're hoping the next one looks like papa," Javier said, his face beaming with pride as he rubbed his wife's growing belly.

Ana turned from the happy couple to hide the stab of jealousy.

With Sofia in one arm, Ana finished setting the table as Elena set out the food in the middle. The four of them sat around the same small table that their family had sat at for years. It had Javier's initials carved on the bottom, along with the date that he finished it twenty years ago. Ana remembered seeing her brother beam all throughout dinner the first night they ate at it. Finding something he was good at was never a problem for Javier.

The table bore the rest of its history proudly; the burn mark from Ana setting a hot skillet directly on the table, the coffee rings from her grandmother and mother across the back left corner, as well as the gouge from Javier trying out a new knife at sixteen. It had seen many birthday parties, Christmas and Easter dinners, and three funerals.

Throughout the years, it stood strong as the core of the house. As they sat together now, Ana rubbed her hands against the smooth corners, touching the places where her grandmother or mother's coffee must have dripped. She was home. Her exhaustion faded away as she held up her glass of wine to toast their small family as the ghosts of those who had gone before them looked on with smiles.

The hours passed without notice as the three of them retold old stories in Spanish, ate niños envuettas, and drank cider. At midnight Argentinian time, they joined their parents' countrymen in a toast. As Javier told his wife the riveting tale of how he and papa created a go kart one summer, Ana tried to imagine Daniel sitting with her family, eating meat pies and niños envuettas and realized that the image was laughable.

"Javi, I think we should open presents now. It's almost midnight and mi niña is falling asleep." Elena also looked as though she might drop from exhaustion.

"Come on, cielo, let's open our presents!" Javier picked the little girl up and twirled her in the air.

"If she throws up, *you* are going to clean it."

Ana laughed at Elena's scolding as they gathered in the small living room next to the tree.

"Great job on the wrapping." Javier held up his present with the generic store wrapping paper. "It looks like Sofia did this!"

Elena laughed with Javier.

"The lady had no idea what she was doing. But whatever. It's better than unwrapped."

The warmth of wine and cider and her brother's teasing made Ana feel like she was part of the family, like maybe she wasn't the burden she thought she was.

Javier replenished their glasses of cider as everyone took turns opening gifts. No gift was ever extravagant in their family, but each gift always had heart behind it. Most of the attention this year was on Sofia, who relished tearing the paper apart. When three layers of paper finally revealed the rocking horse Javier had made, she squealed in delight. The rest of the time she spent between gleefully rocking back and forth on her horse and rushing to help each person tear open their presents. When Sofia opened the large, soft bunny Ana bought for her, she clutched it to her chest and snuggled up against her aunt. Ana could not fathom having more love for her own child than she did for her niece at that moment. When all the presents were opened, Elena sang carols in Spanish and English. Her sweet soprano helped Sofia fall asleep and soon had Elena drifting off as well.

"Tomás brought this back for me from his town in Mexico. You want some?" Javier asked, holding up a bottle of tequila. Many years had passed since she and Javier had spent time alone, drinking together.

"Of course. My throat could use some antiseptic."

They laughed at the family joke. Their mother had believed hard liquor was only good as throat medicine.

"So, tell me more about your boyfriend. When are we going to meet him?"

"Daniel is a professor at the university. Another professor recommended I meet with him to get help with my papers."

"You're dating one of your professors?" Javier pounded the table as he laughed. Ana couldn't help laughing with him. After the cider and tequila and everything else, the truth sounded ridiculous.

"Ok, ok, it sounds terrible," she said, catching her breath. "But we aren't actually dating. I'm not sure what we're doing."

"Papa would kill him if he was still alive."

"Papa would have killed any man I dated."

Javier lifted his glass in a toast of agreement.

"He definitely would have killed Roberto."

Silence followed as their father's ghost, a strong one steeped in old-fashioned values and ideas, sat down next to them. Javier poured a glass of tequila and set it at the spot where their father used to sit.

"So, what's the guy's name?"

Ana furrowed her brow and took a sip of her tequila before answering.

"Daniel," she answered, saying it as she would in Spanish.

"Is he Hispanic?" Javier asked.

She shook her head and laughed.

"No."

"I thought you wanted to marry someone that speaks your language."

"Who said anything about marrying him? It isn't like I have to marry."

Javier shot her a look, his eyes narrowing at her.

"What? I'm twenty-three. I'm finishing my degree and you know I fully expect to set up a business or something. I don't really have plans for marriage right now."

"And babies?"

Ana blushed, some strange anger bubbling to the surface.

"Women don't have to have babies to be actual women."

Javier replenished his tequila before answering. "This is the Ana I do not miss. You get all upset over something I didn't say. But I will say this finally, and you will listen." Before beginning his speech, Javier made a show of handing her the bottle of tequila instead of pouring into her outstretched glass. "I know you and I've never thought of you as the type of girl who wouldn't want a family. You can work. *Obviously*. Don't throw the idea of family away as though it were never important to you for the appearance of being radical or different. It's exactly what you used to do with Roberto. Establish your core values, understand what's important to just you, Ana, and mold your life around those things."

"I don't have to have what you settled for, Javi." The words sounded harsher to her ear than she meant them to, but he didn't even flinch. Nothing ever fazed him. Especially not after bailing her out of jail at two in the morning once and picking her up from the hospital with a black eye from Roberto.

"I know you think I'm too conventional or too conservative, but at least I'm not a hypocrite. A few years ago, papa told me the same thing I'm telling you now. I thought long and hard about it and then wrote out things that were important to me. At the top of that list I placed, 'fearing God' and soon enough, right after that, I wrote 'protecting and providing for my family'."

Ana rolled her eyes at the mention of God, but Javier didn't let up.

"You think God is unimportant, Ana. That's because you've always lived your life to your tune, only caring about yourself and not about anyone else. You don't consider the consequences that your actions have on us. Your family."

Ana tried to protest, but he waved her feeble noises away.

"Life is brutal, Ana. I realized this the night that papa died in that horrible crash. I helped pull his mangled body from the wreck." Ana looked up at Javier in surprise. She had never heard that part of the story. His eyes glistened with tears and for a moment, his throat seemed to close. "I decided then I would try my best not to add to anyone's burden. We all have our hard times and the only way that I see we can ease those times is by not being a burden to others. I play fair, I do business fair, I try to treat everyone with respect, I care for my wife and my daughter and when those feelings of doubt or resentment or depression or bitterness come up, trying to vie for my attention, I get on my knees and pray for strength. That is fear of God. That I mess up daily and should expect no one else to do better than me, but that one man did better and was willing to die for me. If I respect the men who put our military uniform on. Why should I not respect even more the One who died for me?"

"I don't remember God helping me when Roberto started hitting me." Ana flinched at how tight, almost whiny, her voice sounded. The long day seemed to catch up with her.

"Why do you expect help from someone you claim not to believe in, Ana? Just like I couldn't help you leave Roberto until you were ready. Why do you expect help from a God who gave you free will to choose the man you wanted to spend your time with?"

The Christmas lights flickered on and off, their reflection blinking like a heartbeat across the table. Ana didn't move, unable to think of anything to say back. Her breath came easy now. She just sat watching the colored lights flicker. Over the years, she and her brother exchanged many words on their political, world view and religious differences, though they always managed to still love each other afterwards, no matter how fiery their words. For the first time since she could remember, she didn't have a snide remark to seal her thoughts with.

There was no energy left in her to fight her fight. There had never been an exact moment when she had changed her view of the world to be the opposite of how her parents had seen it. Instead, it had been a gradual drip and now she wasn't sure what she truly believed. Right now, after cider and tequila and wine and with her head hurting again, was not the time to ponder deeply.

"You know Roberto is in Chicago trying to get into politics?" Javier rolled his eyes in disgust.

"And he'll probably make it. He was always pretty good at convincing people of his stupid ideas," Javier said, stretching as he stood up. "I'm glad you could spend Christmas with us, hermana. It's always nice to have you around. You should come home more often."

Tears sprang to her eyes when her big brother enveloped her in a full bear hug.

"Now go to bed. It's almost three in the morning and we have to be at my in-laws by ten."

Ana watched as he disappeared down the hall, straight and tall, as though he could drink another bottle of tequila with no effect. In contrast, the room tilted for her as she tiptoed up the stairs. When she passed by Sofia's room, she stopped to listen to the soft breathing of the little girl. In the silence, Ana admitted to herself that she felt the loss of her abortion more than she felt she should have. It wasn't anything anyone seemed to want to talk about, though. And in the end, she had too much on her plate to brood over things already done.

It was time to sleep.

Chapter Fourteen

"Ana, would you get that?" Ellen asked, implying the ringing doorbell.

"Of course." Ana left their game of checkers by the fire to open the door. "Are you expecting anyone?"

"It's probably Marlon, remember? My friend's grandson? She said he might drop by."

"Right," Ana muttered under her breath. "Marlon! Merry Christmas!"

The light from the porch illuminated her frozen breath, and the startled look on his face. Ana realized she was lucky to be there when he showed up. She hadn't put any thought into how difficult it would really be to play Ana-Maria when someone knew both Anas. It was almost enough to cut ties with him completely.

And yet, looking into his dark eyes, she knew she had no desire to cut ties with him.

Not wanting to impose on the festivities with Elena's parents, Ana had come to spend the afternoon with Ellen.

"What are you doing here?"

"It's Christmas Day, Marlon. What are you doing here?"

"I came to check in on Ellen. In case you were busy."

Ana stood back as Marlon entered, suddenly unsure of how to act around him.

"Merry Christmas, Ellen." Marlon entered the living room, handing the Tupperware of food to Ana as he bent to kiss Ellen on the cheek.

"What a pleasant surprise! Ana, we should take out some of those cookies I have in the kitchen. And maybe some hot chocolate."

"That sounds great. What's this?"

"Ana gave me a picture of her for Christmas. Isn't it beautiful? And another one of both of us here. She made me to take about fifteen selfie pictures one day. This one turned out okay. Of course, Ana looked good in all of them, but I think this is the only one with my eyes opened. You know, I don't enjoy having pictures taken."

"I think you both look beautiful," Marlon said, holding up both frames as Ana retreated to the kitchen.

"Ana, come in and stay with Marlon. I'll make the hot cocoa. I need to stretch my back. You two make yourselves comfortable." Ellen said as she took the frames back from Marlon and placed them on the piano, already crowded with old family portraits, before heading into the kitchen.

Marlon followed Ellen to the piano, jumping right into a jazzy version of 'O Come All Ye Faithful' while Ana picked up the checker game to make room for the large tray of cookies and cocoa she knew Ellen would be bringing.

"It's a nice picture of you, Ana."

"Thank you," she said, coming to stand next to him. The way his fingers flew over the keyboard, as though willing the notes to play, was mesmerizing. "I didn't know you knew how to play piano."

"Ever since I was five," he said. "My grandma made me learn."

Suddenly, his fingers stopped and reached towards the top of the piano. Ana froze, her insides reacting as though being jerked about by a rogue rollercoaster. The silence only emphasized impending doom as she watched Marlon pull out a frame from behind three others, then set her picture and the picture of Ana-Maria next to each other. Each movement seemed slower than could be possible. There was no use in hoping Marlon was too obtuse to figure anything out.

"There. That's better," he said.

Her eyes shifted from Marlon to the frames and back to Marlon, but she said nothing.

"While it might be none of my business why you and Ellen are pretending you're Ana-Maria, but it didn't make sense from the beginning. Having known you and Ana-Maria, all I needed was some time to put things together. Like how you lost your grandmother in high school and almost missed our meet in math club because you were so upset. Or that I knew Ana-Maria was a year ahead of you in high school, or that I actually met your parents at the spring musical, which was around the time that Ana-Maria's parents actually died."

Ana had nothing to say. Her body sank into the couch, heavy with dread.

"If you're going to impersonate someone, get rid of all the evidence at least."

"I'm not exactly impersonating her. It's just that Ellen and I-the other day we–I guess we just got nervous. I'm using her scholarship. I'm not stealing her life." Ana sat in dismay on the couch. Marlon seemed unwilling to be anywhere near her, as though she were hot coals.

"Seems like you are to me. Where's Ana-Maria? Does she know you're doing this?"

"My Ana-Maria is dead." Ellen was standing at the door that led to the kitchen, the tray in her hands trembling. In two long strides, Marlon was in front of her, taking the tray from her hands. "Thank you, Marlon. Ana, I think it's time we tell the truth."

Ana sighed, her breath trembling as it exited her lungs. Exhaustion covered her, and fear came along with it. Fear that they could throw her out of the university. Or what Javier would say. Or Marlon.

Her hands shook as several variations of her future passed before her eyes.

"Take some cocoa, Ana. Marlon, please sit down," Ellen said.

They both obeyed, but Ana couldn't bring herself to drink the cocoa. Ana also couldn't bring herself to look straight at Marlon.

"I figured out that you two were lying fairly quickly. What I can't figure out is why?" Marlon said.

Ellen placed a wrinkled hand on Ana's forearm and gave it a squeeze, but Ana couldn't relax. Tears sprang into her eyes at the affection.

"My granddaughter, as you might have heard over the years, developed a problem with drugs after her parents died. I wanted her to come live with me, but she insisted on living with her other grandparents. I didn't see her for many years until about three years ago when she showed up at my doorstep fresh out of the hospital. After swallowing some pills, she took an ice pick and tried to pick out what she thought were bugs inside her thigh. She almost nicked her artery that time."

The story startled Ana. She hadn't known the extent of Ana-Maria's drug problems. Marlon seemed just as surprised.

"I didn't realize she was struggling so much. I never saw her."

"I sent her to a rehab facility after that episode and for a while, she was better. She finally finished high school, and with some wrangling and monetary donations, I managed to get her into the university. Somewhere along the way, she went back to the drugs. Only a few months into school, she ended up overdosing. The doctors had warned her that her heart was weak. She knew she would probably die if it happened again."

Ellen's voice cracked as her grief for her lost granddaughter floated to the surface. She breathed in deeply, gaining control of her emotions after a few seconds.

"I'm sorry, Ellen," Marlon said.

He crossed the room and placed his arms around her shoulders. Ellen patted his hand and took the tissue, but refused more comfort.

"I didn't do right by her. I just didn't know enough. I didn't understand what I needed to do for her. I was still mourning the loss of my son, even after so many years, and I couldn't understand why she didn't just want to stop with the drugs. I should have found more options to help her."

"I'm sure you did everything you could," Ana said, her voice crackling. It wasn't fair for Ellen to take any blame for Ana-Maria's death. She wouldn't allow it if she could help it.

"I think that in the end she couldn't handle the loss of her family and just wanted to forget about it. Or maybe even join them," Ellen said sadly. "Either way, she's gone now, and I've tried to make peace with it. Ana found her last winter, passed out in the cold. She would have frozen to death if Ana hadn't brought her here. I didn't want anyone to know how she died, really I had no one any more to tell. My brother is gone, my husband died years ago, and my son and his wife were also gone. I called Doctor Rossen the moment Ana got Ana-Maria inside the house, but it was too late. Dr. Rossen is the one who took her body away, but Ana is the one who helped me with the funeral and who helped me through the whole dreadful process of burying my last loved one on earth."

"But how does that bring us to Ana impersonating Ana-Maria?"

"I helped Ana use my granddaughter's scholarship to the university."

"But that's fraud." Marlon stood up so abruptly the movement spooked Ana. She looked up to find him staring at her, his eyes wide.

"Oh, well, I guess so. Perhaps."

"No, it's fraud any way that you look at it. If they catch you, they'll kick you out. And they might even blacklist you. They could even sue you to pay back the scholarship."

Ana sucked in her breath, the room becoming slightly tilted.

"But I mean, they don't need to find out. They don't really care. They shouldn't care. I mean, I didn't have a way to pay for it and I've always wanted a degree and—" Ana paused, grasping for words but coming up empty.

"Very few people will understand that argument, Ana. Technically, they could say that you're taking the scholarship money you didn't earn from someone who worked hard for one but who didn't get one because you're using it."

"But Ana-Maria didn't earn her scholarship either, or her place in the university. Ellen coerced it."

"I'm not really talking about Ana-Maria. You taking her money might mean that someone else didn't get a scholarship this year. Or at least, I can see them making that argument."

"And, while it's true I pulled quite a few strings, Ana-Maria did somehow bring home good grades. And she went to that community college to catch up on some classes. That was all her doing. When she was sober, she was quite intelligent. It took some finagling for the university to accept her, that's true. She had a record for shoplifting. Anyway, Marlon, after losing Ana-Maria, it just made sense not to let it go to waste," Ellen said.

"At the time?"

When Ellen paused, Ana thought she might scream. Her heart was beating wildly in her chest at what words might come next.

Everything was breaking down, and she was desperate to stop it. But she didn't know how.

"The more I think about it, the more it seems like a bad idea," Ellen admitted, raising her hand immediately to stop Ana from interrupting her. The small amount of cocoa Ana had consumed threatened to come back up. She tried to concentrate on not letting that happen while Ellen continued. "I've been thinking about how you are going to deal with the whole name problem at graduation and with your transcripts and when getting your first job. It seems like a big problem, and I haven't been able to come up with a solution, except that we stop this whole thing. Then you can apply to the university as yourself."

"But I'm supposed to graduate next December."

"What if you get caught before that?" Marlon asked. "What are you going to do? Besides the fact that they could criminally charge you, they'll definitely ban you from the university."

"I'm so old already for an undergraduate student, Marlon. I can't start over. I just can't."

"But at least you'll have the degree in your own name," Ellen said.

"And how am I going to afford it?" Her voice sounded small to her ears. Money was always at the forefront of her mind. This entire problem could have been solved if she just had some money.

"Does Daniel know about this?"

Ana shook her head.

"Ana-Maria was pre-med and I'm in the business school. There are almost fifty-five thousand students here. It isn't hard to stay away from the pre-med building. Besides, she only showed up consistently for one semester. It's been working. I'm careful. It could still work."

"You should think long and hard about all this, Ana. It might have seemed like a good idea at the time that you both went ahead with it, but I think you should start over. Even if they don't catch you, what're you going to do with a diploma that has a different name on it than yours? It won't be any good to you. Whether you get caught and thrown out, start over or graduate with a diploma that says Ana Sanz instead of Ana Lopez, you'll have done all this hard work for virtually nothing. Leave now, start over at a different university, take a full load in the summer, and plow through as quickly as possible. I really think it's your best option."

The last bit of confidence in her deflated. She had no more fight left.

"I could change my last name," she ventured in a small voice, only half-serious.

"You could," Marlon said, his frustration clear in his voice. "Changing one's last name seems like a perfectly reasonable thing to do."

Ana looked as though he had slapped her, but he couldn't help himself.

"Graduation is so close I can almost taste it." Her voice was quivering with frustration and anger, but Marlon refused to feel sympathy for her.

"It's a year and a half away, but anyway, your problems won't stop at graduation. In fact, they'll just get bigger."

There was no way out. In a matter of a few minutes, her future was gone.

"We can talk more about this in a few days, Ana. It's late."

"Okay," Ana said, barely hearing herself. "I work the next few days at the coffee shop, but I'll come by on Thursday."

"Don't worry, dear. We'll figure something out. I got Ana-Maria a scholarship. I will work just as hard for you as well. Don't cry, Ana," she said, as Ana wiped away a stray tear. "I promise we will figure something out."

Ana nodded but had little confidence in what Ellen was saying.

"Do you want me to take you home?" asked Marlon as he followed her into the kitchen with the half-filled cups of cocoa.

"That's okay. I'll call my brother."

"Ana, let me take you home. I have my truck right outside."

Ana spent most of the ride huddled against the truck door with her scarf pulled around her face, looking straight out the window. As he followed the directions on his phone, Marlon couldn't seem to find anything to say. The entire situation Ana found herself in seemed befitting the crime, so to say. He couldn't conjure up much sympathy for her.

"Two more stop signs and then you turn to the right for my street."

The small houses stood in various forms of upkeep. A typical working-class neighborhood. He had grown up a few miles away, in a more middle-class neighborhood where some of his neighbors had pools. His parents had worked hard to get there and be accepted, knowing their parents hadn't had as many choices in where they could live when they were young adults. Of course, when his parents divorced, a move ensued for everyone, but Marlon had already been in San Diego as a freshman. Though his parents lived in smaller houses now, they were still very much middle class.

He pulled up into a small, but well-kept, split-level house. Another truck was in the driveway and bright porch lights illuminated the front.

"Thanks for the ride, Marlon." Ana said, reaching to open the door.

"Could we talk for a minute?"

"I'm tired, Marlon. I have to work tomorrow morning, and I haven't been sleeping much lately. We can talk some other day."

He didn't bother replying. Instead, he got to the other side of the truck before she could fully step out.

For a moment, they both stood still. When she shivered, Marlon couldn't help rubbing her arms.

"Sorry," he said, realizing what he was doing.

"Marlon, I want to go home."

"Ana-Maria had green eyes. That's something you can't change about a person, their eye color."

Marlon continued staring into her eyes, gripping her arms harder when she tried to move away. The street was dark and quiet all around them.

"What did you want, Marlon?"

"I'd like to get to know who you really are, Ana Sanz," he said, bending his head down close to hers. Ana stiffened.

Marlon stepped back, allowing her to move away. Usually if a woman didn't move, she didn't want to be kissed, or so went his experience in life.

"We can talk another day," she said. "I need some time to collect my thoughts."

"Right," he replied. "Let me know when you're ready."

Chapter Fifteen

Daniel hung up the phone with a sigh and looked around his living room. The fire was finally glowing, the freshly bought red roses were opening in their vase and the vanilla scented candles completed the mood he had hoped to create. His small Christmas tree had three perfectly wrapped presents underneath it. Dinner was staying warm in the oven, and she had the nerve to tell him she wasn't coming. He had not only spent Christmas Day alone but also Boxing Day since Ana hadn't bothered to come then either.

He sank onto the couch and let gloom overtake him. How annoying for Ana to take her job at the coffee shop so seriously, when he made it clear she should quit. If she had done as he told her, then she wouldn't need to make excuses about needing to sleep because of a slight cold. Daniel envisioned her with her sore throat and stuffy nose, as his heart sank. To think that she would rather be alone than have him around to take care of her stabbed him in the chest.

A few minutes on the bus and she could be in front of a warm fireplace with a snifter of brandy in hand to warm her up. He was very good at taking care of people. Even Gloria would agree with that.

Daniel blew out the candles, turned on the lights, and picked up his tablet to read the news. No use wasting romantic gestures on himself. The total silence in the house emphasized the tick of the grandfather clock on the other side of the room. It was impossible to concentrate without her next to him. This was the night that he planned to change their relationship, to carry through with what alcohol and lack of self-confidence had impeded him from doing before. For days, he had been building his courage, and he wasn't about to let a little cold bring him down. It was now or never. And never seemed like a terrible option.

Showing her the tender side of him, instead of the hardline professor side he wore every day, could bridge the gap between their relationship as mentor and student and cement them as boyfriend and girlfriend. He jumped up to get his keys. The plan was perfect; he'd go to her brother's house so she wouldn't have to take the bus, which seemed to be her objection in the first place. Once here, and snuggled on his couch, he would make soup and nurse her out of the cold. She'd be astonished at his compassion, her love for him growing until she never wanted to be separated again. He smiled. It was a good strategy.

But then he couldn't remember where she lived. The keys fell back into their place. Calling her for directions was an option, but that would ruin the surprise. And she would probably tell him not to come. It was possible that if he defied her and went anyway, she would perceive his actions as annoying. Women were hard to please when challenged.

But the fact remained that she didn't understand how lonely he was without her.

Daniel paced around the house, glass of wine in hand, wishing he had a hobby to keep his mind busy. Too restless to read, he settled in for an evening watching television like the uneducated masses. The actress, whom he didn't recognize, reminded him of Ana; long, curly hair and a wide smile that masked her sadness.

With closed eyes, he could imagine her in front of him with her curls draped over her shoulders, just as he liked it. He could see her perfectly shaped body outlined by a form-fitting dress and her full lips moving slowly as she said that she would give up everything for him. He smiled at the thought. They would move to an island in the Caribbean, run a restaurant or bar and have a wonderfully calm life in the sun.

Just as his dream drug him further into it, the doorbell pierced through the silent house. His eyes shot open. Such an enjoyable dream near clear blue water only to find himself in his living room.

The doorbell rang again. Followed by soft knocking.

Ana must have come over after all. No one likes to be alone when they're sick.

Soft knocking continued as he set his glass of wine back down next to the other and ran to let her in.

"Well, hello! I didn't think you were home!"

Daniel froze.

"Can I come in, darling? It's freezing out here."

Gloria stepped forward, forcing Daniel to stumble backwards into what used to be her house. She handed her coat and scarf off, which he took automatically, unable to breathe, let alone think.

He hung the coat on the rack while numbly watching. Gloria walked straight into the living room as though having come home from spending years at the grocery store.

All these years when he thought of her, he always envisioned that she had gotten fat or ugly. She wasn't either of those things, which at first confused him, so ingrained was his theory. On closer inspection of her firm curves and brightened face, he found himself drawn to her as a man. He turned on the entryway light and his appreciation turned to awe. She had never curled her hair or worn make-up when married to him. The stylish dress that hugged her waist and the black leather boots were both weather inappropriate and a major change from the usual khaki slacks and buttoned-down shirt she had worn ever since he first met her in college.

"Are you surprised to see me, Daniel?" she asked.

"Very surprised." His dry throat conveyed more surprise than he wished it would. "What are you doing here?"

"I was in town, and I missed you." She shrugged as though her words were the most normal thing to say to him after so long. "I wanted to see you."

"Where is your husband? Aren't you married?"

"No. I didn't go through with that. He was nice, but in the end, he wasn't for me. I realized I had gotten involved with him for the wrong reasons. After the divorce, I was in a state of shock and obviously wasn't thinking straight. It was a strange time for me."

"You asked for the divorce."

"I know. I don't know how to explain what I was feeling." She looked around the room, her eye settling on the wine and roses and unlit candles. "Were you expecting someone?"

Daniel cleared his throat and rubbed his hands on his thighs.

"Yes, but she's sick. She isn't coming over anymore."

He topped off his glass of wine and sat on the couch. After waiting a moment, Gloria moved away from the fire and sat next to him. She reached for the bottle of wine with exaggerated movements, but he grabbed it before she could touch it and filled up the empty glass for her.

"You're seeing someone?"

"Yes."

"That's something I never expected. I guess I should have, but the thought just never came into my head. I always thought of you as a one-woman man."

Daniel sneered into his wine. "I was until that one woman left."

The two of them sat in silence for a moment. He thought back to all the silent moments they had had during their marriage and smiled at the conclusion that they had had too many.

"Okay, Gloria, what's the real reason you're here?"

"I told you, I wanted to see you."

"About what?"

"Nothing," she said, moving closer to him. She placed her hand on his thigh and smiled. "I missed you, Daniel."

A shudder shot through his spine as her hand moved lightly up his leg. When he heard himself groan involuntarily, Daniel jumped from the couch to the fireplace. After so many years, she still had that effect on him.

Gloria threw her head back and laughed; a bewitching sound that startled him. The discordant laugh that used to embarrass and amuse him at the same time was no longer there. Just like everything else about her unfamiliar look, Gloria's laugh had a deep, sexy quality to it. It was too charming to be anything but fake.

"What's this woman like?" she asked. "Anything like me?"

"She's completely different from you."

"Rebound?"

"What?"

"Is she your rebound?"

"No. My rebound was a drunken night with a linguistics professor. She was a little like you. It confirmed to me why I shouldn't date women who are similar to my ex-wife."

"Daniel, that's a terrible thing to say. Isn't there something good about me you would want in your girlfriend?"

"At one point, you were my ideal. Forgive me if my change of mind insults you."

Even his anger couldn't stop the tingling sensation she had given him earlier. He turned away from her, hoping another drink would cool off his emotions. Facing away from her, he took a moment to close his eyes and collect himself. The only reason he felt like taking Gloria in his arms was because he had expected Ana to be with him tonight. It had nothing to do with Gloria herself; it was simply a hormonal reaction. He breathed out slowly, put his head back in control, and poured himself a whiskey.

"Will you pour me a scotch?" Gloria asked.

"I got rid of the scotch the day they delivered the divorce papers. I didn't think there was a reason to keep it around."

Gloria laughed again. He could feel her presence directly behind him.

"I guess I'll have what you're having then."

His back stiffened as her hand reached around and picked up his glass. Once her nearness faded, Daniel took his chance and turned around, steadying himself by gripping his whiskey. To his relief, Gloria was back on the couch.

"Should we light them?" She pointed at the candles, picking up the long lighter before waiting for him to answer. Her questions were never questions. They were statements and demands wrapped up in the package of a cooperative query.

Daniel stood like a statue; his only movement was his right hand as he drank his whiskey.

"When did you become so romantic, Daniel? You never set out candles and roses for me."

"We were never that type of couple, were we?" he said. "It never occurred to you to be romantic either."

"Don't get defensive, Daniel. It was just an observation. I wasn't accusing you of anything."

"There's nothing to accuse me of. *We* are no longer married. I no longer have a responsibility to answer your questions, and you have no right to ask any."

He was panting with anger now. Unable to catch his breath, he decided not to speak until his body temperature cooled down. In silence, he opted to watch her closely.

Gloria slid her hands down her dress and sat down on the couch. Her curves, highlighted by her gracefulness, seemed to encourage his anger to disappear, replaced by an awe of the female power in front of him. It wasn't just his anticipation of Ana coming that made him want to touch her; it was Gloria's raw femininity.

He gulped down his whiskey and sank into the chair behind him. The urge to make another drink was going to have to be pushed aside for the moment; he wanted to be conscious of his actions. She too was keeping her eyes on him; he could feel it. Like two toddlers in their mistrusting stares, but he was not about to be the one to move away first.

It was hard to miss noticing how the candle glow lit up Gloria's face exactly as he had hoped it would do to Ana's, although he wouldn't have minded looking at her like that for longer, the question of how Ana would react if she found out about his ex-wife being over, cranked up his heartbeat. She didn't seem the jealous type, but the subject hadn't yet come up.

He could only imagine what he would say if she admitted to spending a night drinking with an old boyfriend. Marlon's face popped into his conscious flow, his lips curling at the thought of them together. Daniel was so deep in his daydream that he forgot Gloria was sitting next to him until she shifted her hips. Daniel cleared his throat hard to stabilize his emotions back to reality.

"How long are you staying in town?" He wanted his voice to stay stable, but watching her bend over to pick up her purse caught his breath. He wondered if he had ever really noticed how beautiful she was.

"I don't think you even looked at me like that on our wedding day."

"I don't think your breasts were as visible as they are right now." He meant it as a dig, to prod her into an argument, but she only laughed.

"I know. I really was conservative back then, wasn't I? Well, at least in clothing. After I moved a friend of mine took me shopping. She made me realize I had never taken myself or my clothes seriously. It really changed my entire outlook on life."

"I didn't know clothes could do so much for a person."

Gloria shook her head as she handed him another drink.

"You know what I mean. It just happens that changing the way I dressed helped me see who I was. I was going through a time of renewal and that was just a part of it."

Daniel smirked. She might be wearing different clothes, but her manipulation of words hadn't changed.

"You never told me how long you were going to stay in town."

"I don't know, exactly. I'm in between things right now, so I don't really have a time frame. When I leave depends on so many things."

The meaning of her words was unclear, but her velvety voice sent chills down his spine that made him wish to ask her to never leave again.

They drank again in silence as they both, once again, kept their eyes on the other. Daniel observed her body, allowing himself to linger again at her breasts. When he lingered too long, she set down her empty glass and walked towards him. Instead of lecturing about ogling her, she stopped in front of him, pressing her knees against his to spread his legs open more. The hem of her dress brushed lightly over his thigh as she stepped in as close as she could without falling on top of him.

Daniel floated outside of his body, powerless to resist anything Gloria did. He watched as she leaned over him and took the glass out of his hands. His heart beat loudly in his chest, almost wildly, when her perfume wafted past his nose. He pressed his lips together and clenched his jaws in a feeble effort to calm himself.

He would not give in to his physical desires. He couldn't. It wasn't fair. To him or Ana.

The beads from her necklace bumped against each other just inches from his face, making a rhythmic clicking sound that brought a rush of heat over his body. The impulse to bite them escalated strongly as he dried the condensation of his palms on his pant legs. And suddenly, without knowing how, his fingers met her thighs.

Pride told him to pull away, but her smooth thighs peaked his animal curiosity. Besides, she smelled heavenly. The silky fabric of her stockings moved ever so slightly against his index finger, her muscles flexed against his touch, and a soft sigh escaped her mouth.

It was the sigh that persuaded him to continue touching her, to ignore the past or the voice of reason in the back of his head. The soft gurgle in her throat encouraged him until his hands were sliding up the inside of her thighs, not stopping until they touched the lace at the ends of her stockings. He ran the tips of his fingers over the rounded peaks of the silk lace as a blind man would. Wild instinct urged his fingers farther up her thighs to see if anything had changed about her underneath those elegant clothes, but another sigh escaping her mouth, this one admitting impatience, awoke him out of his stupor. He placed his hands back on his own legs and opened his eyes.

"Much of my staying here depends on you, Daniel," she whispered, as she kissed him on the lips.

Daniel sighed, hating himself for not having the willpower to stop her.

Chapter Sixteen

A BLAST OF FREEZING wind darkened Ana's mood. There was nothing worse than wearing an additional ten pounds of clothing only to have the wind seep through it. Grumbling her frustration into her scarf, Ana tried to hug her coat closer to her body to warm it up. The sweater and coat weighed down on her shoulders, which were exhausted from shivering with fever. If the wind could just stop spitting freezing particles through her porous coat, she knew she could fall asleep leaning against the bus stop wall. Javier had dropped her off at five-thirty when she hadn't felt this bad. The medicine she took before had worn off too quickly, but luckily for her, one of her coworkers noticed her fever-blazed face and sent her home. At least she had felt lucky when she hung up her apron, but now she just felt angry for being out in the cold.

By the time the bus turned the corner, her head was swirling, and her mouth was overproducing saliva. She panicked at the thought of waiting for another bus, but possibly vomiting on the bus was just as unappealing. Grabbing some snow, she rubbed it against her feverish face to settle her stomach. The other lady waiting for the bus stepped around her as though she might carry the plague, then warned the bus driver about a potential drunkard loud enough for everyone to hear while pointing at her. Ana gritted her teeth and kept her mouth shut as she tried to march down the aisle in a straight line.

Relief swept through her until she noticed it wasn't the right bus. This was the 56, which passed by Daniel's house, not her own. Nausea threatened again, and tears pricked her eyes, but there was nothing to do about it. Her pride rankled at the bus driver glancing worriedly at her. There was no way she was going to push the call button to admit she'd gotten on the wrong bus now.

All she needed was a bed, three big quilts, and another ibuprofen running its course. Her only options were to get off and walk back to the 72 bus stop or go to Daniel's house. Tears filled her eyes at the thought of waiting in the cold again. Daniel would probably be happy to see her since she bailed on him the last two days, even if she was sick.

The trees blurred before her eyes, then disappeared completely into darkness until the bus stopping swung her head forward. Jerking herself awake, Ana looked out the window and sighed with relief when she saw she hadn't missed her stop. Despite the pain in her sinuses and head and the burning fever, Ana forced her eyes open and her mind conscious. Soon she would be under Daniel's care, in front of a fire with a hot tea in hand.

Guilt stabbed at her along with the shooting pain in her throat. She spent much of her shift the day before planning out how to break up with him, only to get cold feet and make up an excuse to not go to his house for dinner. Unfair as it was to Daniel, Ana felt she would give up everything she could just to be taken care of at that very moment.

When the bus came to her stop, Ana stumbled down the stairs, almost falling face first into the slush below. Unable to stand upright without effort, Ana concentrated on her feet. It would be about two hundred steps from the bus stop to the left. That's where it always was before. Once she even walked there with her eyes closed, just for kicks. But today when she lifted her head at the two hundredth step, she saw a Bentley in the driveway and practically fell into a sobbing heap, thinking she was at the wrong house.

But no, it was the right address with the same crooked tree in the yard. And the same scraggly bushes. Yet there was a red Bentley gleaming in the driveway. Ana hesitated.

Surely, he didn't buy her a Bentley. That would be rather embarrassing. She was almost certain he didn't make enough money. Almost. But then, really, what did she know about how much he made? He was tenured, which meant he wasn't poor, but she wasn't sure he could afford a Bentley.

Ana vaguely remembered a forgettable conversation between them about which very sensible car she should buy once she had enough money saved. He said she needed one with four-wheel-drive that could drive in the snow. That wouldn't be a Bentley, as far as she knew.

The most obvious answer was that someone was at this house. It was Christmas, after all. But who would be there if he had no family? A friend? A colleague? If so, they might recognize her as a student. Her showing up unannounced could get him in trouble.

Ana stumbled, grabbing onto the mailbox to steady herself. Feverish hammers were hitting her temples in rhythm to her high heart rate. If she hadn't been sick, she would leave, but she barely had enough strength to make it to his door, let alone back to the bus stop. All she needed was for him to take her home. Or use his phone since hers had no battery. Daniel would just have to come up with some sort of excuse, and she would go along with it. She had no energy to do anything else.

She pushed her body to the front door and knocked. It took a few minutes, but finally Ana heard footsteps coming.

The door cracked open just enough for slippered feet attached to feminine legs to appear. The hammers on her temples increased their rhythm as she straightened her spine to find herself face to face with a woman. A woman that looked exactly like the picture of Daniel's ex-wife, only better. Slimmer and somehow prettier. Almost as though she'd grown younger.

"Can I help you?"

Ana shivered and felt her fever bring a wave of nausea.

"Is Daniel here?" Ana swallowed hard to keep from coughing. She didn't want to lose any more dignity.

"Yes. He isn't able to come right now, though. He's in the shower. Who should I say stopped by?"

Even in her feverish brain, Ana understood. It was eleven in the morning. Daniel always took a shower right when he woke up. She noticed the ex-wife was wearing the silk robe she sometimes wore when she slept over. Saliva gurgled up her sore throat and the simple effort of having to swallow took all of Ana's remaining concentration.

"I'll come back later." Ana croaked, her confidence shattered, tears threatening to spill out at the idea of going back to the bus.

"That's fine." The woman closed the door quietly without another word.

Left with no other choice, Ana willed her legs to keep moving, but she had no energy to keep the tears back. With her pounding head and her hips and legs feeling as though made of lead, Ana concentrated long enough to remember which way to turn to get to the house with the one person she knew she could count on.

Gloria was shutting the front door just as Daniel walked down the stairs and stopped in front of her.

"Was someone at the door?"

"Just a Jehovah's Witness wanting to give you some pamphlets about Christmas. You look very handsome this morning."

Daniel scoffed.

"Isn't it time you get dressed? Why are you wearing that, anyway?"

"Isn't it mine? I thought you gave it to me for my birthday." Gloria rubbed her hands over the silk robe, exposing her thighs.

"I gave it to you for Christmas three years ago and today is the first time you've worn it."

Daniel turned on his heels and marched into the kitchen. Gloria followed close behind.

"I'm going to make some coffee. You want some?"

"Haven't you had breakfast yet?"

"No, Daniel, I haven't. I heard you moving around down here before the sun came up this morning, but it's almost eleven now, so I'm sure you're ready for your next coffee and maybe some brunch. Should I make waffles?"

"Make whatever you like. You know where everything is."

Gloria smiled brightly as Daniel put his papers up in front of his face and pretended to read. She knew he was pretending because he forgot to turn the pages. Daniel was the fastest reader she knew, able to speed read through every article in less than half an hour. She used to find it ever so irritating the way he would snap the paper each time he turned it. Like he was showing off.

She glanced over her shoulder at him. He was cute reading the newspaper. Endearing, really. A man who refused to allow time to move forward. Besides, it gave him the excuse to watch her, which was fine with her. She swayed her hips slightly more and rubbed her hands over the silk robe as much as she could without looking foolish.

Gloria exaggerated her sashay as she walked towards him with the coffeepot. She paused to lock eyes with him. He looked away immediately. It was fun to play, allowing Daniel to think he still had some power, but she had a timeline. If she wanted Daniel back in a reasonable amount of time, she couldn't leave anything for him to control. He took too long in decision making.

Gloria leaned forward and thrust out her arm to his nose.

"Her perfume smells good," she said. His eyes snapped away from the paper to her.

"Better than yours did."

Gloria laughed. His insults were pluckier than before. And his feistiness didn't stop when his clothes came off. At least, not last night. She wanted to see more of this Daniel. "I can't believe you would let her use my robe."

"Someone might as well use it."

"What else do you let her use of mine?"

"What else of yours is here? I think the movers took everything that was on your list; all the things that you cared to keep. Anything that was left behind I assumed you didn't want, so I did with them as I pleased. Most of the clothes you left I sent to charity. The only reason the robe didn't go with them is because it fell behind your shoe organizer. I found it when I sold the organizer."

Daniel clamped his mouth closed suddenly, which created a torrent of giddiness inside of her. He hadn't forgotten her robe; he simply couldn't part with it. Perhaps she could forgive him then. After last night, she was convinced Daniel was only with that other woman because of loneliness, anyway. She certainly didn't satisfy him in bed. He wouldn't have been so eager last night if she did.

"Are things very serious between you two?" She tried to stay casual, beating the eggs as though just talking to a friend, but Daniel didn't look like he was buying it.

"I'd rather not talk to you about my relationship, Gloria."

"All right. We'll talk about something else. How's work? I read your paper from last year on the need for more diverse voices in literature. I also read your defense of teaching ancient literature. I don't like the idea of watering it down either. On my campus, they tried to put on Shakespeare with no graphic violence or sex. It was despicable. The very idea that students think they can rewrite Shakespeare is the most absurd thing I've heard in a long time."

That comment got Daniel talking passionately for ten minutes, giving her enough time to focus on the waffles. When the batter was ready, she brought it next to him.

"I thought I would plug it in here so we could talk."

Daniel rolled his eyes and put down his papers again.

"What are you reading?" she asked. "Or rather, trying to read?"

"An article by Professor Whiley."

"Is it interesting?"

"It's Professor Whiley; you think it's going to be interesting?"

They laughed at the private joke. The only way they survived his years as director of the English Department was by making jokes at his expense. He was the topic of conversation for many dinners.

Gloria placed her hand on his, but he whisked it away at her touch.

"Did you miss me in daylight at all?"

Daniel's jaws clenched, the muscles in his cheeks firming. She could sense that he was regretting last night more and more. He was slipping away from her, and if she pushed too hard, he would walk away out of pride. She would have to steady herself.

"How long are you staying in town?"

"I told you I wasn't sure."

"If you were planning on staying here, I don't think it would be a good idea. I have plans with Ana tonight."

"Plans here? At the house?"

"It doesn't matter where I have plans with her. This is my house, and you and I are no longer together. I think it would be better if you went to a hotel."

Gloria swallowed a sigh. She didn't want to be too obvious. There might come a time for that sort of thing, but not yet. She contemplated her next moves while supplying him with buttered waffles. As soon as he polished one off, Gloria plopped down another. Just as he always had, Daniel took one after another while reading the newspaper in complete silence.

Recollections of their first months of marriage slowly rolled through her memory, filled with a youthful version of herself, unable to keep her eyes off Daniel, even when he did the most mundane things. The way he squeezed every drop out of the toothpaste had been endearing, the way he lined his shoes up straight had been inspiring, and his ability to never crinkle the binding in a book was praiseworthy. Of course, after a time, all those things became irritating.

She spent three years wondering how that all changed, with no concrete answer ever coming. Not having an answer felt almost like, somehow, she had made a mistake in divorcing him so quickly. Perhaps she had blamed him for more than his fair share. During the drive back, she worked hard to keep from obsessing over all the reactions Daniel might have when he saw her. Last night she tried to stay in control and resist her physical urges, but she'd let her guard down when she saw his alcohol-induced reactions. This morning, Daniel was defensive, which was fine. She was prepared for him.

She straightened her spine and closed the waffle maker lid on the last of the batter. While it would be easier if he would just accept her, it would be more fun to chase him about a little. That girl who showed up was no competition at all, and it would be fun to put her in her place.

It was nice, in one way, to know that other women still desired him. It gave her a stronger case on why she was coming back. At least she wasn't coming back to a pathetic loser who sat waiting for her for years.

"I think I'm going to take a shower. You wouldn't want to come with me, would you?"

The muscles in Daniel's jaws tightened at her suggestion.

"I just thought you might want to recreate the zealous love making from last night," she whispered, leaning into his ear.

Daniel's fork fell loudly against the plate, and for a moment she thought he might take her suggestion, but his body stayed rigid in the chair.

"What happened last night was a moment of weakness on my part and it will not happen again," he said in a low and clear voice.

Gloria straightened herself up and squared back her shoulders. They locked eyes, waiting for the other to flinch.

"I should be out of here in about an hour," she said when Daniel picked up his paper again. Now was the moment to put her next plan underway.

"Where are you going to go?"

"To Sally and Damon Edwards's house. I called Sally yesterday and asked if I could stay until I found an apartment."

"An apartment?"

Gloria finished her coffee and deliberately placed it in the dishwasher.

"I've decided to stay," she said, calling out over her shoulder and laughing inside at the face she imagined he was making.

Chapter Seventeen

ANA ARRIVED AT THE front door and rang the bell, the ding-dong echoing through her head.

"Hi, Abuela," she said, her voice squeaking as Ellen opened the door.

"Ana! You sound terrible! Come in out of the cold," she said, holding the door open for her.

Ana stepped inside and let Ellen slide her coat off. The extra walk had drained the last bit of energy out of her. Once free of the extra layers, Ana stumbled to the couch and laid down before being invited to. Ellen wrapped two quilts around her, propping a pillow behind her head. Ana tried to smile even as her eyes closed.

"Here, take this," Ellen said, pushing an aspirin into her palm.

"Thanks, Abuela."

"Why did you come all the way out here? Shouldn't you be at home?"

Ana shook her head and snuggled into the quilts. "They sent me home from work. I went to his house, but there was another girl."

"Who's house? Marlon's house?"

Ana shook her head but stopped when pain wrapped itself around her temples. Instead, she contented herself with adding impatience to her voice while closing her eyes.

"Daniel's house. But he's busy with that other woman."

"What woman?"

"The one that answered the door," she mumbled. "His ex-wife. She was in a bathrobe."

Speaking became more difficult as her eyes closed. She felt Ellen stroking her hair, but soon sleep mixed Ellen's touch with memories of Ana's grandmother and the evenings she used to spend with her as a child, until she was taken away to a dreamland where her grandmother still lived and strange women answered doors in bathrobes and Marlon seemed always too far away to touch.

Ana startled awake, her body heavy and hot. "What time is it?"

Ellen looked up from her knitting. "How are you feeling?"

"Not good." Ana's voice cracked into a whisper.

"You might have to go to the doctor, Ana. I don't think this is just a cold."

"He'll just say that I'm over exhausted and that sleep would take care of it."

"You probably shouldn't talk, you sound terrible."

"I'm fine," she squeaked. The sides of her throat burned.

"Would you like some warm tea?"

Ana nodded, her body shivering with fever. She snuggled back down into the blankets, relieved to have someone take care of her. The sound of Ellen in the kitchen was comforting, lulling her back into a restless sleep. A burst of cold air followed by whispers woke Ana out of a dream where she was late for a math test. She tried desperately to open her eyes, but the light was too bright.

"Marlon!"

Ellen's voice echoed, followed by Marlon speaking somewhere nearby.

"Come in and help me make some coffee for us. We'll have to have it in the kitchen though; Ana is asleep on the couch."

"I'm—fine," Ana mumbled, willing her lips to move properly, but her brother kept trying to interrupt using Marlon's voice.

"Why is she asleep on your couch?"

"She's sick."

"Just a—cold." Ana pushed herself into a sitting position in her dream, where she found herself in a theater waiting for a movie to start. Except that she was alone and everyone in the audience kept talking about why she was late.

"I'm sick," she told them, but no one seemed to hear her.

"Why did she come all the way over here if she's sick? She lives on the other side of town." This seemed to come from the audience, again sounding suspiciously like Marlon. Ana shook her head, blasting pain through her temples. She didn't get to think about Marlon. She had deceived him and Daniel. Everyone. She didn't deserve any of them.

"—another girl in a bathrobe," someone was saying.

"Yes, a bathrobe," Ana repeated. The bathrobe. Her bathrobe. But not hers. Daniel's ex-wife's bathrobe. Gloria.

Ana gasped as she sat up on Ellen's couch. Her nose blocked air from coming through, giving the sensation that she was drowning. She gasped in air to catch her breath, using all her strength to sit back into the pillows. Next to her was a cup of lukewarm tea that she gulped down, too thirsty to care what temperature it was. Voices floated out from the kitchen. Ellen's voice and a male voice. With every ounce of strength she had left in her, Ana threw back the covers and stood up.

"Ana, get back under the blankets. I'll bring you some hot lemon water with honey," Ellen demanded as Ana stumbled through the door to the kitchen.

"Ana, come on. You're sick."

"Marlon." It was all she could say as he gently grabbed her by the arm and led her back to the couch.

"Lie down."

"No," she said, trying not to move her heavy head. "I should go home. I don't want to give this to Ellen."

"You don't worry about me. Worry about taking care of yourself."

"Marlon, I should go home," Ana whispered, no longer able to keep her eyes open.

"I'll take you home when I leave," he said through a bullhorn as they stood ready to march in protest. Ana smiled at him, happy to have him on her side. Or was she on his side? Looking around at the crowd, she couldn't tell.

Ellen looked around the room as Marlon dealt another hand of gin rummy.

"What are you looking for?"

"I keep hearing a buzzing sound. You don't hear it?"

Marlon stopped and cocked his head to the right. Ellen lifted her finger in the air until they heard the distinct buzzing of a phone. Marlon nodded and walked into the living room. Next to the couch was Ana's phone plugged in, vibrating angrily across the carpet.

"What is it?"

"Her cell phone," he said. "Someone is sending her messages."

"That's Daniel," said Ellen with a firm nod of her head. "What does he want?"

"You think I should read the messages?"

"Why not?"

"Because that would be a complete invasion of privacy."

"Does she have to know?"

"Ellen!"

"Well, on my phone, the messages show up on the screen without even opening them. At least part of the messages."

Marlon tapped his finger on the phone, lighting up the face of the electronic.

"It says, 'I thought you were coming over today after work.' The next one says, 'Where are you?'"

"Maybe you should write him back and tell him she's sick."

"I don't think that would be a good idea."

"But it's her phone, you could just pretend to be her."

Marlon sighed and shook his head.

"He's still wondering where she is. Why doesn't this guy just call her?"

"Ana says that he doesn't enjoy talking on the phone. Are you going to write back so that I can beat you at rummy again?"

Marlon laughed.

"You can beat me at rummy even if I don't write back. Besides, I don't know her code."

"0824," Ellen said, looking Marlon daringly in the eyes. "It's the date her parents died."

"Geez," Marlon sighed, finding the code to be correct. "There. Done."

"What did you write?"

"Can't come. I'm sick. See you tomorrow."

"I can't believe you just pretended to be Ana," Ellen said, so unironically that Marlon couldn't help but chuckle.

"What a lawyer I would make, huh? Doing exactly what I would not advise a client to do." He shook his head as he picked up his cards again.

Ellen tapped her temples with a smile. "I'm betting most lawyers do that very thing. And don't worry, I'll tell her I did it. I don't see the harm in letting him know she is sick. At least that infernal vibrating will stop now."

"Honestly, Ellen, I wonder if you're a good influence on me."

At that, Ellen burst into deep laughter that eventually caused a downturn to her rummy dominance.

Ana opened her eyes slowly. Her head no longer hurt, though the pain in her throat did, as well as her cough. She cursed her smoking addiction as a cough doubled her over. It was time to quit smoking, New Year's Eve or not. A small voice at the back of her mind taunted the vow. Gasping for breath, Ana sat straight on the couch, practically jumping out of her skin in fright at the sight of a man moving near the fireplace.

"I didn't mean to scare you," said Marlon, coming out of the shadows with a glass of cool water. "I just thought you might want this."

Ana nodded her head slightly as she drank the water.

"Where's Abuela?"

"She went to bed."

"What time is it?"

"Nine o'clock."

"At night? How long have I been sleeping?"

"Well, I've been here since about four. Are you feeling any better?"

Ana nodded as she polished off the water.

"I should go home."

"I'll take you."

"I can call my brother and have him pick me up."

"I'm already warming the truck up for you," Marlon said, pressing a button on his key fob. "No use asking him to go out into the cold."

Ana paused, her body tilting slightly. Even after sleeping the afternoon away, she knew she'd be able to fall right back asleep once in bed. "If you're going to go home anyway, then I guess I'll take you up on the offer."

Her body moved as if it were ninety years old. When the cough attacked, she had to stop and double over to get enough breath. She was so grateful for the warm truck after walking so slowly in the icy cold that stung her eyes.

"Thank you."

"No problem. You aren't working tomorrow, are you?"

"No, but now I have to work Saturday when I didn't have to before."

"I have to work tomorrow."

"You work?"

"Doesn't everybody?"

Ana shrugged.

"What are you going to do tomorrow?" he asked.

"I don't know. Depends on how I feel."

"You aren't going to see Daniel?"

Any small bit of energy within her drained immediately. She hadn't thought of Daniel or the fact that she was supposed to have gone to his house that evening. Then she remembered the woman who had been there that morning. She wasn't sure if she had the right to even be angry about it. Thinking about it was tiring. Thankfully, Marlon said no more and was soon pulling into her driveway.

"Thanks for the ride, Marlon."

"Why did you come to Ellen's house when you felt so sick?" Marlon asked suddenly, before she could open the door.

"I got on the wrong bus from work. I went to Daniel's first, but there was a woman there in a robe. She basically shut the door in my face."

"He doesn't treat you right, Ana."

"I don't treat him right either." Exhaustion was pulling her to the ground faster than gravity. "I'll see you later, Marlon."

Chapter Eighteen

ANA HAD THE DISTINCT feeling that someone was staring at her. Before she could open her eyes, a small, pudgy finger poked her in the nose, followed by the squeak of a collapsed silicone nipple refilling with air. Ana looked straight in the soft, brown irises of Sofia, so close Ana could clearly make out the flecks of gold. The powder scent of a clean diaper along with graham crackers was so homelike it overwhelmed her. Ana smiled and lifted her niece onto the bed to snuggle, hoping to push her longing away.

"Where's your mama?" she asked, knowing Sofia couldn't answer.

"I thought she'd be a nice wake up for you," Elena said from the doorway.

"Geez, Elena, you scared me."

"Mama," Sofia declared, pointing to Elena.

"Weren't you supposed to work today?"

The implication was barely veiled, but Ana didn't have the energy to be offended.

"They send me home sick yesterday and gave me today off."

"You didn't come home yesterday until late."

"I ended up at Abuela's house."

A bilingual cartoon blared from the television as they walked into the living room. Sofia ran around in circles, singing along in her baby language with the show.

"Abuela? Who's that?"

"The woman I clean for. I call her Abuela. I ended up at her house and slept the entire afternoon on her couch."

"Who brought you home, then? Not this abuela, no?"

"Marlon brought me home."

Elena sighed, picking up tiny garments from a laundry basket of clean clothes.

"You need to come home more often so that I can keep up with all these people you're talking about. Who is Marlon?"

Ana laughed, which made her double over in a cough. "He's a friend. We attended the same high school, and we ran into each other a few weeks ago. His grandma is friends with Ellen, the lady who's house I clean. Abuela."

"Right. Okay."

The end of the conversation left them in silence for the rest of the time to fold the clothes. After waking up much better, Ana's head was pounding again.

"What are you going to do today?" Ana ventured to ask. She had a free day and was hoping she and Elena could hang out. Back when Ana was in high school and Elena and Javier were dating, they would watch movies together or South American telenovelas. Those days seemed so far away now.

"My sister is coming over to make tamales. You want to help?"

"You want my germs in your tamales?"

Elena laughed, waving her hand dismissively.

"Your voice sounds sexier than usual, but if you're up to it, I'd love to have you with us. I'll give you some cough syrup and you can wash your hands a lot. Besides, I know you aren't going to really do much more than make tea and eat the meats."

Elena poured out some cough syrup and handed Ana a glass of water with lemon and honey along with an aspirin. She was lucky to have such a nice sister-in-law, but Ana was certain she was a burden. After all, Elena had two and a half people to take care of already.

"What are these for?" Ana asked, pointing at the pile of flattened moving boxes in the hallway.

"Just packing some things up we want to get rid of," Elena said, waving her hand at nothing.

"What kinds of things?"

"I'm heading out with Sofia," Javier called out, coming around the corner with his daughter in his arms. He paused when he saw Ana next to the boxes. Had she not seen the look Javier and Elena exchanged, she would have accepted Elena's explanation.

"There are a lot of boxes here," Ana said, eyeing her brother. "What's going on?"

"We didn't want to worry you."

"About what?"

"We might be moving," Javier said, picking through the drawer for Sofia's mittens.

Ana nodded, remembering the real estate listing she had seen. "You're selling the house."

"Ana, we'll talk about this later. Don't be angry, okay?"

"I'm not angry. I mean, I love this house, but I don't expect you two to stay in it forever. I understand."

"Okay, so we'll talk later? I gotta go." Javier kissed her on her forehead.

"Sure. Later. I'm going to take a shower and I'll meet you in the kitchen, Elena."

"Hmm? Yes, sounds good."

Elena seemed distraught about the conversation, but Ana left her with Javier to smooth things over. It didn't upset her they wanted to move. The house was getting too small for all of them. What scared her was that she had no place to go.

A quick calculation in the shower helped calm her down. She had learned in one of her classes that the best time to sell was in the springtime, which gave her a few months to find a better job and figure a few things out. Plus, once sold, the owners usually had ninety days to move out, which would push it into summer. She should definitely have a plan by then.

Once clean and feeling more refreshed, Ana headed downstairs where Elena handed her an apron and directed her towards the counter. Elena's sister, Maria, was at the stove stirring the contents of two different pots.

"Your first job is to make the coffee."

"Sure, but I really can help with other things too, Elena."

Elena laughed. "I know, hermana, but you're the expert at making coffee and we want some from the new machine."

"New machine?"

"It's right over there."

Ana turned to find a professional grade X505. There were options for espresso, single servings, tea, and cold brew.

"When did you get this?"

"Your brother got it at the Black Friday sales. It finally arrived a few days ago. He felt bad about making such a big deal about not buying one, especially since we decided we would all get a say on what to purchase since we're all paying the bills. I convinced him it was two against one, which meant we should buy another coffee maker."

Ana opened the cupboard to find a brown paper bag of her favorite coffee from Argentina. Javier always complained that it wasn't worth the price. Seeing it forced Ana to pause for a second. She should call Javier later and thank him, but verbalizing gratitude and apologies were not her strong suit. And Javier would get weird about it, too.

The smell of chicken and pork broth filled the house, awaking Ana's hunger. She hadn't eaten in twenty-four hours. She walked over to Elena with a large slice of cornbread and butter once she had served the sisters steaming cappuccinos.

"What are you doing?" she asked.

"Just preparing some things. Maria cooked the pork and the chicken earlier this morning, and now she's warming up the broth. We need to put warm water over the corn husks to make them soft and then the three of us will shred the pork and chicken. Why don't you set out the coffee mugs on the table? The pork and chicken are already over there."

Ana knew she was being given the easiest tasks for a reason, but just being in her mother's kitchen again warmed her, making her willing to do any job they gave her.

"Okay, take a piece of pork and shred it into small pieces like this."

Ana followed orders, proud of herself when Elena nodded with approval.

"See? Things aren't as hard as you always thought they were. It just takes some time, that's all."

"Is that the masa? That looks hard. It's so sticky."

"It is. But messy doesn't mean hard. Here, you pour about half this bag into a bowl, add some chili powder, garlic powder, cumin and paprika and then the broth that I made earlier with the meat."

"You made the broth yourself?"

"Ana, broth is just the water that the meat boiled in with a few spices," laughed Elena. "It makes itself."

Maria and Elena giggled, their heads leaning in so close they almost knocked together. She had always seen them as twins, though Maria was three years older.

"Okay, maybe I think cooking is hard. But I won't learn if you keep laughing at me."

"You're right, Ana. We'll try to keep our giggles to a minimum," Maria said, winking at her sister.

Ana picked up her coffee mug with her meat drenched hands as she watched Maria slowly pour in a cup of broth. Then she stuck her hands into the bowl to massage the ingredients, making sure everything was mixed properly. Her movements were those of someone who knew what to do without thinking about it.

Watching Maria brought back memories of her mother cooking in the kitchen, making niños envuettas and other savory treats for the Christmas holidays. Realizing she couldn't remember the names of most of the everyday items her mother used to make brought a sudden wave of grief that left her motionless.

"Ana, what's wrong?"

"Sorry, Elena. Nothing, really. I was just remembering my mother."

Elena nodded in sympathy, but she didn't know what it was like to miss her mother. Not wanting to drag the day down, Ana moved on. "What's next?"

"Okay, so now that we have the meat done, we have to mix it with some spices, and then we will start putting the tamales together."

Ana watched closely as Elena added the right seasoning to the meat and mixed it up between her fingers until she nodded to herself after tasting another finger full.

"Perfect," she said.

Maria brought over the corn husks and laid ten out on the kitchen towels, dabbing off the excess water and taking her time to make sure Ana laid them out to her satisfaction.

"After Maria spreads the masa on the corn husks, you put the meat in the middle. Then I'll roll them and place them into the steamer," instructed Elena.

Ana smiled, a bit hurt to know she was still doing the least complicated task until she watched how carefully Maria spread the masa and how skillfully Elena rolled the tamales shut. Ana eyed Maria as she took away or added meat, learning to be exact in the portions. Maria and Ana worked silently, listening to Elena gossip about their family and people they knew in common. When she brought up their brother, Alfonso, moving to Los Angeles, a heated discussion ensued. Maria said she had little faith their brother could take care of himself. Elena listened patiently, then tried unsuccessfully to convince Maria Alfonso would be fine.

"Is that someone's phone?" asked Maria, putting an end to the discussion around Alfonso.

Ana ran into the living room, but by the time she finally found it she was too late. She knew who it was. Her heart fluttered nervously as she tapped his number. Daniel answered right away.

"Hello?"

"Hi, did you just call?" Ana asked quietly.

"Yeah, are you coming over today?"

Ana looked back toward the kitchen at the sound of Elena's voice. "No."

"Where were you yesterday? I thought you were going to come over after work?"

"I went over after work. You were busy."

"I was busy? Or I wasn't home? The only time I left was in the afternoon to help a friend of mine look for an apartment."

"You mean the woman that was at your house yesterday morning in a robe? I'm guessing she's your ex-wife?" Ana tried to keep her voice steady, but the shaking came through. She bit her lip and closed her eyes to give herself courage, proud of herself for daring to say something at all.

Daniel sucked in his breath. "You stopped by yesterday morning."

"She told me you were taking a shower; which was strange because it was after eleven in the morning already and you always shower right when you wake up. Anyway, I wasn't sure if I should come over today. I didn't want to catch you with your pants down."

Elena, who was eavesdropping from the table, burst out laughing. Ana looked at her with widened eyes, clamping her hand over her mouth. On the other side of the phone, Daniel stumbled over a few words, producing only strange noises, before he was able to respond.

"Just come over tonight and I'll tell you all about it," he said, finally getting a hold of himself. "By the way, are you feeling better?"

"Yes. How did you know I was sick?"

"You sent me a message yesterday."

"Oh," Ana answered, surprised at not remembering. "I'll see you tonight. Bye." She hung up before she heard Daniel say goodbye and hurried back into the kitchen.

"Are you leaving?" Elena asked. There was a note of disappointment in her voice.

"No, Elena. I'm staying. I need to help finish the tamales. I never thought cooking could be fun."

"And your man?" Maria asked.

Ana shrugged as she blew her nose. The spices in the air were certainly helping her sinuses clear out.

"I guess I told him yesterday that I would see him today. I can bring him tamales as a break-up gift."

"A break up gift?" Maria asked.

"Okay, maybe you just sit down with your tissues and tell us the story from the beginning," Elena said, guiding Ana to a seat. "It sounds like this will be better than watching our favorite telenovela."

Chapter Nineteen

"I'M SO GLAD YOU came over." Daniel opened the door wide, a smile plastered on his face.

Ana tried to smile but failed. There were a million other things she would have preferred to do right then. Ever since stepping foot on the bus, she had been battling an inner storm. Her only reason for coming was to end things, no matter how hard it was. Although an apology from him for accusing her of cheating when he was the one cheating would be nice.

Daniel leaned over and planted a kiss on her lips. The movement was too quick for Ana to move away. His nerve to kiss her on the lips after she found his ex-wife at his house in a robe enhanced her desire for him to apologize.

"I brought homemade tamales. I helped my sister-in-law and her sister make them today. They're delicious. We can have them for dinner," Ana said, slipping past any more embraces.

"Would you like me to make a fire?"

Ana shrugged and pushed down any emotion that was vying to come up. She took some deep breaths as silently as she could, determined not to devolve into the woman she used to be; the one who couldn't have a grown-up discussion without screaming at, and sometimes hitting, the person in front of her.

"What's her name? Your ex-wife?"

"Gloria." Daniel froze at the fireplace for a moment before continuing to place the logs. "Nothing happened between her and me, Ana."

The way he said it, the quickness to say it perhaps, flagged something in her brain. He was lying.

"What is she doing in town?"

"She's moving back."

"And she wants you back?"

Ana's heart beat faster as he tore the sheets of old newspaper and shoved the balls he made underneath the wood. "I guess they hired her at the university again or something. I don't know. She showed up the other night because she didn't have anywhere else to go."

"She couldn't have stayed at a hotel?"

Daniel grunted, obviously wanting to be done with the conversation.

"It's only natural that she would come here. Things are over between the two of us. Nothing is going to happen. Besides, she didn't know I was dating anyone, so she thought I would be available."

"Available for what?"

Daniel laughed, but it sounded desperate, not joyful.

"Come here. She left me, remember? Now that she's gone, we can spend some time to ourselves."

"I thought you said she had nowhere to go."

"That was the first night. Now she's staying at some friend's house while she looks for an apartment."

"Couldn't she have gone to their house first?"

"They weren't in town." His words tripped over themselves in a rush to leave his mouth. He glanced out the window, waving his hands about. "It was Christmas, you know."

A queasy feeling came over Ana as she remembered the voice of the woman who answered his door in the silk robe. His eye twitched and his feet shifted the weight of his body back and forth. She shouldn't care that he was lying, but she did care. Perhaps it was pride, or perhaps it was vanity. Ana shook her head. Perhaps she just wanted a good fight.

"What's wrong?" He stepped closer to her, but she deliberately walked away. Control was necessary in a fight. And she was determined to be the one who kept it.

"Why don't we open a bottle of wine?"

Daniel stood up to help her select one, but she moved her hand away before he could take the bottle.

"Ana, not that bottle, it was a gift, and it's worth a lot of money."

"Are you saying I'm not worth it?" she asked as she picked up the corkscrew and scored around the seal with ease. Roberto's sinister voice echoed in her head from the night the girl he was cheating with tried to punch her: *She isn't worth it.* Ana shook her head hard and waited patiently for Daniel to answer.

"No, I'm not," he protested. "It's just that we should save it for a special night, a special dinner."

"Spending the day making tamales for us doesn't make tonight special enough?"

Daniel grimaced as the cork slid out of the bottle with a crisp 'pop'.

"Well, we might as well drink it now," she said, bitterness and anger trembling in her belly. "It's already open."

Ana held her glass up in anticipation of a toast, but Daniel didn't notice.

"What?"

"You're beautiful."

Ana rolled her eyes and downed half the wine.

"It's so dark you can barely see me," she said. "Are you actually thinking about her and how beautiful she is?"

Daniel jerked his eyes over to look at her.

"No, I was admiring your figure."

"Where did she sleep when she was here?" Ana asked as she polished off her first serving of wine.

"Upstairs in the guest room."

"Where did you sleep?"

"What?"

"Where did you sleep?" she repeated.

"What kind of question is that?"

"Fine. What did you two do, talk?"

"Why the third degree?" he asked. "I told you I did nothing. A friend stayed at my house. That's it."

Daniel slumped into the overstuffed chair, raising his eyebrows in cold indignation as he stared into the fire. Ana snorted before swiping the bottle of wine from the table. She filled her glass almost to the top before setting it back down again next to her. Drinking after taking the cold medicine was probably not a good idea, but she was too angry to be reasonable. Angry at her own cowardice. At Daniel. At Marlon. At her situation. At her cold.

She sniffed, pushing away her self-pity. Anger was a better emotion to feel.

"If this situation was reversed, you'd be furious."

Daniel guarded his silence.

"Don't you have anything to say to me?"

"Yes," he drawled. "I want to tell you that there is no reason for you to be angry. Nothing happened between Gloria and me."

Ana stared at him hard, willing him to keep digging.

"In the morning I told her she had to stay somewhere else, that I didn't want her in my house. She still seems able to manipulate a situation into how she wants it to end, and I hate her for that. She always had control over our relationship because of that power."

"Don't change the subject."

Daniel sighed. Ana wondered if he was frustrated with her or that his distraction method didn't work.

"I'm trying to tell you that nothing happened, and nothing ever will. You're the only woman in my life right now. You're the only one that I want."

His last line, as well as the pleading in his wide eyes, startled her. Everything about his demeanor said he was sincere, which told her she had approached the entire conversation the wrong way. Instead of showing her fury, she should have played up her hurt to break things off with him. The entire opportunity was wasted because she hadn't bothered to think for a minute.

"Are we okay now?" He reached out to her and pulled her close, his fingers massaging her thighs.

"No. We're not okay. Nothing's ok," she said, pushing away from him.

"What's wrong?"

"Everything. Everything is wrong. I've lost my scholarship. My life is falling apart. I just can't do this anymore."

"You've lost your scholarship?"

"I don't know," Ana mumbled, wishing she had said nothing.

"I'm sure your grades will be fine, Ana."

"It's not that. It's just, I don't know. This isn't working, Daniel."

"But it could work," he said, his voice trailing off. He looked confused and dejected, but Ana had no energy in her to comfort him. She didn't wish to do anything to comfort him. She just wanted to go back home.

"Are you staying the night?"

Ana tried hard not to sigh out loud.

"No, Daniel. I think we should stop seeing each other. And if that means even on a professor and student level, I think it's for the best."

Silence fell between them as Daniel sat back on the couch, as though thinking. But the seconds and then minutes passed by with no response, fueled Ana's irritation.

"I think I should go. Would you mind taking me home?"

Her headache was coming back with a vengeance and the thought of the long bus ride home was very unappealing. She had little hope that he would take her home after she just broke up with him. The way his face clouded with irritation gave her his answer before he even spoke.

"Isn't the bus system working?"

"Yes, it is," she said, biting back the reply she would have liked to give. "I'll take the last bus. Do you want me to put the tamales in the fridge?"

"I'm sorry?"

"I told you I brought tamales over for you. My sister-in-law made them."

"Oh, that's okay; you can take them with you."

"These are for you. We have a ton in our freezer at home."

"Yes, but you should take them back with you. I won't eat them."

Ana opened her mouth but shut it again before saying anything.

"And to answer your question from before, I think we can still have a professor-student relationship, Ana. I don't want you to think that I'm not here to help you if you need it."

"Thank you, Daniel," Ana said as she wrapped her scarf around her neck, preparing herself for the bitter cold outside. "I'll keep that in mind."

"Oh, and here, don't forget the tamales."

He held the box out through the open door.

"Good night, Ana."

"Goodbye, Daniel."

"Ana? Is that you?" called Elena from the kitchen.

"Yes, it's me."

"We weren't sure if you were coming home tonight or not," yelled out Javier.

"Well, I'm here." She stopped short at the trio sitting at the kitchen table. Her brother was in his usual place, drinking beer. Elena sat knitting next to him and Marlon was sitting where she usually sat.

"Hi, Ana." He smiled as though expecting her, then took a swig from his beer bottle.

"Hi." She stared at him, willing her face not to blush. The idea of coming from Daniel's house to meeting Marlon in her kitchen was not how things were supposed to work.

"What're you doing here?"

"I was going to call you, but I realized I didn't have your number. I went over to Ellen's house to ask her for it, but she didn't have it either."

"Seems you don't give out your phone number too much," teased Javier. "I don't even have it."

Ana looked at Javier for a second without comprehending him, then turned back to Marlon.

"But what are you doing here?"

"When I couldn't call you, I decided to come over. I had nothing else to do and I know where you live. Javier invited me in, and we've been hanging out for the last two hours."

"Two hours?"

"Sit down, Ana," coaxed Elena, giving her a sympathetic smile.

"I'm going to make some hot tea. Do you want some, Elena?"

Everyone at the dining room table shook their heads. Javier turned back to Marlon to finish their earlier conversation about cars. Ana forced her body to move into the kitchen. After breaking things off with Daniel, she was exhausted. On the bus ride home, she had almost fallen asleep, but with Marlon at the house, she wasn't comfortable heading to bed.

With the water set to boil, Ana snuck a peek under the hanging cabinets to the three sitting at the dining room table. Marlon had said he came by to see her, but he seemed very comfortable exchanging stories about camping with Javier. It wasn't until she heard the sizzling from the stove that Ana realized she had been staring at the creases that appeared at the corners of Marlon's eyes and mouth when he smiled instead of making tea. Ana jerked herself out of her trance. She went back to making tea, though she no longer needed it to warm up. She was sweating.

"Javi, I'm a bit tired. I think I'll go to bed," Elena said, rising slowly from her chair, rubbing her pregnant belly.

"I'll go with you," announced Javier, as Ana finally joined them at the table. She looked at him in surprise, but he ignored her as he shook hands with Marlon and helped Elena up from the chair. "I have a long day tomorrow delivering things and I want to get an early start."

"It was nice meeting you," Marlon said.

"You too, Marlon. Good night, Ana," said Elena with a twinkle in her eyes.

Ana mumbled her reply, but no one seemed to notice. In less than two minutes, she and Marlon were alone.

"You free New Year's Eve?" asked Marlon.

"Wide open," she said. "The only plan I have is to quit smoking the next day."

"A judge I work for invited me to a party. It's at a friend of his in Ann Arbor. Says they always have a big bash for New Year's Eve. I thought it would be fun to dress up and go, eavesdrop on the people who run the world. Or at least the city."

She smiled. "That sounds really fun. I've never been to a fancy party."

"No protesting," he teased, leaning in close to her. She could see the flecks of gold in his irises. A deep desire to kiss his lopsided smile rose in her chest.

"I broke things off with Daniel. I mean, as far as there was anything between us," she blurted out.

"Did you find out who the woman in the robe was?"

The hot tea threatened to go up her nose when she snorted her annoyance at remembering Gloria opening Daniel's door.

"His ex-wife. Her name is Gloria. She's back in town."

"I came to see if you were better," he said. "You don't mind, do you?"

"No, Marlon. I don't mind."

Marlon reached past his empty beer bottle and grabbed a hold of her hand. His long, strong fingers swallowed her small ones, covering them in warmth.

"Your hands are ice."

"Always," she admitted, the safety he brought her lulling her into relaxing completely.

"I better get going," he said, his voice still low. "I have to be at work at eleven."

"There's night court during the holidays?" she asked, wishing he was still holding her hands.

"The twenty-eighth through the thirtieth. Then there's a break until January third. America just never stops working," he said with a smile, his white teeth gleaming at her. He pushed back a stray lock of hair from her face as they stood at the front door. She didn't want him to go and would have tried to convince him to stay if he didn't have to work. But before she could voice her desire to convince him, a small voice in her head reminded her she had only just broken up with Daniel. There were a few rude words she could think of for women who moved on that quickly.

"Good night, Marlon."

As he slowly zipped up his coat, Marlon stepped close to her, staring without blinking. Every pore in her body churned with heat.

"I'm sorry I make you uncomfortable," he whispered. She attempted to look back calmly, but the rise in her body temperature was making it difficult to breathe properly.

"Good night." He moved towards the door, pinning her between him and it. He dropped his left arm as it reached for the doorknob and within a second slid it around her waist and drew her to him. The touch of his lips against hers heated her blood even more.

She could have fallen asleep in his arms. His fingers running through her hair finally calmed the quick beat of her heart. The safety he brought to her lulled her senses until he pulled her in closer and tugged harder on the skin behind her ear. Ana pressed her hands firmly on the back of his head and returned his kisses with a passion that had been untapped in her for years. Above all the emotions that swirled within her belly, the one that rose to the top was the desire to never be out of his embrace.

"Good night, Ana," he said in a hoarse voice. "I'll see you tomorrow."

Ana only nodded in reply, unable to speak any words for fear of letting the tears loose. She closed the door and locked it behind him.

Chapter Twenty

"Hello, Daniel."

The voice from behind his office desk pricked Daniel's nerves, causing this arms and neck to jerk as he entered his own office.

"How did you get in here, Gloria?" he asked, hoping she didn't notice the way his body reacted to her as he closed the door behind him.

"I'm sorry, I didn't mean to scare you." She sat at his desk as though she owned the office.

"Would you mind giving me my chair?"

Gloria smiled as she slowly rose from his desk chair and slid her body out from behind it. She paused for a moment just inches in front of Daniel before sitting herself down in the chair in front of the desk. He stared at her for a moment before taking his position at his desk.

"Okay, relax. I still have your key from years ago. You never changed the lock."

"Why would I have to change the lock?" The name on the open folder she had left on his desk caught his attention. "What were you doing looking at that profile?"

His class grade books were also open and his computer was on a page he didn't have the authorization to open.

Gloria crossed her legs, the slit in her skirt exposing more thigh than he had ever seen on her while dressed.

"I just wanted to find out what students you had last semester."

"And to find out which one I was dating?"

"Oh, that was easy to find. The little heart next to her name was a dead giveaway. I thought you said she was twenty-three."

"She is. She worked for a few years before going to college. Why?"

"Well, from the data in the computer she's twenty-four."

"Twenty-three, twenty-four. It's a glitch, I guess. How did you access her records?"

"My new job allows me to see the records of all students," said Gloria, moving towards the window.

"What new job is that?"

"Didn't I tell you? I'm Director of Student Affairs and part of the board of student advisors for R-Z in this department. I guess no one else wanted the extra work. It's about the new initiative to make sure the students are receiving the best experience here. It's funny how I'll be the advisor to your teeny-bopper girlfriend, isn't it?"

Daniel sighed. His heart rate was still racing from the image of her naked thigh just inches away from him. There was an inner urge at the pit of his stomach to pull her towards him and once again take his sexual frustration out on her, as she seemed to be a willing subject. It would be a scene right out of a novel. But his life wasn't a novel.

Instead of trying something he could only pull off in his head, Daniel took out papers from his bag and pretended to focus on them.

"Why don't we go out?"

Daniel shook his head.

"Come on, Daniel. Have you had lunch yet?"

"We had lunch during the meeting."

"Oh, well. You can come sit with me while I eat."

"I don't think so."

Gloria leaned over the desk, her breasts just inches from his face. They bounced firmly within her bra with each movement, her long, pearl necklace swung back and forth, grazing their flesh. A breeze from the radiator brought the smell of her perfume to his nostrils and made his knees buckle slightly underneath him. He pressed his thighs down hard onto his chair, keeping his view on the wood of the desk, and away from her blouse.

"Daniel, there's no reason for you to avoid me. We're colleagues. That's it. We have a lot to talk about."

"Like what?"

"Well, it seems Ana has had some problems in the past and I need to know if they've cleared up or if I need to be worried about them."

Daniel laughed at the suggestion.

"Are you accusing me of lying?" she asked, sinking into the chair behind her.

"No, but Ana isn't the type of girl to have been in trouble. She comes from a hard-working immigrant family. She's worked from age fifteen. She hasn't had time to get into trouble."

"She has a record for possession of drugs and spent some time in rehab. Looks like she got into the university through a program her grandmother donated to, which allows young addicts a second chance."

Daniel stopped sorting his papers and stared hard into her eyes.

"Gloria, I don't want to hear any more. I don't know why you're so interested in Ana, but lying about her won't get me on your side, whatever your agenda is. I care about Ana and for that reason you should have a little more respect for her."

"Perhaps I looked up the wrong Sanz." Gloria shrugged, walking around his small office as though interested in the knick-knacks he had around it. "It's possible that there's more than one student named Sanz at the university. I'll check again. At any rate, I'll see you later. You're coming to the party tonight at the Rossen's house, aren't you?"

Daniel took a glance at his calendar and sighed. The box had the New Year's party at Dr. Rossen's, clearly printed on it.

"I completely forgot. What time does it start?"

"Eight. Are you going to bring Ana?"

"Yes, Ana will be coming with me," he lied, unwilling to tell Gloria that Ana had dumped him a few nights prior. He was tempted to call Gloria that night, but never went through with it, afraid she might see him as a loser for not being able to keep Ana's interest.

"Good, I can't wait to meet her. Bye, Daniel."

He heaved a sigh. There was always the option to feign being sick and not go to the party. Or go to the party and get drunk. Or pretend Ana stood him up. He considered the last one a moment longer. It held the most possibility of winning him some sympathy points from Gloria. But then, it could make him a loser to her as well. More than anything, he wanted Gloria to find him appealing. He just wasn't sure how to accomplish that.

Chapter Twenty-One

Ana frowned at the image in the mirror staring back at her. She had a feeling that the rest of the women at the party would be wearing elegant dresses; much more elegant than this five-year-old navy-blue dress. It had cost her fifty dollars at the time, marked down from eighty, and so far, she'd only worn it once for a wedding.

"Wow, qué guapa!" exclaimed Elena as she passed by the bathroom. "Do you want help with your hair?"

"I was hoping you would offer. My hair up would make this dress fancier, won't it?"

"The dress is already pretty good for me," answered Elena. "But having your hair up will make you maybe more elegant."

Ana settled down on the top of the toilet as Elena took the curling iron to her hair. They talked about the other women in the neighborhood as Elena pulled and twisted strands of hair over one another and Ana told her about her visit to Ellen's house earlier that day after work.

"She was so exhausted, I might have given her my cold."

"Was she running a fever?"

"No, and she wasn't coughing, but still. It's almost like the beginning stages, you know?"

Well, don't party too late so you can check on her in the morning," Elena said, as she stretched out her lower back. "There, I'm done here."

Just as Elena was putting the last strand in place, the doorbell rang.

"Is that Marlon?" asked Elena.

"Should be. How do I look?" Ana asked, nervously touching her curls. It was just a party with people she didn't know. She shouldn't care who judged her since they probably wouldn't remember her name in the morning, but she couldn't help it.

"Wait right there. I have some earrings that would pop with that dress," she said, hurrying out of the bathroom.

Ana listened through the open door as Javier and Marlon fell into a simple conversation about some motorcycle show they had both watched.

"Sounds like they get along well," Ana said, looking down the hallway towards the living room.

Elena looked back as well and smiled. "Javi really likes him. He says he's a good guy. Here, put these on," said Elena, handing her two earrings with blue crystals in the shape of a flower.

Ana shook her head and took a last glance at herself in the mirror.

The minute Ana walked in, Javier let out a low whistle.

"Didn't know my sister could actually clean up so well," he teased, only to accept a punch in the arm from his wife. "Ouch! That's my cue to leave. Have a good time, you two. Except, don't have too good a time, if you know what I mean."

Elena pushed him out of the room, rolling her eyes back at Ana.

"I'm leaving, I'm leaving," Javier called out as he walked down the hallway.

"You're beautiful, Ana," Marlon said, standing still in the middle of the living room.

"Thank you, Marlon. Is the dress fancy enough?"

"I think you look amazing."

Marlon wore dark blue jeans, a black t-shirt with a thin gray hoodie on top, with a jacket to round out the outfit. On his feet were yellow and red sports shoes. She had to admit; he looked good.

"You're a very handsome date, Marlon," she said, grinning with excitement. They were going on a date. And not to a coffee shop. She hadn't gone out in so long, the excitement was almost too much.

"Ready to go then?"

They listened to folk music as Marlon drove and told Ana about his five-year-old niece.

"Do you have a picture?"

"I got better than that," Marlon said, pulling his phone out at a stoplight. "Here's a video I uploaded of her talking to her dog like she's hosting a reality show."

Ana laughed, delight filling her at the little girl's dramatic flair.

"She's so cute! Oh, is this one of your videos?" The next video shifted into Marlon, speaking about citizen rights when confronted by the police. "Wow, Marlon. You're very good on camera."

"Thank you. That means a lot, Ana."

She laughed at the next clip featuring Marlon sliding glasses onto his nose. "Nice glasses."

"They're from a sponsor," he said with a wink as they pulled up the driveway of a custom, two-story brick house. "But thank you.

"Whose party is this?" Ana asked. "It's the biggest house I've ever seen."

"Dr. and Mrs. Rossen's. They're old friends of Judge Kubson and I'm pretty sure my dad played golf with Doctor Rossen, though he probably doesn't know me."

Ana froze at the mention of the doctor's name. They hadn't seen each other since the night Ana-Marie passed, when Ellen called him. While there was a possibility that he wouldn't even recognize her, there also existed the possibility of him exposing her.

"Hello, there Marlon." Doctor Rossen's voice was just as soothing and deep as Ana remembered from the year before. "It's been years since I've seen you. How's your father?"

"He's good, thank you. I wasn't sure if you'd remember me."

"Of course, I remember you. Judge Kubson says you're a bright young man. He has high hopes you might become a judge."

Marlon smiled, but shook his head. "He and I have had that disagreement many times, sir."

"There isn't much you can do to change his mind once he's made a decision."

"Hello, Marlon." The voice came from a woman in her sixties with shoulder length brown hair and smiling blue eyes. She wore a long-sleeved red dress that showed off her curves, which seemed firmer than most women half her age. "And who is this? I'm Karen Rossen."

Ana took the woman's hand with a smile. Out of the corner of her eye, she saw the Doctor raise his brows for a moment but hide his surprise by taking a drink of his wine.

"I'm Ana."

"It's so nice to meet you, dear. You two are going to bring young life to this party," she said, her laugh like the clinking of crystal glasses. Ana couldn't help laughing with her.

"Nice to meet you, Ana," the Doctor said, taking his turn to shake her hand, winking as he did. Ana could finally relax. "Go on in. Get yourself a drink and enjoy the party."

A large Christmas tree stood against the wall, perfectly decorated in gold and red in what seemed to be the living room. A bar was set up next to the tree with uniformed waiters ready to serve anything a guest wanted. Waiters also walked around with silver platters offering food to the guests, who were milling about. Ana walked slowly through the guests, taking in the scenery. Every party she used to attend with Roberto featured cheap alcohol, drugs, and loud music.

"I've never been to a party where people serve drinks from silver trays," she whispered to Marlon after they accepted two glasses of champagne. "Have you?"

"My father moves in circles like this in California, so I've been to a few," he said with a nod. "The Rossen Christmas party is pretty famous around here for being very elegant."

"Well, it is elegant. Everything is so pretty. But I feel a bit, um, out of place. There isn't going to be some sort of twelve course meal with weird forks, is there?"

Marlon squeezed her hand and said, "Don't worry. There's no dinner and you are not at all out of place."

"Marlon! I'm glad you made it!" A large man with a gray, bushy mustache was charging towards them. Ana stepped back instinctively, but he stopped short of running them over. His big, booming laugh accompanied a hard slap on Marlon's upper back as Marlon introduced him.

"This is Judge Kubson," Marlon said, not seeming at all annoyed about the man's demeanor. Ana stepped slightly to the side to keep herself from receiving any back slapping, but the judge simply held out his hand with a smile. "And this is Ana Lopez."

"A pleasure to meet you, Ana," he said, giving a quick bow. Ana giggled as he turned her hand and kissed it. "Do you mind if I take this young man away from you for a moment? There's someone I want him to meet."

"Of course not," Ana said, already relaxed with the champagne and warm atmosphere. "I'll mingle."

Marlon gave her hand another squeeze before dropping it to follow the judge. Ana sipped her champagne and meandered through the crowd, enjoying the jazz quartet.

"Ana, what a pleasant surprise."

Ana tried not to let her smile wobble as she turned. "Hello, Daniel."

"How do you know the Rossen's?" he asked, sipping his drink as he searched through the crowd.

"I don't know them. They invited Marlon."

"Marlon. Of course. Listen, Ana, I need you to do me a favor."

"What kind of favor?"

"Just go along with it. Please."

Before Ana could answer, Daniel's arm slipped around her waist. When she tried to move away from Daniel's grip, his fingers dug in.

"Please, just stay here for a second," he murmured.

"Daniel, who's this?"

Ana started at the loud voice behind her. It was the same voice that answered Daniel's door the other day. His ex-wife, Gloria. Ana gritted her teeth before turning to face the woman decked out in a hip-hugging red satin dress, her hair left to flow down in soft curls over her shoulders.

"Hello Daniel. Oh, and hello to you again. We were never formally introduced. I'm Gloria."

"Yes, I've heard about you," Ana said, as she shook Gloria's hand.

"All good, I hope?" she asked, flashing a smile. "No, probably not, since you've heard it mostly from my ex. Did you two come here together?"

Daniel answered before Ana could say no.

"Yes. This is the Ana I've been seeing."

Ana eyed him, but he kept his attention on Gloria. His fingers dug into Ana's side, begging her not to fight him.

"Professor Donahue is here," Gloria said. "He wanted to talk to you, Daniel."

"Did he?" He looked in the direction Gloria was indicating. "Shall we go talk to him?"

He directed the question to Ana, who stood gaping at him.

"Um, well, if you want me to go with you," she stammered.

"No, you're right. Professor Donahue can be intimidating to talk to. I'll let you on your own for a moment," Daniel said, his voice sing-song. The entire episode baffled Ana, leaving her wide open for the wet kiss he planted on her cheek. "Don't get into any trouble."

He winked at her and downed his drink before heading over to the other side of the room. Thankfully Gloria spent only a moment more sizing Ana up before following Daniel. With a great sigh of relief, Ana walked around the room again, in the opposite direction of where Daniel was.

Everyone seemed already involved in a conversation with someone else, which suited her just fine. She took her time looking at the paintings on the walls, the family portraits sprinkled around the furniture and biding her time until she came to the bar.

"What are you having?" asked a man beside her.

"Something strong," she said with a smile.

He laughed and tilted his glass towards her.

"How do you know the Rossen's?"

"Tequila on the rocks," Ana told the bartender before turning to the gentleman. "I just met them tonight. I came as someone's date."

"Where is he?"

"Who?"

"Your date?"

Ana looked around until she found Marlon. Talking to Gloria, of all people.

"He's over there talking to that beautiful woman."

The man smiled at the tone in her voice and looked at where she was pointing.

"If you think he's having an affair, I could help you. Vengeance is my middle name."

"And how would you do that?" she asked. Flirting again after avoiding men for so long was fun. She looked over at Marlon. Flirting was just for fun, and Marlon didn't seem the jealous type.

"We could leave together, making it obvious to everyone here, and I wouldn't bring you back until morning. That way, he would assume the worst."

Ana laughed at the suggestion and sipped her tequila. The man winked at her as his body swayed a bit to the right.

"I could make you very happy," he continued on with the game. "I can afford to buy you all the diamonds you want."

"Really? All I the diamonds I want?"

"Maybe not all, but I bet I could buy you more than he does."

"But what if I don't want diamonds?"

The man laughed. "Well, if you want handsome, I'd go for him. He's much better looking than me. And honestly, since he's talking to a bunch of judges, I'd bet he'll soon be able to buy you diamonds as well."

Ana stuck her right hand out with a laugh.

"I'm Ana."

"Todd Dunkett, nice to meet you."

"So, what do you do, Todd, that allows you to buy so many diamonds?"

"I own two restaurants and am opening the third in May."

"Which ones are yours?"

"The first one I opened was Johnny's Steak House on the west side of town. That was about fifteen years ago and went so well that five years ago I opened another one, Cucina Bella."

"Oh, I love that restaurant!" exclaimed Ana. "I've only been there once, but the food was great."

Todd's grin became even broader at Ana's compliment.

"Have you been there recently?"

"No, I was there years ago.

"Well, you'll have to come in sometime. I just got the wine cellar decorated. I had this team of guys that do metal and woodwork put it in, it's gorgeous. I was so happy with their work that I'm having them do the work for the Brazilian restaurant that I'm opening in May."

"I think it was my brother and his friend that did that work for you."

"You're Francisco González's sister?"

"No, I'm Javier Lopez's sister."

"Well, it's a pleasure to meet you," said Todd, his smile even wider. "Javier's very talented. He did the best woodwork that I have ever seen. I'm recommending him to all my other friends. He works hard and gave me a great price. Plus, he had the work done when he said he was going to have it done. That's something you don't always get."

"What don't you always get?" Gloria's throaty voice cut into their conversation with ease. Ana downed her tequila, trying to keep her face neutral.

"Gloria! How are you?"

"Fine, Todd. How are you and the restaurants?"

"Doing great. You need to come visit the Italian one sometime. I'm opening the wine cellar on Valentine's Day. Ana's brother here did the work for me. It's stunning, if I do say so myself, but you'll have to come in and give me your opinion on it."

"I would love to come in and see it. I'm sure it's lovely. Your brother did the handy work for Todd?"

Ana nodded. She tried to wet her suddenly dry tongue with some tequila, but it didn't seem to help.

"Interesting. I didn't know you still had a brother alive, Ana Sanz."

Ana choked, the tequila burning the back of her throat and nose. She held her breath for a second to keep the liquor out of her lungs.

"Your drink a little strong for you, Ana? Want some water?" Todd looked genuinely concerned, but Gloria smiled in amusement.

"Don't worry about it," Ana wheezed. "I'll be fine."

"I'm sorry," Gloria finally said. "I didn't mean to catch you off guard."

"Oh, it wasn't anything you did. I just swallowed wrong."

Gloria continued smiling as though she could see right through Ana's lie.

"Will you excuse me?" Ana asked. "It was nice meeting you, Todd. Goodbye, Gloria."

Todd said something as she excused herself, but Ana didn't bother paying attention. She needed to go home. If she stayed much longer, she might have nightmares of Gloria staring at her.

"Ana, there you are!" exclaimed Daniel. His body swayed violently to the left when he opened his arms to greet her. "Where have you been?"

"I've been around, talking to people. It looks like you've already had too much to drink."

"No way! I'm fine! Having fun, like the young people do. You should try it, Ana. You're always so serious." Daniel pouted out his bottom lip at her before bursting into drunken laughter. "Come on! Let's dance. The night has hardly even begun. I forgot how fun these parties are."

Daniel wrapped his right arm around her shoulders and swayed drunkenly as he pulled her towards the dance floor. She turned away at the overwhelming smell of whiskey that engulfed her as he spoke, but didn't resist moving to the dance floor. She didn't want to make a scene in front of people she didn't know.

"How can you be so drunk already?"

Daniel stopped dead in his dance move and straightened himself up. People were starting to stare at them.

"I am not drunk," he said, pronouncing his words carefully.

"Right. Some water would be good, though."

"Or we could have a drink together. Like old friends. That's what we are, right?"

Ana shook her head, painfully aware now that Gloria was staring at them. A cigarette would be nice to calm her nerves, but she reminded herself that she was quitting, which was why she hadn't bought another pack and had left her vape at home. When Daniel started off in the bar's direction, Ana breathed in deeply and followed slowly behind, while looking around desperately for Marlon. Thankfully, he found her, twirling her away from the direction of the bar and guiding her towards a corner of the room.

"What's wrong?"

Marlon looked around, his face tense. "I would say a few things, though some of them I'll leave for the moment."

"What?"

"Daniel," he answered, his voice hard.

"He's drunk," Ana said, nodding.

Marlon shook his head. "We'll talk about him later. You have bigger problems. Have you decided to leave the university?"

Ana pulled back in surprise.

"I haven't figured that out yet. I guess I was waiting for my grades and to figure out a way to just stay there. I mean, I really only have a few semesters left—"

"Leave the university," he said. "Gloria is the new Director of Student Affairs and is on the board or advisors or something to the advisors of students R to Z, which means something like she's your new student advisor's boss."

"That shouldn't really matter. I never saw my old student advisor, so there's no reason to see my new one."

"Except that she mentioned wanting to get to know every student to help them with all their needs. And she was looking at you when she said it."

Ana looked towards the bar where she had last spoken to Gloria, remembering her conversation with Todd earlier.

"And because she's already caught me," Ana said, before relaying the mistake she had made. "I feel like she has something against me."

"Possibly the fact that you're with her ex-husband."

"Well, she can have him back. I broke up with him."

Marlon's eyebrows raised. "He doesn't seem to remember."

Ana blushed. "He was drunk, and I didn't want to make a scene."

Before Marlon could answer, Doctor Rossen approached them.

"I've just received a call from Ellen. She says she isn't feeling well. Would you go over there and see how she is? I don't want to ignore her call since she rarely complains. I asked if she needed an ambulance, but of course she said no."

"We'll go," Ana said, panic rising in her chest, grateful Marlon was nodding in agreement. "She seemed tired earlier today. I was going to check on her tomorrow, but you're right, she rarely complains."

"We'll go right now," Marlon said.

"Are you fine to drive?"

"Absolutely," Marlon said, as they walked to the foyer. "I haven't been drinking. Didn't even finish the champagne."

"Please, call me if she needs medical attention. I'll come right over." The doctor's eyes were sincere, calming Ana as she slipped into her coat. If he wasn't worried enough to go himself, Ellen must be fine. Still, she had taken care of Ana when she had a cold. The least Ana could do was take care of her if she wasn't feeling well.

"I'll call you either way," Ana said, hurrying to open the door. "Thank you for letting me know."

"Of course," the doctor said.

Ana didn't look behind her as she left the party and hurried towards Marlon's truck in her pumps. Snow seeped into them, freezing her feet almost immediately, but she didn't care. The most important concern right then was Ellen.

Chapter Twenty-Two

For an hour, Daniel fought consciousness, but the persistent sunlight bursting through the windows forced him to give up. His head throbbed and his stomach did somersaults as he turned over, trying once again to move away from the light. The grandfather clock in the hallway chimed the hour, sending a shooting pain through his teeth with every throb of his head. Teeth, he was fairly certain he didn't brush the night before.

Daniel groaned, then stopped himself as the noise brought more pain to his body. Finding slight relief in his cooling pillow, going over the previous evening. Just as he found a comfortable position, Daniel shot up out of bed, his body cold with fear and a hangover. He was naked, and he had no recollection of why.

The walk to his bathroom was short, but difficult. When he finally stood next to the mirror, Daniel barely recognized the reflection; it was one he hadn't seen since his early college days. His eyes were bloodshot, with large, black pools underneath them; his lips were pink and puffy, and his skin was translucent. He sighed in frustration as he struggled to squeeze the almost empty toothpaste tube. All he wanted was to clean the stink of alcohol out of his mouth.

"Daniel!" a voice yelled from downstairs. "Are you up?"

The noise pierced through his temples. Unable to yell back for fear that his head would explode, Daniel whispered yes to the mirror and hoped Gloria wouldn't push the subject.

"You're up!" she exclaimed from the doorway.

Daniel waved a limp hand in surrender, silently pleading with her to lower her voice.

"Are you hungry for anything?" She hovered just outside the bathroom door as though afraid his hangover might be contagious.

"No," croaked Daniel. "I'm going to take a cold shower and then I'll see what I can do. Maybe I can keep down some tomato juice for this miserable headache."

The bathroom door was almost closed before Daniel realized something he hadn't before.

"Why are you here?" he asked.

"Darling, I made sure you got home alright."

Daniel's eyes narrowed.

"You brought me home? Where's my car?"

"It's still at the Rossen's house. I drove us home in mine. We'll have to pick it up later today."

After a few seconds of silence, Gloria turned around to go down the stairs, but stopped herself.

"Daniel, don't you remember anything about last night?"

Daniel shook his head.

"I remember talking to several people, dancing a lot, and drinking. A lot. Most of the night is fuzzy."

"You don't remember introducing me to Ana?"

Daniel snapped his head up, instantly regretting the movement.

"Was she there?" he asked, but his memory sharpened, and he answered his own question. "Oh, yes, I remember introducing you two."

"You introduced her as your girlfriend, but she left with that handsome young man, Marlon. And you didn't seem to miss her."

"What do you mean by that?"

"Let's just say that by the end of the night, you wouldn't let me out of your sight or out of arm's length. It was like when we had first married, and we would stay by each other all night long. By the time we got home, you were even acting as if we were back on our honeymoon."

Daniel's body stiffened.

"Don't worry, darling, you weren't up for it, though you certainly tried. Alcohol got the best of your biology. What would it have mattered, though, anyway? You already cheated on her once. But seriously, Daniel, can you really say that you two are still together when she left with that young man, and you can't keep your hands off me?"

With that said, Gloria's voice disappeared, leaving Daniel in silence to vomit his remorse into the toilet.

Ana stepped off the bus and hurried towards High Oak Road. It was nine-thirty in the morning and Ellen had told her not to worry or come rushing over in the morning, but Ana couldn't help herself. She hadn't been able to sleep very well all night long after Ellen had finally convinced Marlon to take Ana home.

When they had arrived the night before, Ellen tried to make them go home. Marlon left, while Ana stayed behind, ignoring Ellen's complaints that she had only called Doctor Rossen to ask about the dosage of her headache medicine. Ana took Ellen's temperature and found she didn't have a fever, but that had only calmed her a little.

After calling Dr. Rossen, Ana got out the right medication, made tea and finally put Ellen into bed. Ana tried to stay the night, but Ellen wouldn't hear of it.

Ana tried not to think about the party as she trudged down the icy sidewalk. She was embarrassed about not putting up a fight with Daniel. Marlon didn't bring it up again last night, but she knew her behavior bothered him. Had the situation been reversed, Ana knew she'd be hurt.

Turning onto High Oak Road, Ana stopped. The same shiny Bentley that was previously in Daniel's driveway the week before now sat in Ellen's driveway. Gloria was walking up the walkway, her high heels slapping the pavement and echoing into the cold air. Ana ground her teeth, debating if she should confront her. Luckily, Ellen opened the front door before Ana could decide. She hurried behind one of the trees that lined Ellen's driveway and hid.

"Mrs. Sanz?" Ana heard Gloria say. "I'm here to see Ana, your granddaughter."

"She isn't here."

Ana was relieved to hear Ellen's voice was stronger than the night before.

"Well, maybe you and I could talk then. I work with Ana's student counselor. I'm visiting all my students before classes start. To get to know them a little better."

"I'm not sure what I could do to help you. My granddaughter doesn't tell me much about her studies."

"Do you expect Ana back soon? I could come back."

There was silence for a moment before Ellen spoke again, this time too low for Ana to hear.

"I guess I'll come back another time. Here's my card with my office hours and phone number on it. Please give it to your granddaughter when you see her. I'd like to help her register for classes. I hear she's eager to finish her degree."

Ana ducked down as Gloria's heels clicked back in her direction. Suddenly, Ana felt like an idiot. If Gloria wanted to speak to her, she should find out what she wanted.

Straightening herself up, Ana stepped out from behind the garbage and walked up to Gloria, who caught her image in the darkened glass of the car window.

"Hello, Ana."

"What are you doing here, Gloria?"

"I wanted to talk to you," Gloria answered, her voice as sweet as saccharin. "I'm part of your student advising team, so to speak, and I thought I could meet with you to see how you are doing in school. I've taken a particular interest in your file."

"And why is that?"

Gloria shrugged and looked away for a moment.

"I was looking for information about you and came across a video that looks a lot like you. Strangely enough, the name attributed to the woman in the video is Ana Lopez."

"People use aliases all the time."

"Lopez is the last name you told Todd last night."

"It's the name I give guys who I don't want calling me."

Though her answers were coming quick, Ana was almost out of breath. She wasn't sure how many more lies she was going to need before the end of this conversation. Trying not to panic, Ana smiled, hoping she looked serene.

"I noticed your grades are much better these last few semesters. Is that because you found a certain late-night help?"

"I moved to the business school because it interests me more."

Gloria nodded. "How old are you?"

"Twenty-three."

"Your file says you're twenty-four."

Ana froze. "What do you want, Gloria?"

"The truth. You aren't Ana Sanz, are you? See, things about you don't match up with the student named Ana Sanz. She's younger than you, with a drug record, and she had a reputation as someone who didn't take her classes seriously. Then, suddenly, a few semesters ago, she moves to the business school where she becomes known as a reserved, serious student who makes sure no one takes notice of her. Of course, there is an Ana Lopez who looks like you and she too has an interesting past. I found some fascinating reading about her on the internet."

Ana stared at her, pretending the words didn't faze her.

"Well, Ana, do you have anything to say?"

"Just to ask you again, what do you want?"

Gloria smiled with satisfaction. She was back to being one hundred percent certain she was right.

"I want you to give up Daniel," she said, keeping her gaze steadily on Ana. "And leave the university."

The last sentence sent a shock wave through Ana, though she tried her best to keep her jaw and gaze firm.

"And if I don't?"

Gloria shrugged. "Then I report your fraud to the university and to Daniel. Either way, you'll lose. I'm just giving you a chance to leave without hurting your name. At least this way you could attend a different university. No university would take you if you had a fraud charge in your history."

"I've already broken things off with Daniel."

"It didn't look that way last night."

"I don't care what it looked like. We're not together. Isn't that enough?"

Gloria laughed. "No, it's not enough. He could still become embroiled in your scandal, which would devastate him. He isn't perfect, but I know he's worked hard for his position and, quite frankly, I think it's terrible that you dragged him into this."

"Into what?" Ana asked, her heart beating so fast she had to breathe through her mouth to catch a breath.

"Your fraud. I don't know what's going on, but I know you aren't Ana-Maria Sanz. Part of my job also is to make sure the scholarships are being used properly. I'm obligated to report anything that looks fraudulent. And you, Ana Lopez, have several elements that appear fraudulent." Gloria lifted her hand and started ticking off fingers as she began her list. "You have taken over money that isn't yours, but besides that, you're using a name that isn't yours and you're at the university not on your own merit, but on the merit of Ana-Maria. How did you think this was all going to work out?"

Laid out in front of her so coldly, Ana could see what everyone else seemed to see before her. Still, she didn't want to give Gloria the sense of winning. Or that she was as clueless as she felt.

"Well, I should go. I have a dinner date with Daniel. Your 'grandmother' has my card. Call me tomorrow and we can set everything straight. Who knows, maybe I'll be nice and give you a recommendation letter," Gloria said as she slipped into the car.

Ana stood in the cold, watching Gloria drive away, knowing she was right about everything. Not until the Bentley was long gone from view did Ana turn towards Ellen's house. Ellen was standing at the living room windows, watching.

"What did she want?" asked Ellen as Ana kissed her on the cheek before shrugging out of her coat. She couldn't trust herself not to burst into tears if she spoke. All she could muster was a shrug of her shoulders. "She knows you're not my granddaughter."

Ana ushered them both away from the windows. She turned on the electric heater near Ellen's favorite chair and guided Ellen to sit down. "Yes, she knows. But I don't think she'll do anything about it."

"No?"

Ana shook her head as she sank into the couch. "Not if I drop out of school and disappear."

Ellen nodded. "Well. That's that."

"Looks like it," Ana said, the image Gloria painted for her still pestering her thoughts.

"Would you pour me some tea? I was making it, getting things ready, before that woman showed up."

Ana looked at the coffee table, more irritation choking her. "You weren't supposed to be out of bed this morning."

"Don't be telling me what to do. I woke up feeling much better and Marlon's grandmother came by with a coffee cake." Ana opened her mouth to argue, but Ellen lifted one eyebrow almost as a dare. Ana shut her mouth and poured two cups of tea. "I don't see any way out of it, Ana. You're going to have to do what that lady wants of you."

"I know, Abuela, I know. I just—" Ana paused to think. "I guess I can't believe I thought this plan would work. Like, really believed it. And maybe the worst part of it is what Gloria said, because it's true." Ellen waited while Ana struggled to control the tears that were threatening to pour out of her. "She said, '*you're at the university not on your own merit, but on the merit of Ana-Maria.*'"

Ellen grunted as Ana handed her a cup of tea. "That wasn't very nice of her."

Ana looked up, no longer trying to keep the tears back. They rolled down her cheeks freely. "It's mean because it's true. You and Marlon were trying to warn me the other day, but I didn't want to listen. I guess," Ana's voice trailed off as she searched for the right words. "I guess I wanted it too badly. I refused to even consider the possibilities of it backfiring and hurting anyone but me. She pointed out that Daniel could be in trouble if this comes out as a scandal. And, I, I never meant for anyone to get into trouble. I just wanted to go to the university."

Ellen sighed as she slowly sliced the cake.

"Let me do that," Ana said, watching as Ellen's hand seemed to go in slow-motion.

"I'm fine. Just didn't sleep much last night, as you know."

Ana snorted and gently took the knife away from Ellen.

"Did you break things off with the professor?" Ellen said, patting Ana on the cheek.

"Yes. A few days ago, though, I don't think it convinced Gloria."

"She's the one you encountered in the robe before Christmas?"

Ana jerked her head up from her cake.

"You talk in your sleep when you have a fever," Ellen said, her thin shoulders shaking as a coughing fit took over.

"Yes, she's the one," Ana murmured as Ellen sipped some water. She couldn't help laughing as she thought over the last week. She wasn't bitter about breaking things with Daniel, but she couldn't bring herself to be anything other than pessimistic now.

"I'm betting he'll be back with his ex-wife in no time," Ellen said, her voice hoarse,

Ana ignored the statement, though it was probably true. "Should I call Dr. Rossen?"

Ellen waved her away. "No. I told you last night it was just a scare. I hadn't taken my heart medicine. I'm fine now."

Ana nodded. There wasn't anything else to do but agree with Ellen, even though she wasn't sure she believed her. "Try to eat some of this cake."

Ellen took it, her hands shaking slightly. Ana decided not to comment on them. "What are you going to do, Ana?"

"I'll have to call Gloria later to tell her I'll drop out of school," Ana said, the words stirring resistance within her. No matter what Gloria had said, it didn't feel fair that she had to leave the university. "I'm sure she'll be delighted to draw up whatever paperwork it takes to do that. She is my student counselor, after all."

"Don't be so bitter, Ana," said Ellen. "We didn't consider everything in the beginning. Had we done so, you wouldn't have ended up going. And if you hadn't gone, you wouldn't have reconnected with Marlon."

The statement surprised Ana. "Marlon. Yes. He's a good guy."

"What's wrong with being a good guy?" Ellen asked, setting her empty cup down.

"Nothing," Ana said, shaking her head. "He's a good guy. But I don't know. I feel like everything is falling apart and like I should stay away from a good guy. At least until I know for sure this won't blow up into a scandal."

Ellen shrugged her bony shoulders.

"I think he's strong enough to see you through this."

Ana contemplated Ellen's words. Around Marlon she felt wanted, attractive. It would be fun to be his girlfriend. The very idea of it stirred a warmth inside of her, but there was also a small voice in the back of her head told her to stop and consider being alone for a bit. To take charge of her life again and become the Ana with dreams that were her own, not someone else's.

"You're a good girl, Ana Lopez, you know that?" Ellen said quietly. "Even in the circumstances that brought us together, I'm still glad to know you. And be your Abuela."

Ana sniffed away the tears that had sprung up in her eyes.

"Thanks, Ellen."

Ellen smiled. "You're gonna be fine. Everything will work out."

"I'm sure you're right."

"Of course, I'm right. I usually am." Ellen chuckled at herself as Ana shook her head. "Why don't you read my book to me? My eyes are too tired to read the small print."

Ana sat in the chair next to the couch and began to read. It wasn't long before Ellen's breath became rhythmic with sleep. The morning gave way to afternoon, leaving the living room in winter shadows. Ana got up to turn on the lamp next to the chair, smiling at Ellen's peaceful face, and instinctively leaned down to kiss her on the cheek. Lifting her head, she realized that Ellen's raspy breathing no longer filled the room. Ana dropped to her knees beside the couch, placed her head near Ellen's mouth, and felt no air coming in or out. Shocked, Ana jerked her head up and stared at Ellen.

"Abuela?" she asked, quietly.

No reply came.

"Abuela!" she shouted, jumping to her feet. Ellen didn't stir.

Ana stared at the peaceful way in which Ellen held her mouth and choked back tears. A black hole started growing in the pit of her stomach, threatening to overcome her. Grief and despair coiled around her like a snake and choked every hope and will to live straight out of her soul if she would let it.

Before the hole got too large, Ana ran to her bag and grabbed her phone.

"Hello?"

"Marlon?"

"Ana? What's wrong?"

"I think Ellen's dead," sobbed Ana, unable to keep her emotions from overwhelming her. "What should I do?"

"Just stay there. I'll be right over."

Ana hung up the phone and sat down next to Ellen. It didn't scare her to be the only other living person in the house next to a lifeless body. It wasn't the first dead body she had seen. She sat stroking Ellen's lifeless hand as she waited, thinking of all that she owed this woman.

"Ana?" shouted Marlon from the front door. Ana ran to greet him, bursting into tears as she pressed her face against his chest. His hands rubbed her back, his murmurings bringing her a calming effect. "It's okay, Ana."

Ana nodded as she pulled away. A tall woman in her late fifties, with tawny skin and curly, brunette hair, stood at the door. Ana recognized her from some local political ads.

"Ana, this is my mom, Amelia."

"Hello."

"Hi, honey. It's gonna be okay. Where is she?" asked Amelia, taking Ana's shoulders in her hands. The tender touch was enough to fill Ana's eyes with tears again.

"She's on the couch. In there."

Marlon chewed his bottom lip as he considered Ellen's body, looking to his mother for answers. "What should we do now?"

"I called Dr. Rossen already," Ana said, her fingers frantically pulling at the blanket she had picked up. "He was a good friend of hers."

Amelia nodded. "Well, then we'll start with him. Maybe he'll know the name of her lawyer. Now, don't cry. She went just like old folks hope to go, peacefully and in her sleep. She led a good, long life and now she's with her husband and all her family."

Ana nodded, though the words didn't bring her the comfort Amelia probably meant them to have. Dr. Rossen soon came, followed by an ambulance. Amelia and Dr. Rossen took care of almost everything as Ana stood by and watched.

After closing the door behind the paramedics, Dr. Rossen and Amelia, Ana sighed with relief and walked into the kitchen. She swallowed the sobs that threatened to come again as she placed the coffee grounds into the filter and turned on the coffeemaker.

"Can I join you?" asked a soft voice behind. She jumped at the sound, though she should have known Marlon was still at the house.

"You startled me."

"Sorry about that. Do you mind if I stay?"

"Of course not, Marlon. I'd like it."

Marlon sat down while Ana prepared the coffee in silence.

"Mr. Richards said he needed to talk to you soon to arrange the funeral."

Ana stared; her mind blank.

"Ellen's lawyer."

"Okay. I'll remember," she said, quietly.

"If you don't want to handle the funeral, I'm sure my mom would do it."

He leaned across the counter as though reaching for her. Ana stayed where she was, not trusting herself to keep from crying again.

"It's okay. I want to take care of the funeral. I'll meet with the lawyer."

"I'm glad that you were here with her. I'm sure she liked that," Marlon said after a moment of silence.

"I'm glad, too," she said, shuddering at the thought of Ellen dying alone. "Oh, it seems like a year ago already, but when I arrived this morning, Gloria was here. She knows I'm not her granddaughter."

"Is she going to tell the university?"

"No, not if I break up with Daniel, which I told her I already did, and drop out of school."

"What are you going to do?" he asked, pulling her hand closer to him, causing her to lean into the counter. For a moment they looked into each other's eyes in silence, and Ana remembered what Ellen had said about him.

"I'll have to drop out of school. Just don't say 'I told you so' right now, Marlon. You can do it later," Ana said, surprised to find enough energy to tease him.

"It didn't even occur to me," he said, kissing her fingers. A shot of nervous energy went through her as his lips touched her skin. "I'm sorry that this is all happening at once."

"It is a lot."

"Come on, let me take you home. You need some rest."

Marlon's dark eyes were full of compassion, like a refuge. Without wasting a second more of that haven, Ana flung herself into his arms and wept again. Tears of sorrow for Ellen and for the emptiness that Ana felt growing inside her. One more part of her family was gone. Marlon held her until the sobs ceased, stroking her hair, and murmuring that she would be alright.

"Oh, no. I can't believe it. What time is it?"

"Almost four."

"I have to go to work," Ana moaned, swiping the tears from her eyes.

"Call in sick, Ana. They should understand."

"Nathalie won't. I've screwed things up with her too many times. She won't believe me. At this point, she's looking for a reason to fire me and I can't afford not to have a job."

"Fine," Marlon said, leading her to the front door. "Get your coat and your things. I'll take you."

Chapter Twenty-Three

THE MORNING CAME TOO quickly once again after another dreamless sleep. Between working and the funeral arrangements, sleep was hard to get. The last two mornings in a row greeted her with a cold sun and the immediate realization that something was wrong. The first morning it took her foggy brain almost half an hour to realize why a heavy black hole was eating away at her insides. Today, it only took three minutes to burst into tears.

Before she could finish brushing her teeth, her cell phone buzzed with a reminder of the meeting with Ellen's lawyer. Ana sighed heavily. She wanted to climb back into bed and cry. Her body carried the same heavy feeling she remembered having after her parents died. Perhaps not as heavy, but the same type of exhaustion and stress.

Of course, when her parents died, she didn't go in to work. Her boss at the factory gave her two weeks off, but once those were gone, she decided she needed more. They fired her by text message after she didn't show for seven shifts and didn't answer their calls for over a week. Ana could still taste the rage that filled her at reading the text. Even as her hands shook from her anger, Ana wrote up an article about worker's rights after a family death that an online journal eventually published.

The house was quiet. With the remnants of her cold shower still on her skin, Ana tip-toed down the hallway as though being quiet might make her wish come true.

"Javier? Elena?" she called, embarrassed as she did it.

No one answered. For the first time in ages, she found the entire house empty. Ana made her coffee with the new machine and sat down to allow her emotions to roll over her as she sipped the scalding liquid. All alone, she had the time to think about Ellen, Daniel, herself, and the mess she'd gotten into without fear of someone asking her to explain the tears rolling down her cheeks. She could allow herself to endure the embarrassment of her weak, insipid relationship with Daniel and revel in the love that had grown between Ellen and her.

A time for mourning. A time to live and a time to die. One of her grandmother's favorite sayings. Each time after saying it, she would sit for a moment, then rise with a heavy sigh and get to work around the house.

The vision of her grandmother's tenacity brought Ana to her feet. Before Marlon drove up, Ana already had her coat and scarf on and was outside waiting. Underneath the warm layers, Ana was overcome with a sense of resignation for the day. It was work that had to be done each time a person died. Death, after all, was what they all succumbed to in the end.

"Good morning, Ana." His deep voice carrying over the rumbling of the truck somehow comforted her. It worked like a magnet on her heart, drawing her to the truck without a fight, resigned to what she needed to do. She was glad he would be there, as her brother had been there with her after their parents died. Doing it alone seemed like frightening work.

Soon they both sat in a large office, that was much nicer than the building from the outside. As the lawyer droned on about Ellen's wishes for burial, Ana tried to listen, but found herself lost in the lawyer's monotone words.

"Coffee?"

The small voice snapped Ana out of her thoughts. She looked up at the secretary, who had blond curls and a sympathetic smile.

"Yes, thank you," Ana said, taking the mug.

"Thank you, Deborah," the lawyer, Mr. Richards, said once everyone was served. "Now, Ana, I feel I'm keeping you too long. I'll send Ellen's wishes to the funeral home and leave you a copy of her ideas for the wake. Now, on to the fun things."

"What about this is fun?" she asked, her old defiance bubbling within her.

The lawyer smiled. He clasped his hands together and leaned his aging face forward so that Ana could make out each of his laugh lines.

"As you know, Ellen didn't have any family left. No blood family, at any rate."

He paused. Ana nodded, though her desire to hit the man hadn't yet diminished.

"A few weeks ago, she came in here, wanting to change her will. Before that, all her belongings were to be transferred to a charity, but that day she changed almost all of it. I gotta say, it's best that she was the last living relative. I've seen this before when there are still children alive, and it can be a mess."

"I don't understand what you mean."

"She left the house and most of her bank account to you, one Ana Lopez."

A muffled thud from her coffee mug hitting the carpeted floor registered quicker than the words the lawyer had just said.

"I'm so sorry!" Ana jumped out of the chair, staring at the damp spot growing larger by the second. "I'm sorry. I'm sorry. What did you say? Maybe I heard you wrong."

Mr. Richards called his secretary instead of answering. It was just as well, since she wasn't paying attention. She was too busy trying to soak up the coffee from the plush carpet with tissues from her purse. Deborah came charging in, armed with paper towels and dry rags and a stain remover spray.

"You just sit down," Deborah said, "and I'll bring you more coffee. Not that big of a deal, see? Believe me, you aren't the first and you won't be the last."

Ana did as the secretary ordered, trying to smile at her reassurances. Mr. Richards and Marlon sat quietly, waiting for Ana to settle. When she sat again, Marlon grabbed her hand and held it reassuringly in his while Mr. Richards shifted the papers on his desk and cleared his throat.

"Where were we? Ah, yes, I was telling you that Ellen left you the house, everything in it, as well as what's left in her bank account."

Ana looked at Marlon, then back to Mr. Richards.

"And what am I supposed to do with a house?"

Ana climbed down slowly from Marlon's truck, her mind still in overdrive with the information she received during the last few hours. First it was Ellen's death, then her giving up the scholarship and leaving school, and then this meeting with Ellen's attorney with the news that she now owned a house. So much had happened in such a short time. She was constantly on the verge of crying. Either from missing Ellen, remembering she couldn't go back to school or the stress of not knowing what to do with her life.

Ana looked at the heavy manila envelope. Countless emotions bubbled up within her. Ellen's death meant possible financial relief for herself. She had forgotten about Javier and Elena moving, leaving her to find another place to live. This inheritance from Ellen supplied her with just that, but at the expense of not having Ellen.

A thought that brought her guilt back.

"You want to build a snowman instead?" Marlon asked, his velvet voice breaking through the icy cold air.

"I'm sorry. I didn't realize you got out of the truck with me," Ana laughed, trying to shake off her tension. "More than anything, I would prefer to run away to Alaska and build an ice hotel and pretend none of this happened."

Marlon turned to face her. Already one step up, he towered over her more than usual. He was a wall of strength covered up in a puffy coat. She leaned her heavy head against his chest as his arms wrapped tightly around her.

"Ana, I know this is a lot, but I'm here for you," he said, as his fingers stroked her hair. "I really am here for the good and the bad. There's just something about you I'm not willing to let go of. It's okay to cry with me or rant with me. It's okay to show that you're pissed off around me or confused. I'm here for you."

A staggered sigh escaped her at his words, but she refused to allow the tears to well up right then. It was time to go into the house and figure out the small details for the funeral the next day.

"Thank you, Marlon. Come inside with me."

"Of course."

"Is that you, Ana?" called Javier from the kitchen as they walked into the warm house.

"Yeah, it's me."

"Why aren't you at work? You didn't quit again, did you?"

"Funny. I took the next few days off for personal reasons."

"What personal reasons could you possibly have for taking off work for a few days?" asked Javier, his mouth full of food. "Marlon!

Hey, man. I didn't know you were here. You guys want something to eat?"

Ana shouldered her way past her brother to the sink.

"Why don't you sit down at the table to eat your lunch like a normal person, Javier?" Ana poured herself a glass of water and took down a bottle of aspirin from the cupboard. Exhaustion was settling into her bones. The idea of figuring out the funeral and wake made her want to crawl into bed and pretend to sleep forever.

Her brother shrugged and took another bite of food.

"I don't have time. I have to go back to the shop and work on some shelves for that new restaurant of Todd's. He's thinking of opening earlier than he had planned before and said he would make it worth my while if I could hurry with the order. Some people in this family have to work," he said.

Though he was smiling, the words stabbed Ana.

"Javier, I just took a few days off."

"The woman Ana used to clean for died the other day, Javier," Elena said, coming into the kitchen. "Be nice."

"How was I supposed to know?"

"I told you," Elena said, tapping his forehead.

"Anyway, not that it's any business of yours why I'm taking a few days off, but I had to sort some things out."

"Why do you have to do it? Doesn't the family usually do that stuff, not the maid?" His jolly mood gnawed at her nerves.

"Her family is dead already and she and I became like family to each other as I worked with her. She and I got really close, so it's only right that I take care of the few things left to be taken care of."

Ana saw her brother look at his wife, whose eyes must have put him in his place because he said nothing else.

"Well," he said, kissing his sister on the forehead and his wife on the lips. "I'm off. I'm just going to give Sofia a kiss and brush my teeth. What's that?"

Javier pulled the legal papers from the manila envelope before Ana saw he had them. His first reaction was a low-pitched whistle, his eyes wide when he looked up.

"She gave you a house?"

"I inherited Ellen's house," Ana said, snatching the papers back from her brother. "She left the house and everything in it to me, along with some money."

"Nice. And in a rich neighborhood, too. You'll get quite a bit of money from the sale."

"I haven't decided what I'm going to do with the house yet, Javier. I was thinking I might live there."

Javier shook his head. "You can't live alone in some strange neighborhood, Ana. You belong here, near us, near your family."

"Your family is growing, Javier, and living alone at my age isn't as scandalous as you make it out to be. Besides, it would be nice to have a place of my own. I'm only in your way here, especially with the new baby coming. It would be the best thing for all of us."

"We'll talk about this later."

When Javier was out of earshot, Elena patted Ana's hand.

"Javier will come around. He's only trying to protect his little sister," said Elena with a strained voice, before leaving the kitchen herself.

Ana stood still for a moment. Her head pounded rhythmically into her temples. Javier's reaction wasn't as bad as she had expected, although that could have been because Marlon was in the house.

"Would you like something to eat, Marlon?"

He shrugged and sat down at the table.

"If you're going to eat, I will. You really going to move into Ellen's house?"

"Why not?"

Marlon tapped her chin with a smile.

"Don't be defensive. That's what I would do, though there isn't any cultural opposition to me doing so. Well, my mama would have loved for her kids to always live with her, but other than that, there's no opposition. Personally, I love living alone. As much as I love my sister, I could never live with her."

"It might be nice. I've never lived alone before. Javier is just overly protective, like papa was. I think he still sees himself in papa's place."

"You can't blame him, right?"

Ana's mind flashed back to the night she showed up after Roberto's punch sent her to the emergency room. No, maybe she couldn't blame him.

"Besides, it isn't like you are moving out of state. It's just a few minutes away from here."

"That's true, isn't it?" she reflected as she prepared their plates. "And it isn't like I'm going to ask him to pay me my part for this house, if that's what he's worried about."

"You don't mind moving?"

Ana shrugged, trying to collect her thoughts. She ran her hand over the kitchen table with all its burns and dents and marks.

"Honestly? It might be hard to live alone. But here, I'm in the way. I should have moved out a while ago."

They sat in silence for a moment. The more she thought about living in the large house on High Oak Road, the more excitement bubbled up within her. She let her thoughts run wild with how she would spend her days fixing up the house and the garden; how wonderful it would be to have something that was completely hers.

Her daydreaming ended once Marlon finished his plate. They set to work at the kitchen table, making the last arrangements for Ellen's funeral, then deciding how to arrange the furniture in the house for the wake. They had just finished everything when they heard Sofia whimpering in her crib.

"I'm going to make a snack for her and some coffee for us. You want some?" Ana asked, coming back into the living room with her niece on her hip.

"Of course."

Sofia gazed at Marlon for a long moment, then raised her arms for him to take her.

"That's funny. She rarely goes to people she doesn't know."

"Ah, she just knows I'm gonna be the fun one while her aunt makes coffee," Marlon said, setting Sofia down on the floor with him, already busy with trying to teach Sofia the concept of rolling a ball back and forth before Ana could even enter the kitchen.

When Ana snuck her head around the corner to see what made Sofia squeal with delight, she found Marlon pretending to be a bear. Sofia squealed and threw the ball at him. Though it missed him by a mile, Marlon fell dramatically, clutching his chest.

"Your niece is funny," said Marlon, without looking up. "She sure likes thinking she's hurting me."

His voice startled Ana.

"How d'you know I was spying?"

"There were too many people in my house growing up. The minute there was silence, you knew someone was spying," he said. He picked Sofia up with one hand and made her fly across the room before she crash-landed on the couch. The little girl dissolved into contagious giggles.

"Cocho!" exclaimed Sofia, waving her arms in excitement. She giggled at Marlon's tickling, but pushed his fingers away to get to Ana and the snack tray.

"Toddlers are fascinating. They're so smart and yet have so much growing to do."

They both looked at Sofia as she shoved a large bite of cake into her mouth with slobbery fingers. The doorbell rang suddenly; the sound making Ana jump nervously. She placed Sofia into the highchair with shaking fingers.

"Do you want me to get it?" Marlon offered.

She wanted to say yes, but it was her house.

"No, it's fine. Will you stay with Sofia?"

But when Ana opened the door, she immediately wished she could shut it again. Daniel stood on her front steps. The small amount of food in her stomach swirled and for a moment, she thought she might be sick.

"What are you doing here?"

"I heard about Ellen Sanz," he said, stepping closer to her.

"How did you hear about it? The obituary comes out tomorrow."

"I was talking to Dr. Rossen today, and he told me. I'm so sorry. He told me that her granddaughter was with her when she died and I took that to be you, so I came right over. How are you doing?"

"I'm fine. She died in her sleep, so—it was peaceful."

"I'm sure she appreciated it. You being there with her, I mean." Daniel's eyes roamed past her into the house. "It's kind of cold out here. Can we go inside and talk?"

Daniel charged forward, leaving Ana with no other recourse but to move out of his way. She turned slowly and walked up the stairs to the living room. There was a cold exchange of hellos between the two men.

"What are you doing here, Marlon?" Daniel asked

Ana busied herself with Sofia, wishing she could disappear.

Marlon cleared his throat uneasily, shifting his weight away from Sofia as Ana took over cleaning up the highchair.

"I've been helping Ana out with the funeral arrangements. My grandmother and Ellen were good friends and Ana called us yesterday when it happened."

"Ana called you?" Daniel repeated the word almost to himself, more than to anyone in the room.

"Are you going to the funeral? The reception is at Ellen's house afterwards." The words were stilted, and Ana immediately regretted them. She had no desire to have Daniel anywhere near her.

"Yes, I'll be at the funeral. Dr. Rossen asked me to accompany him. His wife can't go, and I knew Ellen Sanz once, a long time ago."

Marlon shot her a hard look before picking up Sofia, who pulled on his pant legs for attention. Ana busied her hands by filling a mug full of coffee for Daniel, who sipped it noisily, made a face, and carefully set it back on the tray.

"I should probably go," Daniel said, moving towards the door. "I should go. I just wanted to see how you were. I didn't mean to interrupt."

His voice trailed off thoughtfully. He stood transfixed for a moment before his body jerked back into motion, then he hurried down the stairs and out the door before Ana had time to accompany him. Ana looked at Marlon, but he just shrugged and picked up another piece of cake.

"Who was that?" asked Elena, entering the living room.

"Daniel."

"Your Daniel?" asked Elena. "What was he doing here?"

"Not Ana's Daniel, just... Daniel," said Marlon, rolling the ball to Sofia. "This cake is delicious, by the way."

Chapter Twenty-Four

"WHERE'VE YOU BEEN?" ASKED Gloria as Daniel walked through his front door. She was leaning against the wall in a black pencil shirt and an angora sweater, looking ready for a photo shoot. Daniel deliberately turned away and hung up his coat, keeping his mouth closed as he walked past her and into the kitchen. The click of her heels followed directly behind him. He tried to take in deep breaths but found clenching his teeth was a better option to keeping himself from saying things he might regret. Like asking her how the hell she got a house key.

"Would you like some hot tea? It's my recipe that you used to like, the one with the cinnamon and allspice."

Daniel finally turned and looked at his ex-wife. Her offer filled him with loss and gratitude. Memories of sitting in the kitchen alone, wishing to taste her spiced tea again, sprung up. While her presence irritated him, the truth was, he didn't want to be alone.

"That would be nice."

Daniel tried to let go of the bruised pride that had hung on his shoulders since Ana's house. She had clearly moved on quickly. Or worse yet, had moved on before breaking things off with him. Perhaps she had been involved with Marlon for weeks now, as he had suspected before Christmas.

Gloria placed a steaming cup of tea in front of him and was mercifully quiet for a moment as they sipped. A strange, comfortable, thought-filled silence, like they used to have when they were married. One thing he found so exhausting about dating anyone was the amount of talking that always seemed involved. With Gloria, he had been able to brood or mope or just pensively pass the time without a need to fill it with words.

Talking with Gloria was also easy. They used to have so much in common with each other between their studies, their students, the other professors, and the university. When they first got married, they created their own mini book club, just the two of them. They would read the book aloud while giving each other massages, which typically turned into more mature activities. For their second Christmas together, Gloria signed them up for a couple's massage class taught by a seventy-year-old couple who always showed up wearing matching spandex outfits.

"What're you laughing about?" asked Gloria.

"The old couple in spandex." Daniel tried to say more but couldn't hold his laughter. Once Gloria started giggling, Daniel let his laughter loose. Soon they both had tears streaming down their cheeks as they retold each other the stories the old couple used to tell about their sex life.

"We had some great times, didn't we?"

"We did," he said.

"We could have them again. It isn't too late."

Daniel said nothing for a moment. He tried to rummage around in his heart for what he wanted, for feedback on what those words meant to him. But he found nothing.

"I'm not sure. It might be too late."

Gloria grabbed his hand in hers and looked earnestly into his eyes.

"It isn't. I swear it isn't. We're still young. If we're able to forgive, then we could still make it."

"You left, Gloria. You wanted something bigger and better than what we had. You left me alone and just when I'm finally over you, you decide to come back and tell me we should try again? What am I supposed to say to that?"

"Are you really over me?" she asked, stroking the back of his hand.

"It took so long to push you out of my head. I was so comfortable being married to you. When you left, it was as though I had a vast hole in my life. For months, I hated coming home, so I stayed at my office for hours on end. Sometimes I didn't leave until the sun came up just because I didn't want to see the empty closets and drawers and cabinets."

Daniel looked out the window as he spoke for fear he might start crying if he looked at her. That would be the end; he would have to admit he wasn't over her. Even to himself. Slowly, Daniel took his hand from hers to sip his tea, still averting his eyes.

"I wasn't really leaving you; I was leaving a dead end. We had so much fun the first few years, but eventually it all just became a routine. Do you realize that we didn't sleep together for six months before I left? And we hardly had sex in the six months leading up to those. Not only that, but we also stopped communicating. We were more like roommates," she said.

"That was around the time we had that fight about having kids."

Gloria nodded. "But that fight wasn't the reason we stopped sleeping together."

"No, you were the reason we stopped. You acted strangely every time I tried to touch you."

"I had just had a miscarriage. I wasn't the same for a little while."

"The understatement of the year, right there. The reaction you had after the miscarriage was not what I expected of the woman I loved."

"What do you mean?"

Daniel pressed his mouth into a hard line to get control of his anger before speaking. “I remember it clearly. When I looked at you to see if you were okay, you showed no grief at all. I was trying not to break down right there in the doctor’s office, and you just started getting dressed even before the doctor finished talking.”

“I don’t remember sighing. I only remember trying to control my crying because I knew that if I did, I’d be a sobbing mess. I didn’t want to cry in the doctor’s office. I wanted to go home and cry into my pillow with you holding me, but that never happened. When I reached for your hand in the car, you pulled away. I felt like you blamed me for losing the baby. I used to spend the nights in the guest room crying until the sun came up,” Gloria said, her voice escalating as she stood up to pace. “I needed some time. I wasn’t sure I was ready to try for another baby. That’s no reason to shut down on me. You were angry for months!”

“You controlled everything in our marriage. Whatever you wanted, you got. It didn’t matter that I wanted kids; if you didn’t want them, we weren’t going to have them. End of discussion.” Daniel’s fist came down against the table to make his point.

“I told you I wasn’t sure I wanted to have kids two days after having a miscarriage because I wasn’t sure if I was willing to go through that again, especially since I couldn’t trust you to be emotionally available if it happened. You shut me out and made me deal with it myself.”

“Only because you seemed happy about it, and that scared me. I tried to talk about Samuel, but you got angry every time I brought him up.”

“Talking about him was so difficult. Each time I tried, it was as though I was strangling myself,” she said, her voice several decibels higher now.

Daniel shook his head to clear it before he responded. Half the things she was saying seemed false. Or at least, not fully true. But the speck of doubt made his thoughts swirl into a jumbled mess.

"It isn't just about losing the baby, Gloria. I've had a lot of lonely nights to remember you and us and our marriage, and the truth is that even before the miscarriage, you started to change. You were always ripe for battle. About everything. If I got a class that you wanted, you would claim it wasn't worth your time, anyway. If I got a paper published, you would critique it beyond what was necessary. You tried to change the structure of our marriage; you tried to change my habits: you tried to change me."

Gloria glided towards him, her heels silent, her stance as stealthy as a tiger's. Her eyes were wide with venom at his words. When she spoke, she hissed, as though unable to both control her emotions and speak at the same time.

"Change you? I couldn't even be me! I wasn't allowed to change at all from the twenty-two-year-old you met in college. You're so quick to blame me, Daniel. What about you? For years, you were harsh on my papers, my teachings, and my opinions. Sometimes I would hide and cry over what you said. For you, it was as though criticism was the way of encouraging people. And yet here you are now, telling me that when I resorted to being just like you, you resented me and my ideas. I guess the teacher couldn't take what he dished out."

The bitter truth was a cold slap in the face. It was true he had always ranked himself as a better professor. When the department started to recognize her more, right before she got pregnant, his jealousy made him feel out of control. When he found out they were going to offer her graduate courses before offering him, Daniel sent an anonymous letter to her boss, convincing him she wouldn't be right for the job. When they let her go as part of the downsizing, she never found out he had a hand in it. He hoped she never would.

"I'm going to lie down," Gloria said. "Maybe we should pick this up later or try to start over, but we should talk about this again."

"Whatever you want. I wouldn't want you to feel like I wasn't being nice."

He couldn't help himself, as immature as his words were. He braced himself for Gloria's rebuttal, expecting a colorful rebuttal she had been known for, but much to his surprise and agony, she said nothing. After a few seconds of silence, Gloria simply turned and walked away.

Chapter Twenty-Five

Ana opened the door to Ellen Sanz's house and stepped into the now cold, lifeless entryway. A few tears welled up in her eyes as she looked around at the place that she used to come to for comfort and warmth. They started out over a year ago as two strangers, neither one knowing they had just found the companionship that they needed more than anything. But now Ana was alone again, one house richer and one loved one poorer.

The living room, where they spent so much of their time, now seemed uninviting without Ellen's presence. She walked to the center, hoping something would happen. A spark to add some life. But everything was still. The piano with all the pictures on it, the sofa where Ellen's quilt lay, the coffee table with Ellen's glasses, the fireplace with the ashes still piled high from the last day Ellen was alive. It was all Ellen, and yet empty of life.

She jerked into motion. First, she cleaned out the fireplace and made a new fire. With that finished, Ana assessed the rest of the house. By tomorrow, she needed to clean the house and carve out space for the food and coffee. Plus, more chairs needed to be brought in, the wood needed to be polished, and the floors needed a good mopping. Ana sighed as the clock struck eleven. All her body wished her to do was to lie down and snuggle into Ellen's quilt. Gathering up what little energy she had and all the willpower she could muster, Ana took out the dusting supplies and set to work.

When the doorbell interrupted her, Ana was relieved to see it was almost one o'clock. Suspecting Marlon was at the door, she ran to open it.

"Hey, I was just about to have lunch!" Ana's excitement froze. Marlon wasn't standing at the door, Gloria was. "What do you want?"

"Could I come in?"

"Why?"

"I heard Ellen died, and I thought I could pay my respects." This Gloria was a diminished version of the one Ana knew. Where usually she was confident, now she was fidgety and seemed not to have enough words.

"You can pay them tomorrow at the funeral."

"I don't go to funerals, so I thought I would pay them now. Perhaps I could help you? I read in the paper that you were having people over here after the funeral tomorrow." Gloria's hand shot out and stopped Ana from closing the door.

The move seemed desperate to Ana, but she still hesitated before speaking again. "I have some tuna salad and chips. Would you like some?"

Gloria was stepping through the door before Ana could finish the question. Though Gloria's confidence seemed to be diluted, Ana was still intimidated. She turned briskly away from the door, leaving Gloria alone to figure out where to put her coat, and hurried into the kitchen to ground herself before having to host a woman who should be her enemy.

"I'm sorry that Ellen died. Daniel said you were with her when it happened."

"How did you know her again?"

"It seems like everyone knew Ellen a few years ago. Everyone in our small group, anyway. She was a very active member of the alumni of the university, always at the dinners and fundraisers. I saw her a few times after her son- and daughter-in-law died in that awful car crash, but by then all her fire was gone. It's not as though we were close friends, but I admired her energy. One year, probably over ten years ago, she spoke at one of our conferences. When she was younger, she used to speak all over at the high schools and middle schools and set up a program for a rural library bus that would drive a circumference of, I believe, twenty-five miles. She funded the whole thing. I thought it was a great idea, being a girl from the country myself."

"I didn't know," Ana said, stung with jealousy. She placed a sandwich on a plate and passed it to Gloria, at a loss for all small talk.

They ate slowly in silence.

"I bet you have a lot of work to do. I could help you. If you want," Gloria said.

"I think I have everything under control," Ana answered, finally finishing her sandwich. Ana willed the words to be true, but when she looked around, it was obvious she was lying. Just clearing the kitchen and setting it up for the caterers was going to take her most of the afternoon.

"We wouldn't have to talk. I just need to keep my mind busy. I'm good at cleaning, despite my choice of dress."

Ana couldn't help smiling as Gloria motioned to her slacks and perfectly oversized sweater.

"We aren't friends. And we don't have to become friends. But you need help, no matter what you say, and I need to keep busy. It's a win-win."

"Right. But see, there really isn't that much to do. I'm trying to arrange it better for when people come over after the funeral. The actual work will start in a few days when I have to separate everything to either sell, give away, or keep."

Ana shut her mouth suddenly, realizing she was becoming too comfortable talking to this woman who cared nothing about how she ruined her dreams of graduating from the university.

"She left you the house, then? She must have really admired you." Gloria murmured. "Isn't it funny how the death of someone brings back memories you haven't thought of in years, even memories that have no connection with that person?"

Ana squeezed the broom to keep herself steady. She hadn't thought of it that way, but it was true. Each time she attended a funeral, it wasn't just the memories of the person who died that would overwhelm her senses, but memories in general.

"By the way, I think I owe you an explanation. You're nicer than I assumed you were. Daniel told me that going to the university was important to you because you hadn't been able to go before."

Ana blinked to wet her eyes. A few years before, she might have thrown a punch at this woman for her audacity, or at least a few curse words. Now, though the same anger vibrations were still active in her chest, she no longer had the energy to fight.

"I don't know the circumstances that led to you pretending to be Ellen Sanz's granddaughter, but I can try to understand it. I probably would have done the same in your position. When you wait for something for so long, any opportunity to take it seems like a good idea."

Gloria paused. Her eyes looked past everything in the house and moved towards something Ana couldn't see. "Anyway, I didn't do it all out of malice for you, though I admit I had little regard to how you'd feel about it. When I found out you were involved with Daniel, I was angry. And I made—assumptions after seeing those videos of you."

For a moment, Ana felt an inkling of compassion for the woman.

"Yes, well, those videos don't' show me in the best light," Ana said, placing all the frames from the piano into a box while Gloria wiped up the dust.

"I assume you're taking me up on leaving the university?"

"Yes. It's my only choice, really," Ana said, remembering why she should be angry.

"That's good. I got a call before Christmas break asking about a rumor on whether Ana-Maria Sanz was dead. The veteran group that granted one of her scholarships wanted answers."

Ana tried not to believe her, but Gloria had no reason to lie. She already had everything she came to get.

It hadn't been all Gloria's fault that she couldn't go back to the university. Marlon had been right.

"Ellen was afraid that I would get caught. She was trying to convince me not to go back. I tried to convince her everything was fine, but had she pushed it further, I would've had to do as she asked. She had a reputation to lose, after all. I just never thought anyone would find out."

"I don't know who started the rumor or questioning, but it probably has to do with the audit they're doing on the scholarships. I'll do my best to make sure they don't take it any farther. Especially because I don't want Daniel to become connected to it. He'd be devastated if they fired him, being the guy who plays by the rules."

"Oh? Well, he's the one who made the first move between us. And he knew perfectly well I was a student."

Ana breathed in slowly to calm herself. There was no way Daniel was a victim in this situation. Before she could say something, the doorbell pierced through the house.

"I'm sorry I'm late," Marlon said, walking in before Ana could reach the door. "I hurried as much as I could. Should we get started?"

Marlon froze when he saw them, but Ana was in no mood to explain anything to anybody.

"Marlon, you know Gloria, right? Well, she came to help us. Why don't you tell her our plans for the funeral while I make the coffee?"

Chapter Twenty-Six

As Ana prepared her coffee the morning of Ellen's wake, she couldn't help feeling like Ellen would peek around the corner at any second. She shuddered as the coffee percolated, knowing what the day held in store. Open caskets didn't scare her, but she wasn't keen on having her last memory of Ellen being that stiff, lifeless figure that the casket always held. Memories of her parents' funeral drifted through her thoughts as she pulled her toast from the toaster and spread Ellen's homemade jam on top. There was no open casket with them. The car accident did too much damage to their bodies to have one. Usually she avoided those memories, but this time she allowed them to come.

She could remember standing outside the small Catholic church with Javier, feeling dead herself as they received the guests. The line of people filing in seemed interminable, and she became more and more anxious about the service. Each time someone offered her their condolences, she had to fight hard to not turn away. It seemed unjust that she and Javier had to stand there and comfort those coming to pay respects when everyone should have been comforting them.

The worst were the women who broke down in front of them, their tears wetting the shoulder of her black dress. They were the worst because she didn't wish to cry in front of everyone, but their sobs seemed to fill up her tear well again. She hated them for it.

Although a few tears fell from her eyes, she hardened herself against sobbing, setting her jaw so tightly that it ached for days later.

After the funeral, she purposely avoided anyone who had known her parents. She funneled her anger into social activism, moved in with Roberto and down the path that eventually left her broken and dejected.

Such a waste of time, she told herself again, shame filling her.

Ana poured herself a cup of hot coffee and pulled the robe that she had taken from the guest room tightly around her. At least Mother Nature was cooperating with her mood, covering the sun with dark grey clouds. The day she buried her parents, the sun shone brightly in a blue, cloudless sky and the smell of lilacs had filled the cemetery. The contrast had been too blunt, only infuriating her more.

The grandfather clock in the hallway struck nine o'clock.

"Hello?"

Her voice drifted into the empty house, falling flat. No one answered, and she felt ridiculous having spoken at all. Heading upstairs, Ana remembered how excited her mother was each day when she and Javier came home from school. Perhaps it had something to do with the oppressive quiet of the house. Her mother used to lament that in America, women did so many things alone. When she was in Argentina, she used to go to the market, or the stores, or even the doctor with a neighbor or friend. Anyone. And it was normal. No one enjoyed going places alone.

Stepping into the shower, Ana realized she might be more like her mother than she thought.

"How're you doing? Tired?" Marlon asked her quietly as they rested on the couch after the reception.

"Exhausted," she admitted. "These things are always exhausting. Funerals, I mean. They just zap the energy from you, no matter who it's for."

"True. And you've had a lot of changes in the last few days that you haven't had time to get used to."

She moved just enough to reach out her hand and bring back her coffee and cake.

"I invited Javier to come back for dinner and now I wish I hadn't."

"Why?"

"I don't know. I guess I felt bad not inviting them over, like they would be alone if I didn't."

"Maybe you don't want to be alone."

"You can be annoyingly perceptive sometimes, Marlon." Ana swatted at him playfully, but the way he looked back at her stopped her from any more touching. She wondered if Marlon had meant to spend the evening with just her and him.

"How was your first night in the house?"

"It was strange at first, and I had trouble falling asleep, but I enjoyed waking up alone. Getting my coffee and not feeling like I had to talk to anyone was nice, but then I got all self-conscious about being alone and felt weird that I hadn't even spoken." Ana shrugged, unwilling to give all the details.

"You'll get used to it. I love living alone now. I can go visit my mom or my sister and then I go home where it's quiet. You'll do the same with your brother. And anytime you feel too lonely, you can call me."

Ana looked away as she nibbled on her cake, avoiding Marlon's stare. His comment was perfect, and if she wasn't careful, she would blurt out an invitation for him to move in with her.

"I could fall asleep right now," she said, after she couldn't stop a yawn.

"You could get in a good nap before they come. I'll stay and wake you up after half an hour or so."

"I was hoping the coffee would help."

"Probably won't."

"Why? Because I drink too much of it?"

"No, it's decaf."

Ana groaned at the confession.

"It was the only thing left. Either that or I just couldn't find the regular."

Marlon raised his eyebrows as she dunked her cake into the milky coffee before biting off the soaking half.

"What?"

"I didn't say anything. You're just funny, that's all." He smirked as she continued to dunk and eat her cake, but she ignored it, enjoying the cake too much. She polished off the last bite with flair, then wiped off each finger with a napkin.

"How am I funny?" she asked, moving closer.

Instead of answering, Marlon placed his lips on hers and kept them there for a few seconds.

Ana stayed motionless as his hands reached behind her head, pushing her gently forward until she was prone on the couch. She closed her eyes and allowed him to cover her face and neck in his little pecking kisses. Marlon kept kissing her as Ana felt herself transfer into sleep.

"Ana?" Marlon whispered. "Are you falling asleep?"

His words pulled her consciousness away from dreamworld and into reality, but all she could muster was an affirmative grunt.

"Would you like me to go?" Marlon asked.

Ana knew she should give him permission to stay or go as he pleased, but if he chose to leave, she would be all alone. She grunted a flat note, leaving the decision to him, and allowed herself to fall into a dreamless sleep.

Suddenly, her body jerked upwards, but something heavy kept her from sitting. That something grunted as the sound that had awoken her pierced through the air again. The doorbell. Ana checked the old grandfather clock, her mind still wondering what time it was and where she was.

Ellen's house. Four-thirty in what seemed like the afternoon.

"What?" Marlon mumbled when she pushed against him. "Why're you pushing me?"

"Someone's at the door." Finally free to stand up, Ana left Marlon alone to open the door. She really hoped it wasn't a salesman. She wasn't sure she could keep her temper in check.

"Yes?"

"Ana, hi." Daniel stood at the door, looking as though lost.

Still half asleep, it took Ana a minute to understand where she was and wonder why Daniel was there.

"Were you sleeping?" he asked.

"Actually, yes." She smoothed her hair over her shoulder, resisting the desire to shut the door in his face.

"I wanted to talk to you. Can I come in?"

Just like the last time, Daniel stepped forward before she could say no. And just like last time, Daniel stopped mid-step when he saw Marlon.

"I guess this is a bad time. I'm sorry. I'll come back later."

"Later?"

"It really isn't anything important. I can come back at a better time."

"Daniel, why are you here? Whatever you have to say, you can say in front of Marlon. He's around so much he hardly counts as company anymore." She had meant it to loosen the tension, but the words fell flat. No one even flashed a smile.

"Hello, Marlon," Daniel said awkwardly as he entered the living room.

Marlon stood up and shook Daniel's hand, offering him to sit down in the chair.

"I'll make us some hot cocoa."

"I think I'm going to go, Ana." Marlon's voice sounded distant as he stood. Ana panicked at his indifferent look.

"Why? I thought you were staying for dinner. Javier and Elena are coming over with Sofia."

"I'll come back," Marlon said, shrugging into his coat as the two of them walked to the front door.

"When? For dinner?"

"Sure. I'll come back around seven-thirty. I'll come if that guy isn't here." Marlon leaned close to her ear as he put on his jacket. "But only if he isn't here."

His anger was palpable. Her ear tingled with it, but Ana felt helpless to soothe him with Daniel in the next room. Before he slipped out the door, she placed her hand on his chest, which stopped him for a second, but when their eyes met, she could tell he wasn't about to be pacified by a simple touch.

"I'll see you later?" she repeated, hoping it would be enough to convince him to come back. "I promise I'll get rid of Daniel."

"You shouldn't have let him in."

Ana sighed.

"I didn't know what to say."

"Okay. I'll see you later."

Ana watched helplessly as Marlon walked into the hallway and left the house. The blast of cold air that entered with his departure aptly fitted her emotions.

"Did Marlon leave?"

"He had to go. Do you want a coffee?"

"That hot cocoa would be nice."

"Fine, let's go into the kitchen. You can tell me why you're here while I heat the milk."

"I don't really know where to start. It's about Gloria."

"I don't know why you'd come here to talk to me about Gloria."

Daniel's face crumbled slightly, but it didn't stir up any compassion within her. His presence was grating on her nerves, though she tried to hide it and be pleasant. As she made his drink, Daniel sat silently, his face looking as though several emotions were wrestling for dominance inside him.

"Daniel."

"Yes?"

"Are you going to tell me what's going on or just sit with your thoughts all by yourself?"

"It has to do with how and why Gloria and I broke up," he said. "I think it might have partly been my fault."

"Isn't divorce always the fault of two people?"

"How can you say that? If someone cheats, then it's that person's fault."

"Did she cheat?"

Daniel sighed, his shoulders slumping. "No."

"She says I was too overbearing and critical. She says that I never had anything nice to say about her papers. I thought I was helping her. That's how people get better, by seeing what they did wrong, not by being praised for what they did right."

Ana rolled her eyes at the steaming mug of milk as she poured in Ellen's homemade chocolate sauce. It occurred to her that she wouldn't know how to refill the jar once it was gone. She had to blink several times to keep her tears away. The last thing she wanted right now was to cry.

She set the hot cocoa in front of him, but Daniel stood to pace the floor and recounted what sounded like a fight he and Gloria had a few days before about misunderstanding their entire relationship.

"I don't understand why you're telling me this," Ana said when Daniel took a minute to collect his thoughts.

Daniel stared at the fire for a moment. "I guess I want to know if—if I'm wrong. Did you think I treated you unfairly?"

"You're a kind man, Daniel. And you helped me enormously, though you were harsh sometimes. More during the last few months."

He seemed genuinely surprised at her agreeing with Gloria.

"But your grades went up, right?"

"Yes, they went up. Mostly because of your help and suggestions. But there was a point when you seemed too eager to only find problems in my paper. It was as though you couldn't recognize I had gotten better or something. You became harsher, I think."

"But as you get better in one area, you have to move on to the other things to improve."

"Maybe," Ana said. "But at what cost? It sounds like it became too much for Gloria if you were never willing to recognize her good points? I don't know, Daniel, I wasn't there."

Daniel didn't answer right away. Ana waited with her jaws clenched to stay patient. She checked her watch discreetly, not sure why she bothered to be so careful with his feelings.

"Gloria wants to get back together," he intoned, as though saying the words for the first time aloud.

"So?"

Daniel turned around quickly from the fireplace to face Ana.

"This isn't something to be taken lightly, Ana."

"Seriously, Daniel. You're being so dramatic. The answer to that problem is simple: Do you still love her? I would say you do and that deep down you want it to work out. But that isn't the real problem. The real problem is whether you can admit to her and to yourself that you were wrong before and that perhaps your break-up was just as much your fault as it was hers. And if it was just as much your fault as it was hers, then you'd have to let go of the anger that you've kept towards her since she left. Ridding yourself of that anger is the real problem. I know-" Ana stopped short, unwilling to share her experience with Roberto. "Well, anyway. You need to bring yourself down a notch."

Daniel stared at her as though she were a stranger.

"I don't know what to say. You've never spoken to me like that."

Ana shrugged. "There's a lot we never talked about. So, what is the answer? DO you still love her?"

"I don't know."

"I think you do. Love her, I mean."

"Why do you think so?"

"Seems to me that when you can't seem to let go of someone, you still love them. And you can't seem to let go of her."

"What do you mean?"

"You want to be near her. The first night she was here, you could have sent her away. But you didn't. At the New Year's party, you were with her almost all night, except when you wanted to make her jealous of me."

"So, I should give her another chance?"

"Seems to me it's about giving your relationship another chance. It's clear that the two of you were to blame for the breakup. It isn't any more her fault than it is yours, but you keep looking at it as if most of the blame points to her."

"That isn't true. I told you just a minute ago that some of it was my fault."

"No, you said that she thought some of it was your fault. And I agree with her. Sounds like you're trying to convince us that you aren't really to blame at all."

Daniel looked away.

"I have to admit, Ana, I'm a little disappointed. Just a few days after we break things off between the two of us, you're willing to give me advice as a friend, as though we have never been involved. I thought maybe you'd be jealous."

The change in discussion caught Ana off guard. It was almost time for Javier and Elena to arrive. She didn't have time for another discussion.

"How do you do that?" Daniel asked, turning towards her from his position of staring at the fire.

"Um, I guess it's because we've always been more like friends in our relationship. We never started being really involved."

Daniel pulled himself back up.

"We could change that."

"What?"

"We could see how compatible we are, Ana. Making love."

His eyes traveled down to her breasts, then back up to her eyes. Before she could react, he cupped her face in his hands and kissed her. Ana yanked herself away, almost falling in her desire to get away.

"You need to leave, Daniel." Her voice was low, almost inaudible, but he received the message, though he seemed not at all ashamed of kissing her.

"You want him, don't you? Marlon?"

She opened the door before Daniel even had his coat on, waiting for him.

"What I do with my life, who I'm with, is none of your business, Daniel."

Daniel grunted his answer as he slipped into his winter coat.

"I hope you're happy with him, Ana."

"Goodbye Daniel."

She made sure he got into his car and drove away, then slammed the door behind him.

Chapter Twenty-Seven

MARLON WALKED BRISKLY DOWN the dark sidewalk. After leaving Ana to deal with Daniel, he had stomped his way to Grandma Rue's house, who greeted him with a hug and cookies. Thankfully, she hadn't asked him why he was there, though she made a comment about his sour attitude. He joined Grandma Rue in her living room, watching reruns of MASH, though he barely paid attention. Instead, he ate his cookies and brooded over the situation with Ana, wondering if she was worth pursuing at all. This was the second time Ana just let Daniel in and take over as though his problems held precedence.

He had planned to confront Ana about Daniel's behavior at the Rossen's, too but then Ellen died, and it seemed inappropriate. He even let the first time Daniel barged in on them go, but now she'd done it again. She let Daniel come in as though he had priority over him. Ana was attractive and fun. He'd always thought so, but he wasn't about to share space with Daniel in a relationship with her.

The arctic wind burned his nose and eyes. Marlon tucked his chin into the wool scarf bundled around his neck and picked up his pace, wishing he just gone home before. When he finally arrived, Ana was outside staring into the night. Daniel's car was no longer in the driveway.

Marlon slowed his pace and thoughts. He took a deep breath, choking on the cold, then swallowed until his emotions flattened so they wouldn't show.

Ana lit a real cigarette, the flame bursting through the darkness. She jumped at the sight of him coming up the driveway.

"You came back," she said, the cherry of her cigarette burning brightly as she sucked in the chemicals. "I was afraid you wouldn't."

"I just came for my truck."

"You're not staying for dinner?"

"I'm not sure I should."

She threw the butt on the ground and stepped on it, shaking her head as she did. "I swore I would quit these this year."

"It's been stressful lately," Marlon said. The moonlight cast a romantic glow over her face and hair. It was a perfect moment to kiss her. Remind her he was a better choice for her than Daniel. But he stayed still.

"Will I see you tomorrow?"

"Probably not. I leave in a few days for a conference. I've been wondering if I should go or not, but tonight I decided I probably should. It'll be an excellent networking opportunity for my website and law channel."

"What?" she cried out, the moonlight now emphasizing panic in her face. "Don't you dare do this to me."

"Do what?"

"Leave me all alone!" she cried out, grabbing his arms, shaking him in frustration.

Cigarette smoke and perfume filled his nostrils as he looked at her. The desire to hold her, protect her, be whatever she needed him to be, electrified him.

"Ana," he said, but there weren't enough words to tell her what he was feeling. So instead of speaking, he pulled her to him, his lips meeting hers with a desperation he didn't have the words to express. She made a small sound, like a surprised mouse, but he didn't stop. He pulled her closer, cradling her in his arms, his lips pulling hers in, refusing to let hers go. Demanding that she see him and only him.

Headlights turning into the driveway tore them apart. Ana jumped away as Marlon turned to find Javier's truck. He'd forgotten about them coming. Everything suddenly felt very exhausting.

"Hola!" called Elena, as she tried to keep Sofia from wiggling out of her car seat.

Ana sidestepped away from Marlon. She rolled her shoulders back and smiled as Sofia toddled over for a hug. Javier clapped Marlon between his shoulders, his smile sheepish.

"Sorry, bad timing, huh?"

Marlon laughed the comment away and tried again to give his excuses to not stay.

"Come on, man, stay for a bit. You can't leave me with all these girls. I'm always with girls," Javier complained. "Come on, let's get some food and go inside. It's freezing out here!"

Javier playfully shoved Marlon forward, giving him no choice but to enter the house. Marlon resisted the urge to tell Javier off, knowing he was just being friendly.

"Don't leave tonight until we talk, please?" Ana whispered as they all entered the house.

The pizza delivery cut the discussion short. Javier called him over to have a beer while Ana and Elena got out the dishes.

"Pissa!" Sofia exclaimed, holding her arms up to Marlon. He couldn't resist the cute smile and insistent arms.

"How do you like living in your new house?" asked Javier.

Marlon sat at the table to occupy himself with Sofia, who enjoyed shoving pizza directly into his mouth. Her tiny fingers smelled like goldfish, but she kept his thoughts away from Ana and the kiss they just had.

"It was a little weird to wake up in a big empty house with no one to say good morning to today."

"You'll get used to that, hermanita," said Elena.

"Maybe. This morning I considered giving myself a few weeks to see if I can come to like it. I mean, there is an advantage to being alone. When I go back to school, I'll have room to study and I won't need to go to the library all the time, plus it'll be fun to fix up this house until then. I'll just come over to the house and visit you guys when I need noise."

Javier and Elena exchanged looks.

"What?"

"You're always welcome at our house, but it'll be in a different place. We're moving at the end of the month."

Javier looked through the dark windows as he spoke, ignoring Ana as she coughed out the pizza she had choked on.

"You decided to sell the house?"

"I never said we were selling the house, Ana."

"You just said you were moving."

Javier and Elena tried avoiding Ana's gaze.

"We're moving because Tío Luis sold it, but to someone else. He made some deal with a guy he knows or something. His real estate agent told us to be out within six weeks. We thought we had a rent-to-own deal with Tío Luis, but he changed his mind without even speaking to us."

"But he can't do that! Mama and Papa left us the house!"

Elena and Javier turned their focus to her. Marlon tried to make himself invisible. Ana looked lost and confused, like a wild animal caught in headlights.

"Mama and Papa had some sort of agreement with Tío Luis. He owned the house, and they paid him. The idea was that when they finished paying, he would hand over the deed. When they died, he allowed us to keep up with those payments."

"He's done it for many people in the community. Unfortunately, lately he's also been changing his mind about a few of the properties," Elena added quietly.

"How can he do this? Where are the papers that Mama and Papa signed? Isn't there a contract?"

Javier shrugged his shoulders, and Elena shook her head.

"If there is, we don't have it. Now we gotta move."

"How can you just accept that? So many people get exploited because they don't understand their rights and they can't access the same services that other citizens do. How could Papa know what he was doing if he wasn't even given the information about what his rights were? Tío Luis is running a scam, and no one is stopping him."

"I think papa knew exactly what he was doing with Luis. He wasn't stupid."

Javier's voice dropped low. He stood calm, collected, and straight-backed, daring her to continue. Ana sat back down, retreating under Javier's glare.

"There's an immigration lawyer at the homeless shelter I did community service at," she said, picking at her pizza.

"We talked to a lawyer, Ana. There's no written document or contract between Tío Luis and Papa. There's only the mortgage that has Tío Luis's name on it. Punto. Luis can do whatever he wants with it. It's his house. In the eyes of the law, we are just renters, and he gave us the mandatory three months to leave."

Sofia climbed down from Marlon's lap and walked over to Elena, looking wide-eyed at Javier, whose voice had become grainy with emotion.

"What if we buy the house from him? How much did he sell it for?"

"He offered the option to us a few months back. He wanted two-hundred thousand."

Ana's mouth dropped.

"Well, maybe we can figure something out."

"No, Ana, he was making a deal with us just to be nice." Javier paused when Ana made a murderous noise at that description of Luis. "Fine, nice or whatever. He ended up selling it for almost four hundred thousand."

Ana's shoulders slumped at the number. Marlon tried a change of subject to ease the tension.

"You have a place already?"

"Near King Street."

"That's a terrible neighborhood!" Ana squealed.

"No, it's just that it's on the edge, between the good and the bad. It'll be fine," Javier said, visibly calmer at the change in subject.

"My friend lived over on Hyber Road and Ohio for a few years," Marlon said. "He said it was okay, but he moved because he didn't want his kids growing up there."

"We just need to be there for one year while we save and then we can move into a better place. Being there is temporary."

Ana switched her weight continually, like a bull pawing the ground.

"Why didn't you tell me any of this before?" she asked, the words blurting out louder than anyone else was speaking.

Javier turned his attention back to her as Elena moved to sit down in the far corner, as though afraid of what Ana might do when this angry.

"I told you a few weeks ago about Tío Luis wanting to have an inspection in the house and that he had been over with some realtor in order to appraise the market's worth."

Ana wrinkled her nose. The movement made her face more doll-like. "I thought you were going to sell it after buying it from Luis."

Defeated in her argument, Ana sank into a chair and put her face into her hands.

"Your brother wanted to go to the lawyer first and see if he could stop Tío Luis, hermanita. When he couldn't, he decided that he was going to take care of getting us a place to stay all by himself. I only found out about this a few weeks ago. It was like pulling teeth to get him to talk."

"Well, you can't move to King Street." Ana's head snapped up, her eyes bright again. "You'll move in here."

"No, Ana."

"Why not?"

"This is your house. We'll be fine in the apartment. Don't worry about us. Just like Javier said, it's only temporary until we can save enough to move into a bigger place."

Elena's voice was firm from the corner.

"Fine. Move to King Street."

"Should we start going home?" Javier asked his wife, kissing her on the forehead. He moved stiffly, as though the conversation had aged him. Marlon stood to leave; grateful the evening was being cut short.

Elena nodded and stood up, rubbing her pregnant belly.

"All right," said Ana. "Can you take me to work tomorrow?"

"Of course. What time should we be there?"

"Could you pick me up around eleven?"

"Muy bien."

"You know, Ana," said Javier as they put their coats on. "You're going to have to renew your license."

"You're right," she said, the smile on her face weary and forced. "And you need to help me find a car to buy."

"Anytime, hermanita," he answered, kissing her on the cheek before taking his family out the door.

Marlon watched Ana hesitate before closing the door behind her brother. When she turned towards him, Ana's eyes blazed with anger, ready to fight.

"I cannot believe Tío Luis. What a bastard."

"He seems like one, yes. I can talk to Professor Tuden about it and maybe Judge Brisko would have some insight into what you can do. But honestly, it doesn't sound like the law is on your side, Ana."

"Stuff like this keeps my people down in this country. People who don't keep their promises and help each other out. We become so attached to this idea of capitalism being the only way to do things we're willing to betray our own kind. Maybe this is a sign. All this change. Like getting kicked out of school and inheriting this house."

Ana angrily shoved the glasses and plates into the dishwasher. Growing up in a house full of women, Marlon knew full well to wait.

Ana ranted and muttered about Tío Luis and the oppression against the Hispanics until everything was cleaner than it had been before dinner. Any other day, Marlon would have offered to help, but he was too annoyed. Plus, if he opened his mouth, he might put her in a place she didn't want to be. For a few long minutes, he focused on the clock and tried to think about anything other than the counter arguments running through his head.

"Maybe it's a sign that I need to go back to activism and fighting for my people."

Marlon couldn't stay quiet any longer. "You talk as though the Hispanic community would collapse without you going back to activism."

"What?"

"Don't you think you could do more in the world if you got your life in order before going out and fighting people? Straighten yourself out first, Ana, then you can straighten out the world."

Ana stared at him for a moment, blinking as though he were a poor-quality mirage. Then the emotion lining her face changed from confusion to rage.

"My brother can't wait for that! And he's probably not the only person getting screwed over by people like Luis! I care about this happening, even if you don't. If I do nothing, and they do nothing, then this will just keep going and more people will suffer."

Marlon tilted his head at her pause, waiting for her to say more. He had learned that people will fill the silence and typically fill it with the truth.

"You know all about this! Or do you think we should sit down and be quiet because we haven't been here as long as you?"

"As long as who?" Marlon asked, knowing well what she was implying but unable to not amuse himself with her answer.

"Your people!" she shouted; her face scrunched impatiently at his question. "You're from two groups who have had to suffer under the stifling laws of this government and the indifference of its people, who only fight for justice when it affects them."

"Do you fight for justice when it doesn't affect you?"

The first poke only partially deflated Ana for a second. She puffed up again almost immediately.

"I have to fight first for the justice of those who are like me. It is we," she said, moving her finger between herself and him, "who suffer more than anyone else. Once our justice is equal, then we can fight for all justice."

Marlon couldn't help his deep sigh. Ana jerked her head in shock at his reaction.

"What?"

"I just don't believe that you're more morally superior. I've seen you in the activism field and I've listened to you speak when you're in it. You're passionate about a lot of things, Ana, but if you allow anger to be your guide, you end up saying things you probably don't mean. At least I hope you don't mean."

Her passion at that deflated substantially. He was referencing a particular video in which Ana can be heard saying she didn't care after being told a child had gotten hurt, before claiming that the parents would be taken to jail for placing their kid in danger.

"After that, I have little respect for people who demand an intact, shiny, perfect new law for themselves because it fits them at the moment. I told you I would help—"

"You also said that the law isn't on our side."

"I'm not a lawyer yet, Ana. It's possible I'm wrong. I'm just telling you my opinion from what I know right now."

"Well, we should! It's our house!"

Marlon exhaled slowly, trying to keep a hold of his temper.

"Laws should be equal and fair. But they're not."

"Ana, I know about unfair. Like you said, my family has suffered under unfair laws. On both sides. Strangely enough, they've also prospered and I, for one, can't ignore that piece of the puzzle. Injustice isn't right, but if you look at the legality of this Luis guy, he probably has every legal right to do what he's doing. I don't know if your parents didn't understand it or if they took the gamble. It's hard to be an immigrant here without credit. I help people like that all the time at work. The system isn't perfect, but all I can do is help people navigate it."

"Well, I guess they couldn't afford a good lawyer, Marlon."

His name snapped off her tongue to goad him, but he didn't take the bait. Being in debate class during high school and college and law school kept him more or less immune to what were supposed to be insults when the opposition had no argument.

"There is still work to be done, Ana. Believe me, I know. But we also have an obligation to step back and take responsibility for our actions and decisions, even when they turn out opposite to what we expected. What Luis is doing isn't morally decent, but it probably is legal."

Marlon stepped towards her.

"That's what you get with me, Ana. It isn't like you're wrong about everything. And it isn't like I'm right about everything. Your heart is good and in the right place. And you're really smart. You should develop your ideas into actual policies that could affect change for all people."

Ana snorted. Exhausted, Marlon moved to end the fight.

"I'm attracted to you, Ana, but I will not play games and I will not sit around while you waste energy and time on stuff that won't help you or your family. I have my own opinions about things. I've listened to my family's stories and watched their actions. I've come to my own conclusions and made my opinions and beliefs for myself. With my own hands."

He spread his fingers in front of her. Ana looked at them and then back into his eyes.

"We all spend years wrestling with who we are, right? I did, just between me and God. I know what I believe and the foundation I live my life from. Doesn't mean I won't evolve from this point, doesn't mean I won't change my opinion on things, it just means I know what kind of man I am, and the kind I want to become. I'm on the road to becoming a man people can trust and look up to, someone his wife respects and who respects her. I know what I want people to say about me when I die and I strive, imperfectly, every day to become that man. I won't ever try to make you think like me or believe like me, but we gotta have a place where we can respect the other's opinion. Otherwise, even friendship won't work."

"You're accusing me of not knowing what I believe in? You think you're so much better because you came to the wrong conclusion on how politics should work after supposedly 'wrestling it out with God'. I didn't have to wrestle anything with God to understand that helping people who are losing their houses is the right thing to do. Where are you going? Now you want to walk away from the discussion?"

"I've seen this Ana before on videos. You wanna insult me and turn my words around so you feel like you won, but I'm not taking the bait. I'm not arguing with you about this. It's a waste of time, Ana."

She snapped her mouth shut. She seemed to chew his words and her response at the same time, but Marlon was drained. He wanted to go home.

"Look, Ana, it's late and I've seen enough today. Seems to me like you need some time alone to figure things out."

"What do you mean?"

"Maybe I'm in your way. Tomorrow I'm hanging out with my family and then I will head to Florida. I'll probably be there for a week or two. I'll see you when I come back. I hope you've figured some things out by then."

Marlon calmly opened the door and stepped into the night. He half expected Ana to come after him and apologize or ask for a better explanation, but she didn't. Which meant he was probably right about her needing time away from him to think and decide what to do. This was a family issue between her and Javier. And he needed to stay out of it. Going to Florida would be a perfect time to do that.

Chapter Twenty-Eight

ANA TOOK A DEEP breath as she exited the community college. She spent all morning with a fake smile, pretending she was excited to attend the open house, like it wasn't the only choice she had without any transcripts from the university, but swallowing her pride was never easy.

Getting into the car, she tossed the application on the passenger seat, no longer needing to hide her frustration. She wished she could talk to Marlon. Over a week had gone by without a word from him. Just like when she left Roberto, Ana felt abandoned. She had to figure everything out for herself, with no one to talk to. Neither Marlon nor Ellen would remind her this was the right decision.

She hadn't told Javier or Elena anything about Ana-Maria or leaving the university and hoped she would never have to. The more she thought about the whole situation, the more embarrassed she became. If Javier ever found out, she knew the first thing he would ask would be, "What were you thinking?" Something she'd been trying to figure out on her own for the last few days but didn't have an answer for yet.

She looked at her phone, willing Marlon to call her. He would know exactly what to say to soothe her anxiety.

As if on cue, the phone buzzed, jolting Ana as she pulled the car out of the driveway.

"Hello?"

"Ana."

"Javier, what's wrong?" An icy dread fell over her at the sound of her brother's voice so high-pitched.

"I'm at the hospital. I had to bring Elena here last night."

"What? Is she okay? Where's Sofia?"

"With Maria. But she has to work. Can she drop Sofia off with you?"

"Yes, of course. Did Elena have the baby?"

"No, but the doctor said she should take it easy for the next couple of weeks. He put her on bedrest. Said she was too stressed out."

"That's good," Ana said, her heart still beating too fast.

"Ana, I'm going to need help from you. I still have to work, and Elena shouldn't be running after Sofia. She needs to be lying down. Can you watch Sofia during the day?"

"Yes," she said, not knowing how she would manage with classes starting and work. But she owed Javier.

"I also need help to move to King Street. Elena shouldn't be doing anything."

"You can't move there, Javier," Ana said. "It's too far away. This is a sign you should move in with me."

Javier sighed heavily into the phone. "Ana, we aren't moving in with you."

"Think about it, Javier," she said. "Elena can be on bedrest and still feel like she sees Sofia. I can clean and I can do the cooking and you will only have to go to work and back instead of driving all over the place."

"I'm not moving in if you make me eat what you cook," he said, laughing.

She smiled, relieved to hear some of the stress gone from his voice. "I'll learn to cook, then. Come on, move in with me. At least until the baby comes and Elena is better."

Silence echoed through the phone before Javier sighed in defeat. "Fine. Maybe you're right."

"I'm always right."

"Yeah, okay. We're going home now. Maria should be at your house soon, and I'll bring Elena over once she's rested."

Just as Ana pulled into her driveway, Maria showed up with a sleepy Sofia in her arms.

"She didn't sleep much last night," Maria explained. "I already fed her an early dinner, but a bath might help her to calm down enough to sleep. Be sure to place pillows or chairs around the bed, to keep her from falling."

Ana nodded, taking Sofia in her arms. Maria kissed their shared niece and drove away, leaving Ana alone with Sofia. Once inside the house, Sofia perked up, ready to play. While Ana fixed herself a sandwich, her food for the last few days, Sofia found magazines to rifle through, ripping most of the pages. After giving her niece a bath and reading a story, she finally fell asleep, leaving Ana free to pick up the mess downstairs.

Again, she thought about Marlon, wishing he would call. Surviving her first evening all alone seemed like a feat worth bragging about a little, but the house offered no one to listen. She picked up the paperwork for the community college with a sigh. Classes started in one week and with nothing more to do in the house, she might as well accept the future and fill out the forms.

Ana ran down the stairs quietly, hoping the doorbell wouldn't ring again before she got there. After an early morning that included

Sofia banging on pots and pans, the little girl was finally napping, and Ana had a pounding headache.

"Shhhhhh!" exclaimed Ana as she opened the door to let in her brother- and sister-in-law. "I just put Sofia down for a nap. Elena! How're you feeling?"

Elena smiled as she wobbled through the door. "I'm better. They gave me something for the contractions. Just tired."

They moved to the living room where Elena stretch out on the couch.

"Are you going to work, Javier?"

"For a bit. There's a project I want done by Friday, so I can take the entire weekend off and move stuff out of the house."

"When will you be home tonight?"

"I don't know." Javier hesitated, ready to argue with her.

Ana narrowed her eyes, her arms crossed.

"What?"

"This is home now, Javier. No arguments."

"I was thinking about it, Ana. Maybe we shouldn't-"

"Javier, come on. We lived together in harmony for the last four years and there's no reason to change it now. Think of it like a change of scenery. This way Elena will get rest, I'll have something to do, and you guys won't be throwing away money every month on a crappy apartment in a sketchy neighborhood."

Ana watched Elena pat Javier's knee, which seemed to sway him.

"I'll think about it."

"Javi—"

Javier turned to Elena. Under the light now, Ana could see the stress under his eyes and around his face.

"You want to stay here, Elena?"

"At least for a few months, Javi."

He sighed heavily, his face softening at his wife's words.

"Fine. We will stay here. At least until the baby is born. But then we'll probably leave."

"Good. I won't want you to stay longer anyway," Ana said, with a wink at Elena, who laughed.

"Well, if I'm staying, I need some food before I go to work. Got anything?"

Ana laughed. "You two tell me what the doctor said while I make some sandwiches."

Javier and Elena recounted the story of the night before through the open door into the kitchen while Ana put together a lunch tray.

"But the doctor says you're not in labor, right?"

"He gave me medicine to make sure I don't go into labor."

"Good, because I'm not sure I would know what to do."

"I'm sure you wouldn't know what to do," Javier said. Ana could hear Elena hitting him against the chest. There was silence until Ana stepped back into the living room with lunch.

"Here we go, sandwiches! See, I told you I could learn to cook."

"This isn't cooking," giggled Elena.

"What's this?"

The change in Javier's tone stopped Ana in the middle of pouring water. Her brother was holding the application. Her heart jumped a beat as she quickly tried to come up with an answer that didn't sound like a lie.

"Why are you applying for the community college? Did something happen at the university?" Elena asked through mouthfuls of tuna and bread.

"I'm switching schools," Ana said, shrugging to show them it didn't matter.

"You put here that your education is just up to high school."

"Did I? I was so tired last night. I'll have to fix it later." She tried to grab the paper from Javier, but he gripped it tightly.

"Ana, stop lying. What's going on?"

"Why do you even care, Javier? You don't want me to go to school at all."

"You spent the last year bragging about being at the university, and now you're going to the community college? I don't have my degree, Ana, but that makes no sense."

Ana looked at Elena for help, but she now stared expectantly at Ana as well, both eyebrows raised.

"What did you do?"

There had been a few times in the past Elena had spoken to her in that tone. There was the night Ana showed up at two in the morning after running from the cops. Ana told her brother she hadn't done anything, but Elena took one look at her and told her to go back home. The day after the debate, when the fights broke out. Elena was ready with video graphic evidence Ana was not just hit in the head, but was active in fighting and deserved the black eye she received.

Ana squirmed. They didn't budge.

"I was at the university under Ellen's granddaughter's name."

"What?"

Dread filled Ana, knowing she was about to disappoint them. She took a deep breath, then told them the story from the beginning, trying to hold back her tears as Javier couldn't hide his disappointment with her.

Hearing the story out loud made it all sound so ridiculous. A headline flashed in her head: *Young Latina Girl Steals Scholarship from Beloved Dead Granddaughter and Takes Her Place at the university.* Her heart skipped a beat at what could have happened.

"Unbelievable, Ana. What a stupid thing to do."

"I swear, it didn't sound like this bad of an idea when Ellen and I put it together. And really, it was Ellen's idea."

“And that makes it ok? Grieving people do stupid things all the time. You stole someone’s scholarship! I knew something was going on.”

“What do you mean?”

“It was so strange how you just were suddenly going to classes. We never saw an application for the university, and you never spoke about going, but then, all of a sudden, you were in. When you finally admitted to dating someone, we assumed he had something to do with it.”

“You assumed I slept my way into the university? Thanks a lot, Javier. Glad to know you have faith in me.”

Javier shrugged, shaking his head at her. “You didn’t deserve to be there, Ana. Why are you upset we assumed something like that when the truth is worse? It’s like you want to hold us to a standard that you can’t even begin to live up to. You got into the university by cheating, but now you’re upset that I always thought you cheated?”

Ana slumped into a chair.

“Yeah, well, I guess I got what I deserved. You happy now?”

No one said another word for a few minutes. When Elena picked up the application to the community college again, Ana fought the desire to snatch them from her hands and stomp out of the room.

“Are you sure this Gloria lady won’t take this any further?”

The question intensified Ana’s irritation.

“She said she wouldn’t.”

“And you believe her?”

“I have to. Besides, there’s no reason for her to bother with me.”

“Well, I guess that’s it then,” Javier said. “I have to get to work. You’re lucky they aren’t making you pay the scholarship back.”

Ana couldn’t keep herself from snapping back. “I think I’m paying enough with having to start over. It’s going to take me a long time now to finish school. Even so, I’m glad I did what I did.

Rescuing Ana Sanz from the snow didn't save her life, but I met Ellen because of it. And we're here because of me meeting her."

"Yeah, well, I guess there's always a silver lining. Does Marlon know about this?"

"What does Marlon even have to do with this?"

Fatigue was setting in, clear in her snappy answers.

"Because you're dating him... aren't you?"

Ana looked away, closing her eyes against the frustrations of living with family. Now she remembered why she had wanted to live alone.

"No, I'm not dating him. And yes, he knew. He wanted me to leave on my own. Just like you, I've pretty sure he's glad I got what I deserved."

Chapter Twenty-Nine

DANIEL ADJUSTED THE PAPER heart wreath on his door with a grimace. It looked out of place on his office door, even if each heart had a quote from a classic novel. Perhaps if the wreath was made using book shapes instead of hearts, he could stomach it. Hearts were just so feminine. He stepped back to eye it again, wondering if he had the guts to tell Gloria the truth. She would go on and on about how fragile his male ego was, thinking she was teasing. The real question was if he could weather through the teasing to convince her it wasn't about his ego, but about the fact that he simply didn't like the wreath. Or really, wreaths in general.

Honesty was the real problem. The idea of a wreath on his door made him shudder.

"Looks good," crooned Gloria, coming down the hall towards him. "I thought you would like it."

"I don't actually like it," Daniel said before he gave himself a chance to overthink his answer. "But you bought it, so I put it up, anyway."

"Why put it up a week early if you don't like it?"

Daniel turned. It was a good question, something Gloria had plenty of these days. That was a change he hadn't expected and was still getting used to.

After the night in January, when Ana so thoroughly rejected him for Marlon, he saw the future held only one option; getting back together with Gloria. Part of him was eager to be back with the woman he had loved since college, but another part of him wanted to run away and live in a hut alone. He didn't have the guts or the know-how to survive in the wild though, so he was left with getting back together with Gloria.

He had sat in his driveway until the car was as cold as the outdoors, determining the next steps. The only idea he came up with was to be more honest. With her, with himself, with their relationship. The idea grounded him enough to leave the freezing car, convinced it was the perfect steppingstone. A small voice had warned him that his honesty might be met with honesty, but he brushed it away with the snow, certain it wasn't anything to worry about. His thought process stopped at releasing an honest statement into the air, not beyond what she might say. She always seemed ready with a question or comment, which then started a long conversation. Like a therapist digging for the root. There wasn't always a root, but the more they conversed, the more comfortable they grew with each other.

The heart with a quote from *Romeo and Juliette* was crooked. He lifted his hand to straighten it but dropped it when he saw his hand was shaking. Daniel hoped the correlation between telling Gloria what he really thought and his nerves firing in all directions would end soon enough.

"I put it up because you gave it to me, which means you thought of me when you saw it. Or you actually went looking for it hoping to find me a unique gift. Either way, I'm grateful. Putting it up is a token of my respect and appreciation."

"Respect and appreciation are exactly what I wanted for Valentine's Day," she said, pressing her lips into his cheek. He slid his hand over her back and buttocks before reaching past her to open his office door. Gloria responded with a pat on his butt before slipping into his office.

"Have you seen Ana lately?"

"Of course not," he answered, waving his hand at the question. "She doesn't attend this university and I've no reason to seek her out at her place of residence."

"Don't be offended, Daniel. I was just asking."

"I'm not offended in the slightest," he answered, eyeing Gloria. "But you're twisting your ring, which means you've something to say."

Gloria's pinched lips spread into a smile.

"How well you know me. But stop looking at me like that. I need to tell you something, and smiling is inappropriate for it."

"About Ana?"

"It's more like a warning. I don't want you to get hurt."

"A warning about what?"

"Robert Manter told me he asked you to substitute for him at the community college. I didn't want you to run into her and be surprised. On one hand, I'd almost prefer for you to run into her to realize whether you're actually over her, but then I thought if you end up seeing her and found out I knew she was attending classes there, you'd get mad at me for not warning you. So, I'm warning you. You might run into her at the community college when you go."

"That's interesting," Daniel said. "But I have another theory."

"What's that?"

"You just wanted to see my reaction at telling me Ana is at the community college."

Gloria burst out in laughter. While Daniel enjoyed the sound of it, there was something about it that caused him to be uneasy.

"And what is your reaction to Ana going to community college?" she asked.

Daniel leaned into his chair away from her and tried to place himself in a position of running into Ana. She would still be attractive, of course, but Daniel had to admit his initial reaction to seeing Ana might be to run in the other direction. Now that several weeks had gone by since seeing her, he realized just how trivial their relationship was. There were even days he marveled at how stupid he'd been for involving himself romantically with a student. Especially after seeing the videos Gloria showed him of Ana at protests. Thinking of what could have happened with his career had Gloria not convinced Ana to leave the university, with no accusations coming his way, made him nauseous. He was lucky he still had his job. And he owed everything to Gloria.

He preferred not to see Ana. There was a slight chance of her accusing him of sexual misconduct. Of course, an accusation would open an investigation into her stealing the scholarship, which would cause her more problems, but sometimes people didn't choose the sensible action.

"I don't want to run into Ana at all, honestly. That chapter is closed in my life. You are my next chapter, and the focus of my attention. But thank you for warning me. I prefer knowing I could run into her rather than being caught by surprise."

"It's good to know our baby has a strong father," Gloria said.

Daniel snapped his head around, his heart racing. Gloria beamed at him.

"You mean, really. Right now? Not speaking of the future, but right now?"

"Well, about eight months from now, but yes. I'm pregnant."

Daniel leapt from his chair.

"I'm so happy," Daniel whispered, pressing Gloria to him. "Though I guess now I have to marry you again."

Gloria threw back her head and laughed.

Chapter Thirty

ANA CLOSED THE DOOR gently behind her. It was only nine-thirty at night, but the house was dark already. She hung up her coat and tiptoed into the kitchen with her books. The first week of classes at the community college had proved fairly easy, though that was probably because they were lower than the classes she took the semester before. Still, between working more at the coffee shop, taking care of Sofia, and getting settled into a new routine, she was glad to have some easy classes.

Where've you been?"

Ana jumped at the sound of Javier's voice. She turned around to find him at the foot of the stairs, his eyes dark with anxiety. Before she could answer, he waved his hand at her and looked up the stairs. "I have to take Elena to the hospital. She's been having contractions all night and now her water broke."

"What? Isn't it too early still?"

"She's almost thirty-seven weeks, so I think the baby's okay. The doctor wanted her to get to thirty-nine weeks but said to bring her in if her water broke. Can I leave Sofia here with you?"

"Of course. Why didn't you call my phone?" she asked as Javier grabbed jackets and blankets and his wallet, his actions rushed and wild.

"I did," he said flatly. "Elena! Why are you walking down the stairs?"

Ana had never heard her brother's voice so high-pitched. She would have laughed at the sound if the situation was different.

"I'm fine, Javier. Sitting is very uncomfortable."

Javier wrapped his wife in a large coat and his arms, guiding her out the door.

"We'll call you later." Javier called back, not waiting for Ana to reply before shutting it behind him.

Ana watched them leave, feeling helpless at the change of events. When the car was long gone down the street, she went to the kitchen to make herself some food and finish up her homework. Just as she was heading up the stairs to bed around midnight, Javier called to let her know his son, David, had arrived and was currently in the neonatal intensive care unit.

Ana flipped through a new recipe book for beginners, trying to fight the temptation to lie down for a nap.

"Nana!" Sofia said, pointing to her art creation on the tray of her highchair.

"Very nice, Sofia," Ana said, glancing at the blue, purple, and red smears on the paper and Sofia's belly. "Don't eat it silly!"

Sofia giggled, but her temper turned the minute Ana tried to wipe her face.

"No!" the little girl said.

Ana sighed but put the rag down, too tired to argue. Taking care of a child was much harder than she ever thought it would be. For the past week, she'd been on her own with Sofia. Not only was David in the newborn intensive care, but Elena still hadn't come home either. After the emergency c-section delivery, Elena developed an infection. Javier slept at the hospital every night. He came home for breakfast to see Sofia, then headed to work, leaving Ana to take over basically everything, including the laundry, cooking, and cleaning.

The smell of roast meat and potatoes filled the kitchen, mixing with the aroma of fresh bread. Ana's ability to cook jumped several levels in the last week thanks to the help of a slow cooker and a bread machine.

"Hola." Elena's sweet voice startled Ana and Sofia. Maria and Elena stood in the kitchen doorway, taking in the scene. Sofia burst into tears. Elena looked ready to cry as well. Maria reached to pick Sofia up.

"Hola! Let me help you," Ana said, rushing to wipe the paint from Sofia's belly. "I leave her in a diaper because it's so much easier than doing more laundry."

"You figured out how to work the washing machine?" Elena asked, holding her arms out for her daughter once she was sitting.

"Hey!" Ana exclaimed. "I did my laundry at the other house, too!"

"You turned a white towel blue," Elena laughed, hugging Sofia close.

Knowing her sister-in-law was teasing, Ana brushed away her defensiveness and laughed. "That was one time, and it happened because I put a pair of my jeans in with it."

"What are you cooking, Ana?" Maria asked. "It smells good."

"Pot roast. Or at least I think I am," Ana said, relieved at the change in topic. "A girl from one of my classes recommended this recipe book."

"Easy Crock Pot Recipes," read Maria. "What have you tried so far?"

“Only a few things. The green chili chicken the other night didn’t turn out so great, but the chicken soup was a hit. I also bought a book on pasta and made a really good carbonara.”

“Javier told me it was good,” Elena admitted, her nose pressed into Sofia’s hair, tears visible in her eyes. Not knowing what else to do, Ana kept up the conversation about her cooking.

“I know that I’m still well below your levels of cooking, but it’s a start.”

“Just a little practice is all you need, Ana,” Maria said, as she took Sofia from Elena, who looked suddenly very drained.

A ding drew all their attention.

“What’s that?”

“The pot roast is done, which means dinner time for Sofia. She usually eats something before we go to class,” Ana explained, taking out plates. With Elena back, she suddenly felt self-conscious in her routine. “I don’t have to take her to class if you don’t want me to. Javier said he thought it would be better for you to rest, but obviously it’s up to you and how you feel.”

“Does she enjoy going?” Elena asked, pain showing in her voice.

“I think so. She never cries when I drop her off and she always has a smile on her face when I pick her up. There are a lot of young kids to play with and they haven’t told me of any problems so far. Do you two want to eat now or later? I’m going to eat something now to hold me over until after class.”

Elena wasn’t up to eating, but Maria politely took a plate, exchanging looks. After watching Sofia take a bite, Maria took one as well, her face changing from apprehension to surprise.

“Está bueno!” she said.

“Bueno!” exclaimed Sofia.

Ana laughed, relieved it was edible. “All I did was follow the recipe.”

Sofia squirmed and giggled, bouncing up and down on her mother's lap in her excitement. Ana grabbed Sofia when Elena winced, who then burst into tears. Two months before, even two weeks before, Ana would have been at a loss as to what to do. After a week of being with Sofia all by herself, though, Ana was ready to show how much she learned. First, she twirled her niece around to get her to giggle instead of cry. Then she raised her above her head and let her drop quickly until they were face to face.

"Cuckoo!"

Sofia erupted into laughter. Once calm, Ana set her on the floor to eat her dinner, away from Elena.

"Crisis averted," Ana declared, smiling, but Elena seemed too uncomfortable to be very impressed. Ana set Sofia down, swallowing back her pride.

"Maybe you should take her with you today," Maria said, helping Elena to her feet.

Elena nodded, limping forward. "I think I'll just go to bed early. I want to be at the hospital early tomorrow morning to feed David."

"That's fine," Ana said, secretly happy to have Sofia go with her. "When can I see him?"

"We're just trying to be careful now with him. They're going to release him from the hospital in a few days, and then you can see him all you want."

"I understand," Ana said. Though she knew Maria had visited David already, she didn't push the subject. "Come on, Sofia, let's eat so we can get ready."

Ana busied herself with wiping down the counters and putting away the kitchen things to hide her rejection.

"Hermanita," Elena said, reaching out to her as Ana walked by to the garage. "I want you to know we really appreciate you looking after Sofia these last few days. I didn't want her to have to see her little brother in the incubator with all those tubes going through him."

"I know, I understand. I'm glad I could help in some way. And, really, she's been so good, haven't you?" Ana picked her niece up, hoping she wasn't blushing too much. "I'll see you tomorrow? Don't worry about tonight. Just rest. I'll take care of Sofia."

"Thank you, Ana."

"Ven, hermana," Maria said, cutting the conversation short. "You're tired and need to sleep."

"And I better get this little girl dressed for class, otherwise we're going to be late."

Ana stuffed some meat between two slices of bread and gathered her things. With a quick wipe down of Sofia's stomach and hands, she stuffed her back into her clothes and called for her to follow her to the car. The looks on Maria and Elena's faces were priceless as they watched Sofia toddle behind Ana to the garage.

Ana had to admit even she was semi-surprised she and Sofia had survived so well alone together. Her vegetables were kind of soggy, and she had almost caught herself on fire while trying to sear the roast, but no one needed to know about that. She had managed with everything, even buying a car and renewing her license with a toddler on her hip. In all truth, it made her feel invincible.

Sofia squealed against her car seat, kicking her legs in some sudden discomfort. Feeling just like a mom, Ana twisted her arm to give the little girl a pat on the knee to reassure her they were almost "at the community college. Sofia accepted the gesture and closed her eyes to sleep the rest of the way, but Ana's eyes filled with tears.

She was happy Elena was doing well and David was leaving the NICU, but she also couldn't help feeling a little disappointed. Sofia no longer relying on her opened a small hole of fear and loneliness in the pit of her stomach. A small part of her was afraid she found her new self-reliance only because of the family emergency. That if they no longer needed her, she would get stuck again, not knowing how to make good decisions for herself.

But then, she also couldn't fade behind Javier and Elena. With school much easier this semester and her new job starting Monday, she should have some time to figure out a new plan. Something more solid than what she had now.

Ana sat still in the driver's seat for a moment after parking the car, absorbing her dilemma. The soft breath coming from the back seat caught up with her own inhale, the sweet breath bringing tears to Ana's eyes.

"This is silly. I'll be fine."

"Ana gave a quick check to her eye makeup in the rearview mirror, then rushed out of the car. Sofia rubbed her eyes and looked up with a confused, sleepy look. Ana smothered her face in kisses as she buttoned up the little girl's coat and pulled her out of the backseat. A few twirls in the parking lot averted tears and some motor sounds as Ana ran them across the parking lot. Down the hall on the left was the childcare center, which Sofia knew well. She wiggled in Ana's arms, kicking out until Ana set her on the ground to run to the doors.

"Sofia!" greeted one worker as Sofia ran in to check on her favorite plastic kitchen set.

Ana signed her niece in, then hurried down the hall, rummaging in her bag for the right notebook. A quick glance at the clock above the lobby told her she had ten minutes to grab a soda and run to class. As she turned the corner, someone jumped out of her way.

"So sorry," she said, her eyes still on her phone.

"Ana! It's good to see you."

The voice stopped Ana in her tracks as she walked down the semi-empty halls of the community college.

"Daniel. What are you doing here?"

He stood tall, his hair trimmed, his beard shaved, and with an energetic vibe to him. Having never experienced breaking up with someone that didn't result in someone throwing things, she wasn't sure what the protocol was when coming back into contact with an ex. The immediate emotions within her were of scorn and disdain, but she wasn't sure that was correct. After all, she didn't regret not being with him and she shouldn't care at all if he was happier with Gloria. The two of them would not have been happy together.

But Gloria had ruined her life, in a way. If she chose not to believe her when she said that the scholarship committee was already looking into the death of Ana Sanz.

"You look well," Daniel said, taking another step towards her before stopping himself. Ana laughed, the tension in her body releasing with the sound.

"I'm sure I look exhausted. I've been taking care of my niece full-time while my nephew is in the NICU. Plus, taking classes here."

"Ah, you sound busy," he said, looking around the halls as he stepped backwards.

"Do you like your classes?"

"They're classes I have to take so I can apply to the university. For real this time. They're fine. The professors are nice, though my classmates aren't too serious about studying. At any rate, I'm where I should be right now. How's Gloria?"

"Pregnant," Daniel said, his voice soft and far away.

The words slammed against her. Suddenly, she didn't want to be there. The honesty was out of the ordinary for the Daniel she knew. Though she had no desire to be with him again, she couldn't help the strange tinge of jealousy that crept over her.

"Congratulations."

Daniel's eyes slowly connected with hers, his face unreadable.

"Thank you. We're getting married in three weeks, just to have everything squared away for the baby. Just a small gathering at the courthouse."

"I'm happy for you, Daniel," Ana said, glad to realize that her words were genuine, that her mind and heart had finally connected to the right emotions. "Listen, my class is about to start."

"Of course, I don't want to keep you. Go ahead. Maybe we'll cross paths another day."

Ana hoped they wouldn't, but nodded anyway, before leaving Daniel behind for good.

Chapter Thirty-One

Ana looked away from the wooden desk she was sanding to check on Sofia. The day was unusually warm for early March, and Ana wanted to take full advantage of it. With her homework out of the way and David and Elena sleeping, she and Sofia had dressed up in their play clothes and marched outside. Ana took on her new hobby of stripping old furniture. She had spent years watching her father and Javier work with wood, but this was the first time she had tried her hand at it.

The week before, she had woken up in the middle of the night with the ingenious idea of starting a business in which she would take furniture she found on the side of the road for free, strip it, paint it, and then sell it. Now, after spending a hundred dollars, she wasn't about to give up. Even if her arms were about to fall off. Even if it took her years to finish.

Stretching her arms and neck, Ana walked over to check on her niece, who was busy filling buckets with grass and rocks and anything else she could find. The little girl concentrated as though the fate of the world hung in the balance of how many items she could fit in her plastic orange buckets. She noticed Ana coming over and endured a kiss, but then pushed her aunt out of her way. Ana pinched her nose but took the hint to go back to her work.

Again, her thoughts turned to Marlon. Several nights since things calmed down with Elena and baby David, Ana laid awake, obsessing about Marlon and how she left things with him. How she could have done things differently; better. When the ache in her chest was too intense from missing him, she looked up his videos and started binge watching them just to hear his voice. Just that morning, her phone buzzed with the notification that he uploaded a new one and she couldn't help but watch it. He looked good. Better than she felt.

A cold snap of wind blew between her and Sofia, reminding Ana of her first kiss with Marlon. The memory left a knot in her stomach.

She should have...

He should have...

If only she had apologized. If only he had understood.

The thoughts refused to leave her alone. Had she never gotten too close to Daniel, then she would have been available to pursue Marlon all along. Why did she think she had to invite Daniel into the house that last night after Marlon had done so much for her?

Another whisper floated into her thoughts. *If only you knew yourself better and found yourself sooner.*

Desperate suddenly for air and a water break, Ana threw down the sanding paper and ripped off the humid mask that covered her mouth. At the sudden movement, Sofia threw her buckets down and toddled over. Ana scooped her up while trying to control the overflow of emotions that were threatening to bubble up. Sofia rubbed her eyes before laying her head on her aunt's shoulder. It was well past naptime for her.

"Maybe you should have taken a nap earlier when your mama put you down," Ana murmured. "But then, perhaps you and I should snuggle together. I could start reading that book that I need to read for history class, which is sure to put us to sleep quickly. Should we do that?"

Sofia's contented sigh answered the question. They walked to the front door, where she handed her off to Javier before turning back to the yard. Every cell in her ran slower, wading through the mental sludge of her treatment of Marlon. She was tempted to leave her mess and go have a good cry on her bed, but the dark clouds on the horizon changed her mind. With all the time she spent working on the desk, she didn't want a spring storm to ruin it.

A truck came up the road as she bent over to pick up Sofia's toys. She didn't bother to look up until she heard the tires pull against the curb and the engine die. The shiver that ran down her spine wasn't just from the wind picking up. It was Marlon's truck. She was sure of it before even looking up.

Panic started swirling in her belly. She was trapped. Javier asked if he could invite Marlon over someday and she had said yes. But truthfully, she thought Marlon would never show up. Or at least Javier would invite him when she wasn't home. She would have to face him, speak to him, see in his eyes that nothing had changed. Running away was tempting, but there was no place to hide. Plus, he'd already seen her.

Time ticked by slowly as he walked towards her. Ana continued placing toddler toys into a mesh bag, hoping he wouldn't notice her trembling. Nothing had changed about him. He still stood tall, confident, exactly what she thought a lawyer should be. In his eyes, she saw just enough pride and always a little amusement, as though he were on the lookout to have fun. Ana noticed his skin was darker than before, perhaps because of the gray weather, or perhaps from the sun in some other part of the world. Her hands shook as she envisioned placing them against his cheek.

"Hello, Ana."

The jovial tone snapped Ana out of her daydream. She almost lost her balance, reaching for the last plastic shovel. The wind snapped through the yard again, helping to dry off the beads of sweat forming on her forehead. She hoped her cheeks looked wind-burned rather than flushed.

"Hi," she said as she scrambled to stand up. "Where've you been?"

He answered only with a raised an eyebrow.

"Looks like you've been in the sunshine instead of waiting out the Midwest winter like the rest of us.

"I had a conference in Florida, remember? I ended up staying longer. Did some deep-sea fishing and snorkeling."

"Did you catch anything?" She was painfully aware the conversation was moving down a ridiculous path.

"I caught a few things. Threw them back in, though. I was just there for the experience and the conference."

Ana nodded, at a loss for what to say next. Marlon also said nothing, and Ana wished the earth would swallow her whole. She tried to keep her eyes leveled to his, but when her arms started quivering, she had to look away.

"I came to see Javier. Is he here?"

"Um, yes, of course." Ana swallowed hard, her disappointment refusing to go down with her saliva. "Javier's inside. Go ahead on in."

The second the last word was out of her mouth, Ana turned on her heel and hurried to the garage. She placed the mesh bag full of dirty shovels and buckets into the worn-down chest and took a moment to take in some deep breaths. Tears of disappointment threatened to fill her eyes, but she sniffed them away. She couldn't stay out in the garage forever and she had no intention of Javier clumsily asking if she'd been crying in front of Marlon.

After rolling her shoulders a few times, Ana marched back to the front, ready to head inside and pretend she was fine. When she turned the corner, she nearly jumped out of her skin at the sight of Marlon standing on the front stoop, as though waiting for her.

"You can go in."

"It isn't my house, Ana," he said, his voice too neutral for her to read anything into it. "I'd rather wait for you."

"Fine." She said it more for herself as she dragged her feet forward until she could smell his familiar cologne. She pushed the door open, then waited for him to go through before she made another move. After placing her shoes carefully on the mat, Ana hesitated at the stairs. Marlon being here had nothing to do with her and it would feel so good to lie down and commiserate with herself on what she had lost with him, but she also knew that her brother wouldn't let her hear the end of it if she didn't show up in the kitchen which smelled of homemade cookies.

"Hey, man! What's up?" Javier said. "I didn't expect you to come today. Didn't you just get in?"

"Yeah, a few hours ago. I had the afternoon off, so I thought I'd just stop by," Marlon answered as the two of them grasped each other's hands and bumped shoulders. "Is this the new little man?"

"Yep, at home and growing big."

"How's Elena doing?"

Ana shouldered her way between the two of them to pour herself some coffee. She slid a mug to Marlon without asking, along with a plate of cookies.

"You want me to take a look at your car? I brought the stuff with me."

"I have time right now. Ana, can you watch David? Elena's sleeping."

Ana rushed over to take the sleeping baby. The chance to babysit David was not an offer she was willing to let go of.

"You know I don't mind, Javier," she said, already cooing him back to sleep.

"Let me just check on Elena and I'll be back down. I need to change my shirt, too."

Ana smiled as her brother hurried from the kitchen, taking the stairs two at a time.

"He misses having his friends living in the neighborhood," Ana said. "I think he's a little bored living here."

Marlon nodded, but said nothing else.

"Have a seat. He'll be a minute. Want more coffee?"

Marlon shook his head.

"How are classes this semester? Have any interesting ones?"

"Some are interesting, but nothing exciting. I just plow through them so I can work on my business. What about you?"

"I'm taking classes at the community college and working part time there in the admissions office. Things have been crazy at the house, with David being in the NICU and Elena in the hospital longer."

"You're at the community college? Good for you."

Ana shrugged her shoulders, her cheeks burning at how she acted when Ellen first suggested she go there. "It isn't as bad as I thought, though Gloria didn't leave me with much of a choice."

"Nothing wrong with that. Lots of people start out at community colleges. They're cheap."

"I guess I never thought I could keep a well-paying job, pay for college, and get good grades. Now I do. I guess I just have more confidence than I used to have."

"Having money definitely helps, I guess," said Marlon.

"Of course, it helps, but I didn't inherit enough for it to change my life."

"I'm glad you decided to keep studying," Marlon said after a minute. His soft tone sent a shiver down her spine.

"Okay, I'm ready," called Javier as he descended the stairs.

Marlon jumped out of his seat, never looking back as he headed out the door with Javier.

Ana waved her hand in annoyance as they left the house. The sound of the car engine turning in the driveway seemed just the right trigger for the tears to flow down her face and blur the image of a perfect baby in front of her.

The clouds opened in torrents just as Elena came downstairs. Ana was in the living room with David wrapped up in a quilt, reading the book assigned for history class. It wasn't as boring as she thought it would be, which, along with a strong cup of coffee, helped keep her awake. At the sound of Elena's voice, David stirred from his position in the basinet, breaking Ana's concentration.

"Where's Javier?" asked Elena.

"He and Marlon have been outside for the last few hours. I heard him come in to get more beer about an hour ago. Come here, Sofia. Want to read?"

Sofia looked at the baby, pointing at him with a slobbery index finger.

"Baby hungy. Sofia hungy."

Elena took the baby to feed him, showing Sofia again how to be gentle with his head, something she had to do several times a day. Bored after a few minutes, Sofia walked up to her aunt and pressed her nose directly into Ana's.

"I hungy."

Ana laughed, giving up on her reading.

"Let's go get something to eat, then. Want something, Elena?"

"Whatever you make for Sofia is fine, and maybe a glass of water. I'll go into the kitchen with you."

"I don't mind bringing it out here."

"I know that, hermanita, but I want to talk about Marlon being here. And I can't wait until you're done making coffee and putting that showy tray together."

"Being a little pretentious never hurt anyone."

"A strange sentence from my hermanita," laughed Elena. Ana laughed with her, noting how much Ellen had changed her ideas about some things in life.

"I was surprised my gossip-loving sister-in-law didn't come downstairs the second Marlon got here."

"I was so tired," Elena complained. "Besides, I wanted to give a chance for the coals of love to burn again. So, spill. Did you two talk? Did you kiss?"

"Elena! No, we didn't kiss. It's awkward between us. He wants nothing to do with me. He came just to see Javier. He had texted him a few times, apparently."

"You don't believe that, do you? I mean, I like Javier, but why would Marlon bother to be nice to him when he barely knows him unless he wanted to see you?"

"Marlon's just a good guy like that. He made a promise, and he's the kind of guy that will stick to that promise."

"Seems to me like an excuse to come and see you," Elena said. "It's what they always say on the telenovelas."

"Pssha. Real life isn't telenovelas."

"It is if you make it. Now, you have to do something dramatic, and he will declare his love for you!"

"Love is a strong word, Elena." Her whole body warmed at the suggestion Marlon might still like her.

"He was practically in love with you a few months ago. You think that he just stopped because you guys had a little fight? I really think you're dense sometimes. What did you guys talk about?"

"I asked him about classes, and he asked me what I was doing this semester. We only talked for a few minutes before Javier came back down and took him away."

"Ugh, so boring. Be more dramatic. That's what he would like. He needs to see that you regret pushing him away. Or whatever it is that you did."

"Why do you think it was my fault?"

Elena raised her eyebrows at Ana as though no answer was necessary. Strangely, Ana felt laughter bubble out of her at the look her sister-in-law gave her. A few months ago, maybe even weeks, the assumption that the fight was her fault would have offended her. Even though it was true.

"When will your auntie admit that she's in love with that tall man out there and stop fooling around?"

"How could I be in love with him when I barely know him?"

"You don't 'barely' know him. You know him and you know you like him and want to spend time with him, and I even bet you've fantasized about living here with him."

Ana's face burned at the accusation.

"See? You're blushing! Seriously, hermanita, apologize to him, and try to win him back."

"He doesn't want to talk to me. It might be too late."

"Even if it is, at least you'll have done all that you could to get him back. According to you, he's already refused you, so you have nothing to lose."

Ana's shoulders slumped at her sister-in-law's words. "Thanks a lot."

Elena shrugged with a smile. "Go out there and talk to him."

"Now?"

Before Elena could answer, Javier and Marlon walked into the kitchen.

"Changed the brake pads!" Javier announced to his wife as he kissed her on the cheek. "Our car is now safer than it was this morning."

"It took you guys almost three hours to change some brake pads?" Ana teased Javier. "I thought that was a simple job."

She snuck a look at Marlon, but he was busy playing with Sofia, who laughed at his childish game of making her apple slices disappear and reappear.

"We had to go to the store because I bought the wrong ones," explained Javier, making a face at her. "And hermana, we looked at your car and changed the brake pads and oil, both of which it needed. So, you're welcome."

"Thank you," Ana said, beaming at her brother. It was a relief he knew how to do those things.

"Marlon, are you staying for dinner?" asked Elena.

"I already asked him, and he turned me down, even though I told him he had to stay and try your enchiladas."

Marlon shook his head. "I have to do a few things after missing so much class."

"But you have all day tomorrow to study," insisted Elena. "It's only Saturday."

"I really shouldn't," said Marlon, looking at Ana for the first time since they entered the house.

Her mind went blank at his look, her hands trembled.

"Javier, will you get me a blanket for David? I think he's a little cold."

"I'll go," offered Ana, needing a moment away to collet her thoughts.

Within a few minutes, Ana was back downstairs, stopping in her tracks when she entered the kitchen. Javier rolled his eyes at her as Elena grabbed the blanket out of Ana's hands.

"Go out there and talk to him," she ordered. "I don't understand why you're making this harder than it needs to be."

Ana hesitated for a second.

"Go, Ana." Elena's face was stern. She stood unwavering, staring Ana down until she finally turned on her heels and ran out the door.

"Marlon!" He was already in his car, even as she shouted. Before he could pull away, Ana knocked on the driver's side window, shouting again.

"What?" he asked, rolling down the window despite the trickling rain.

"I'm sorry. You were right and I'm sorry."

"Sorry about what?"

Ana stood silent for a moment to catch her breath. She visualized the apology note she wrote during two rather boring history classes, but never sent. There was so much that she was sorry for: cheating her way into the university, spending part of her life with another man who never cared about her or who she was, not knowing who she was herself. But that was all irrelevant to Marlon.

"Ana?"

Ana let out a staggered breath as a slow drizzle started again. She willed her brain to visualize her words so that she could make some sense.

"Ana, I need to go. What do you want?" Marlon asked, his voice soft and deep. The vibrations triggering the faucet of tears again.

"I'm so sorry! For so many things," she said, stepping back when Marlon finally opened his door and stepped out. "I needed some time to—figure things out. Figure out what's important and what I needed to learn to let go of, I guess. You weren't there for me to lean on for a bit, and it made me learn to—"

Ana stopped to think. Her mouth had gotten ahead of her brain.

"Maybe to trust myself," she concluded.

Marlon looked at her with raised eyebrows, but kept his mouth shut.

"This time without you made me realize something."

Ana paused, adding the drama Elena told her to, hoping he would ask her to go on. Marlon smiled.

"I'll bite, Ana. What did it make you realize?"

"That I wanted you. I want an actual relationship with someone who will challenge me like you do. It still makes me uncomfortable, but I'm starting to like being pushed. I want to be better, and I know you will make me better."

The wind blew Marlon's hair over his eyes as he started to speak, but Ana rushed on.

"Wait, I'll give you time to speak. But I need to say things, and I don't want to forget."

Marlon closed his mouth and leaned back. "Go on then."

Ana took in a deep breath and focused on a spot behind Marlon. To help her think about something other than kissing him. "For the past few weeks, I've been thinking about calling you to explain that and apologize about our fight, but I just never knew what to say. Then so many things happened, and time passed and then I felt like it was too late. I wrote you a letter, but I didn't mail it, because that seemed just as embarrassing. But now you're here, and you don't want to have dinner with us, and I think that it's because of me."

"It's because I have things to do."

"So, you won't have dinner with us?"

"I can't. I already told you, Ana. It's a family thing. My sister expects me at her house."

Ana froze. She had expected him to come back into the house with her. To tell her he forgave her and wanted to be friends, or more, again. But instead, he opened the door and slipped back into his truck.

"Marlon, couldn't we at least be friends? At least?"

"I don't want to be friends, Ana. I already told you that."

"But I just told you I don't want to be friends either," she said, unable to hide her frustration. "I want to be more. That's what I'm trying to tell you, and now you're walking away."

"I heard what you said, but I just don't see anything, any action, that really makes me believe it."

"What?"

"You say you've changed, but at the same time you're still waiting for me to make things different between us, for me to make the next move. That confidence that you have in everything else just doesn't show where I am concerned."

"I'm waiting for you? I'm the one out in the rain. I didn't apologize so my brother could have a friend to hang out with. I apologized because I thought you deserved an apology. I treated you unfairly and now you want to claim that I'm just waiting for you to make the first move? You're an ass."

Ana turned on her heels and stomped away, frustration and humiliation pressing hard into her lungs. At the front door, she turned around to an empty street and a fading engine hum. The sky still drizzled, washing away the tears that managed to roll down before she could stop them. The hardest part was not trying to control her tears, although that was proving difficult. But she would have to recount this horrible conversation with Elena.

She closed her eyes and took a deep breath. Listening to the patter of the rain helped her gain control over the tears that wanted to bubble up. In her daydreams, whenever she had the courage to apologize, Marlon always accepted her back. Usually with a grand kiss. She never expected him to reject her like he did.

Ana gripped the doorknob, breathing through her misery. She could cry in bed later that night, after she had dinner. With another deep breath she turned the doorknob, just as the hum of the truck once again pulled up to the curb.

The truck sounded like Marlon's but must have been one of Javier's other friends. Ana turned around to greet someone she didn't know, only to find Marlon slam the door shut and march towards her, the rain quickly soaking him as it picked up in intensity.

"I'm sorry."

Hope filled her. "Me, too," Ana whispered.

"I went to Florida to forget you. To move on. The problem is, I couldn't stop thinking about you."

All the tension left Ana's body. She slumped against the brick of the doorway to keep herself standing, the weight of his words too much.

"I think I'm falling in love with you."

Ana stared at his wide eyes, intense with emotion and transfixed by her own gaze.

"I realized all I want is you. I want you to be happy, but I want you to be happy with me. I want you to be with me. I want to be with you."

Marlon closed the distance between them, holding her face in his hands. He leaned his forehead against hers. The heat they breathed out warming the other's nose and cheeks as the temperature dropped around them and thunder started crashing in the distance. All it took was for Ana to tilt her chin slightly up for Marlon to give her what she wanted.

He pressed his lips against hers, pulling her in close against him as though making sure she was really there.

“You’re shivering,” whispered Marlon as he pulled his lips away. “Should I warm you up?”

When she nodded, Marlon pressed his lips against her neck and murmured things she couldn’t understand. All her mind could comprehend was that he was back. He was holding her. She hadn’t ruined everything. When he pulled away, Ana pinched her arm to make sure it wasn’t a dream. Marlon laughed.

“We’re actually going to do this, right?” he asked. Ana nodded.

“If you’ll stay for dinner, we can start right now.”

“I’m not just staying for dinner, Ana," he said, kissing her again. "This time I’m staying for good.”

Epilogue

"YOU LOOK VERY HANDSOME."

Ana watched Marlon focus on her through the mirror, a smile breaking his contemplative face.

"I love the little hat, especially. That's what I'm most jealous of."

"My Oxford cap?" he asked. "You'll have your own soon."

"Maybe," she said, a mixture of pride and a bit of jealousy stirring in her.

Marlon closed the distance between them in three strides. The air shifted, sending a slight shiver down her spine. He swooped her into his arms, her feet lifting from the ground as she squealed in surprise.

"Me, too," demanded Sofia from below, her arms raised towards Marlon.

"You'll get your little sombrero soon enough, Ana."

"Oh, you're speaking Spanish now?" Ana asked, feigning jealousy.

"I've been teaching him Spanish," Elena said as she passed by in the hallway. "Didn't you tell her, Marlon?"

"Am I not allowed to have any secrets?"

"Not in a house of Latinas," Javier said, hoisting a box labelled Ana's clothes onto his shoulder. "Are you sure you guys have to move next week? Why can't you just wait until the summer's over?"

"I told you why," Ana said, following Javier down the stairs, talking loud enough to irritate him. She knew he was moving the boxes because he hated not having anything to do, but she couldn't help teasing him. She was too happy. "Marlon already has a job, and I need to look for one. And seriously, Javier, I don't understand why you have to move boxes around just before we leave for Marlon's graduation ceremony."

At the bottom of the stairs Javier whipped around, flashing Ana a wicked smile. She jumped back before dissolving into giggles with Sofia, who had joined them.

"Not funny, Javier," she said, feigning a pout at Sofia.

"You know what else isn't funny?" he asked as he headed to the side door. Ana waved him away, refusing to take the bait. She had other things to worry about as two cars pulled into the driveway.

Marlon's mother, Amelia, stepped out of the driver's seat. She wore a navy-blue skirt she smoothed down as she left the car, with a matching jacket and silk shirt underneath. Her hair was elegantly coiffed in a pile of curls on top of her head. Ana pulled her long brown hair to one side and wondered if it was too late to put it up.

"Maybe you should have put your hair up," Elena said, watching in awe as the matriarchs of Marlon's family marched up the sidewalk. Behind Amelia was Marlon's grandmother, with a walker, her spine straight as an arrow. Then came Condie, Marlon's sister, who looked like a model straight out of a magazine, even with a baby on one hip and a six-year-old in her other hand.

"Too late for that," Ana said, sighing heavily.

"You're beautiful as you are, hermanita."

Ana flashed her sister-in-law a smile as Marlon swung the front door open.

"Look at this handsome man!" called out Amelia, rushing the last few steps to hug her son.

Squeals and compliments filled the entryway. Ana shifted to the outside of the circle. While Marlon's family was always kind to her, she didn't belong inside the circle of women who now touched his trimmed hair and shaved chin, commenting on the color of the gown and how skinny he was.

"I can't believe you trimmed your hair. You should've let me give you dreads again," Condie was saying, eyeing Marlon as the baby dressed in white lace grabbed at Marlon's tassel.

"You want a lawyer to wear dreadlocks?" Melanie, Marlon's grandmother, demanded. She had a voice that was impossible to ignore and was the only woman of the family to accept Ana with no questions asked. She laughed and pinched her grandson's cheek, looking up with moist eyes. "Ana! There you are. Isn't he a handsome man?"

"Yes, he is, Melanie."

Amelia glanced over her shoulder at Ana. Her eyes narrowed slightly, but she said nothing. Heat pricked Ana's forearms. Despite the beads of sweat forming under her dress, she smiled when Marlon sent her a reassuring wink.

"Turn around," his mother demanded, circling her fingers. "Let me see you. My son. The lawyer."

"I thought Uncle Marlon was a judge." Randal was six and always had questions.

"I'm not a judge. I write and talk about law. Now I'm a dispute resolutions expert."

"He's gonna be a judge someday," Marlon's mother said, ignoring the lift in her son's eyebrows. Normally, a comment like that might start a long, drawn-out conversation, but today Marlon seemed unwilling to argue. Instead, he picked Randal up and perched the Oxford cap on his head.

"Condie, tell Mama to leave me alone."

"You're the one that keeps going to school. I assume you'll be a judge someday, too."

"At least in politics," their mother said with the familiar smile seen about town in her political posters.

"President!" Randal shouted, twisting the cap around on his head.

"Who's gonna be president?"

Javier and Elena joined everyone in the cramped entryway, dressed in their Sunday best, with Sofia and David ready to go. Ana introduced the families, pointing from one person to another and pausing only long enough for them to shake hands. Amelia stood back, her red lips pursed together, smiling only when Ana looked directly at her.

Amelia was unhappy about Marlon moving to Florida, and Ana assumed Amelia thought it was partly Ana's fault. Marlon had always talked about not staying once he finished his masters, but that never stopped Amelia from planning Marlon's campaign for mayor every time they had dinner together. When Ana got accepted to the university of Florida, Marlon didn't hesitate before deciding to go with her.

"I'm not dating you long distance," he told her when she brought up the possibility. His firm stance pacified her since she didn't want a long-distance relationship either, but nothing mollified his mother.

"We better start heading out," Amelia said, checking her watch. "Marlon, you ride with me."

Marlon nodded, shrugging his shoulders.

"Let's not argue about the little things today," he whispered when she raised her eyebrows at him. Just as loudly as they came in, Marlon's family marched out, snapping selfies and pictures as though following a movie star.

"They sure are excited," Javier said, once they were alone in the house. Ana watched from the living room as Marlon's family took pictures before they climbed back into Amelia's Mercedes.

"It's an exciting day," she told Javier, rolling her eyes at him. She refused to make a fuss on Marlon's big graduation day. Besides feeling jealous she wasn't walking the stage that day, Ana was bursting with pride for Marlon. And if she felt ready to burst, his mother must have been floating on a cloud, and Ana refused to be her rain.

***

"Alright, one more picture, folks!"

Marlon's cheeks burned from smiling so much, but he stood tall once again, holding out the diploma and smiling for the camera. He didn't know how much his mother was paying the photographer, probably too much, but he refused to be the one she reprimanded for wasting her money by not smiling.

"There now. You're all so beautiful!" Amelia said, as the cousins relaxed from their poses. "Now, eat up! There's plenty of food."

"Can we have one more, Mama? Just Ana and I?"

Amelia smiled at Marlon as he grabbed Ana from his aunt, but it was what he called her television interview smile. He didn't know if she was irritated with him for wanting to move away or still adjusting to their conversation a few days before.

"There now. What a cute couple." Amelia stiffened at the photographer's words, but Marlon ignored it.

"Mama, come here and get one with me and Ana."

Amelia obeyed, posing gracefully for the camera, then ducking out at the first call of an aunt nearby.

Ana looked up at Marlon with a sigh.

"Is she still mad?"

"She's sad, but she'll be alright. This day was coming."

"Yeah, but now she can blame it on me," Ana murmured. "I'm going to go help your sister. Maybe that'll win me some points."

Marlon squeezed her hand just as Javier and Elena came into the backyard.

"Congratulations, man."

"Hey, Javier," Marlon answered. "Thanks for coming."

"We wouldn't have missed it, Marlon. You're like family to us now."

"He will be family soon," Javier said with a wink.

Marlon thumped Javier on the back in warning. Javier nodded sheepishly, busying himself with David, who was crying in the stroller. Sofia looked over the top of the stroller on her tiptoes to caress her brother's head.

"She's paying a lot more attention to her brother," Marlon said, pointing to Sofia. He'd seen Sofia throwing fits over Elena holding David several times. After not seeing her during all of May because of exams, the change of heart was impressive.

Elena laughed, eyeing her daughter warily. "Yes, it seems her jealousy is finally fading."

"Who's jealous?" Ana wrapped her arms around Marlon as she joined the group, breathing out a sigh of relief. "I escaped from Aunt Tina. She's so much like Tia Teresa. A pill for everything."

Elena and she giggled, but very quickly, Ana straightened up and pulled away from Marlon. Without looking, he knew his mother was approaching them. When his mother got sidetracked by another family member, he felt Ana's muscles relax.

"The sun is setting, Marlon," Ana said, noting the orange sky. It was the moment he wanted to give their announcement.

"Ready?" he asked. She nodded, though she didn't smile. His heart pounded in his chest at what he was about to do. This was the moment he'd been both anticipating and dreading. He could take his mother being irritated as long as Ana said yes.

"Yes." Ana grabbed his hand, her face beaming. Javier winked at them as they set off to the front of the deck. Marlon climbed onto a chair, clinking his fork against a plastic beer mug.

"Hey, everyone! That's right. Settle down. That means you, Camden."

A young man in the crowd yelled back a response that was immediately covered by laughter as he watched his cousins, friends, and family gather around him. Ana stood next to him, just a few feet below on the ground, watching him as well, as though to hide in the crowd.

"That's right. There we go. Thank you all for coming. Let's give my beautiful mother a hand for organizing all of this. For the second time."

His mother bowed to the crowd as they whooped and cheered.

"Just keep graduating from something, Marlon. Your mama throws a mean party!"

"Thanks, Brent." Marlon waited until the claps and cheers for his mother died down to speak again. "And thank you, mama. Okay, okay. As most of you know, I came here to get this law degree, and though mama wants me to stay and run for mayor, I'm still too young."

Whistles and boos burst from his cousins. Marlon laughed, faking indignation.

"Obviously, they should change those laws just for me," Marlon said, allowing the ripples of laughter to die down. "But they won't do it. Instead of staying here to get another degree, I'm going to be moving to Florida with my beautiful girlfriend, Ana, here. Stop it, Camden. She's mine."

His cousins laughed as Camden stopped his whistling to let Marlon continue.

"Ana's been accepted to the University of Florida, so we'll be moving to Gainesville in a week. I'll be working down there and, well, we're excited about this next adventure of ours."

As his cousins hooted and yelled, Marlon jumped down. Now was the time for the bigger announcement. Marlon's hands were clammy and cold, but there was no going back for nerves. Ana smiled up at him, completely innocent of what was about to happen.

A rhythmic thumping started coming from the side of the house. It came closer and closer, low, and just under the surface, until it surrounded them. Ana looked at him, her eyes wide with surprise. The crowd quieted until all Marlon could hear was the beating of his heart in rhythm with the thumping coming from the speakers. He signaled to his cousin Jake, already in position.

The evening burst into color as hundreds of string lights flickered on across the yard. Then came the words of Ana's favorite song and a fizzing sound that magnified as everyone in the crowd lit their sparklers. Ana started laughing. She turned to Condie when she called her name, giving Marlon enough time to lower himself to one knee. He took a deep breath to steady his trembling hand, then nodded at his cousin to turn on the mic he wore on his lapel.

"Ana," he said, his voice surrounding the yard. Ana jumped in surprise, then gasped when she saw him. "I had no idea I would find you when I accepted the scholarship to come here, but fate brought us together that day. You've completely turned me upside down, and I wouldn't have it any other way."

Tears were streaming down Ana's cheeks as Marlon fumbled to open the small box. The overhead string illuminated the pink diamond perfectly, bringing a gasp from his family members at the front of the crowd.

"Ana Lopez, will you marry me?"

Ana gurgled an incoherent sound, trying to control her sobs.

"Yes," she finally said, her voice cracking. He stood up, rubbing the tears away gently with his thumb.

"What did she say?" yelled Camden.

Ana looked at Marlon, her voice still choked with tears, as he picked up her left hand and slipped the ring on her finger.

"She said 'yes'!" Marlon shouted. Then he wrapped his arms around her trembling body and kissed his future wife.

About Kat

Kat Caldwell believes everyone has a story worth telling, and she is passionate about helping those who want to write their story get the tools and support they need. She pursued the indie author route to satisfy her desire to write multiple genres. Her historical romance, *Stepping Across the Desert,* came out in 2017. Her magical realism novel, *An Audience with the King*, in 2019. And her contemporary women's fiction, *Coffee Stains*, came out in 2021.

Kat is also an Author Accelerator certified fiction and nonfiction book coach.

If she isn't writing or hanging out with her writing community, you can usually find Kat interviewing other creatives for her Pencils&Lipstick podcast or volunteering with her local church -- always with a cup of cold brew nearby.

Visit Katcaldwell.comFollow her on BookBub, Instagram and Facebook.

www.ingramcontent.com/pod-product-compliance
Lightning Source LLC
LaVergne TN
LVHW091106080826
845145LV00008B/1832

* 9 7 8 0 9 9 9 5 8 8 1 8 5 *